A PIECE of LAND

MELODY TYDEN

Chapter One

~**Laura**~

The warm Texas sun beat down on the rows of graduates in their black gowns and mortarboard hats as my classmates paraded slowly across the stage at the front of the field.

Somewhere in the rows behind me, my family were proudly gathered to watch, all except my older brother, Dex. He would have been there, but his wife, Shawna, had just been readmitted to the hospital for more cancer treatment and I insisted that he stay with her that day. He'd already attended my high school graduation and my undergrad convocation, so seeing me get my Master's degree didn't qualify as a scenario worth leaving his wife's side.

Their absence cast a pall over the day, but unfortunately, our family had gotten used to it. In the three years they'd been married, Shawna had spent more time in treatment than out of it. How they kept their spirits up, either of them, I didn't know, but they were still just as head-over-heels for each other as ever.

I really didn't know how that felt.

My relationships up to that point had all been short-lived. They started out exciting but fizzled out fast, usually once we got to the point where we'd start talking about the future. Very few of the men I met in Houston had any interest in moving to a small town they'd never heard of before, and the fact that I wouldn't consider anything else made my plans incompatible with theirs. I convinced myself it didn't matter. I needed to focus on school anyway, and at least I had my career to look forward to even if my love life appeared to be a lost cause for the time being.

The kind of relationship Dex and Shawna had, or my parents for that matter, or my sister, Tonia, and her husband, Cam, a true partnership with someone who matched you blow for blow, I hadn't found anything close to that yet.

"Laura Callahan."

The dean called my name as I strode across the stage to receive my degree, and I waved the document in the direction of my family, smiling as they hooted and hollered in reply. In some ways, it felt like my six years in college had lasted forever, but it also felt like they had passed in the blink of an eye. I would have been just as happy to take over management of the family ranch as soon as I finished high school, but my parents had insisted I needed to see more of the world and get an education first.

They were certain that once I got a taste of the big city, I'd never be satisfied with our small town again, but that hadn't been the case at all. What did happen, though, was that once I started studying, I found I liked it, and when I got offered a place on the Master's agriculture program by one of my undergrad professors, I decided to carry on for the extra two years it would take to complete it.

Now that I'd finished, now that I had the piece of paper in my hand that made me exceptionally qualified to bring the Callahan family ranch to a whole new level, I couldn't be more ready to return to the small town I'd grown up in and claim the land that had always been my past and my future. None of my siblings had ever shown any interest in running the ranch, but it had been my dream for as long as I could remember. My parents had been so sure I would grow out of it, but I never did. Everything I'd done for the past six years had been in anticipation of carrying on the Callahan ranch for a new generation.

I couldn't wait to go home.

But first, we went to dinner to celebrate.

"To Laura and her kick-ass future!" Tonia's toast at the restaurant made me and our other sister, Billie, laugh even as my mother winced.

"Tonia, that child of yours is going to get kicked out of preschool if he repeats half the things you say." She shot a worried look at my nearly-two-year-old nephew, who continued to colour away on his kid's menu, blissfully unaware of anything going on around him.

"And where do you think I learned all my best curse words?" Tonia teased back, giving our dad a nudge.

He chuckled with her, but he hadn't been quite himself that night. He looked a little pale, leaving me worried that his heart might be giving him trouble again. He'd had a close call a couple of years earlier, and it always lingered in the back of my mind whenever he looked a little under the weather.

As if he'd heard my thoughts, he cleared his throat to get our attention, and everyone at the table fell silent as we waited for him to speak. "I know this is Laura's night, but I've got some news for all of you too. You know that your mom's been after me to retire fully."

We definitely knew that. Ever since his heart attack, she'd been hounding him to take things easier. He had stepped back a lot, but the ranch still occupied a big space in his head and heart, even when he wasn't physically there. With my degree finished, I would be able to take that burden from him.

"The thing is, I didn't want to pass the ranch on to just anyone. I wanted to make sure the person who took over from me wanted it for the right reasons. I wanted it to be someone who felt that same love of the land that I always did and who would respect what I'd tried to do there."

My heart beat faster in anticipation as Tonia gave me a wink. She knew just how much I wanted this. She'd even given up on trying to get me to join her in her own thriving business, knowing my heart belonged to the ranch, and it seemed the moment had finally come.

My dad carried on, still looking far less comfortable than usual. "It took time to find the right person, but eventually, I did. The papers have all been signed this afternoon. It's done. The Callahan ranch has officially been sold."

An uneasy silence settled over the table, my sisters exchanging nervous glances as I tried to make sense of what he just said. Sold? That couldn't be right. I hadn't bought or signed anything.

"Sold to who?" Tonia finally asked when no words came out of my mouth.

My mom put a supportive hand on my dad's arm as he answered. "His name's Jesse Greenbank. You'd like him. Quiet, responsible young man. I hired him to take over the day-to-day running of the place last year and he'll do a good job with it."

This had to be some kind of nightmare. The words weren't making any sense to me.

"You sold the ranch to a stranger? Without telling any of us?" My temporary muteness seemed to have passed as the words rushed out of my mouth, louder than I intended. Several people at nearby tables turned to look at us, but at that moment, I didn't care. "Is this a joke? You can't sell our home, Daddy. It's our legacy. *My* legacy."

"Now, Laura, there's no need to be upset. A house is just a house. It's the people that make it, and we've got our new home here in Houston with all of you." My mother meant her words to be comforting, but they only reinforced how little she understood about how I felt.

"It's not the house," I insisted, turning back to my father who still refused to look me in the eye. "It's the land. You said you wanted someone who loved it like you did? That's me, Daddy. I've always loved it. I've always planned on moving back there. You know that! I did everything you said, I spent time in the city and got my degree, but the connection I feel with it has never changed. I'm ready to go back."

The more I thought about it, the more I realized that every time I'd brought up the ranch in conversation with my parents over the previous year or so, they always put me off, saying we'd talk about it later. Maybe that should have been a clue, but I had no idea they were even considering selling. Why would I?

"You don't really want that, honey." My dad offered me a tentative smile. "I know you love the place too, but running it all on your own, it becomes your whole life. It takes more out of you than you can imagine. Maybe if you had a husband to help you..."

My mouth dropped open as Tonia and Billie both leaned back, anticipating the eruption they knew would be coming. "There is *nothing* a man could do that I couldn't. I know that ranch inside out. I know the town, the people, all the connections, and now, I've got a fucking Master's degree! Can Mr 'Quiet and Responsible' say that?"

"Fuck-in Master!" Little Charlie's voice piped up from the end of the table before Tonia quickly shushed him.

Her husband, meanwhile, jumped in on my behalf. "Mr Callahan, you know I respect you and your right to do what you like with your land, but Laura's capable of making her own decisions too, and she's been working hard to prepare for this. I personally can't imagine anyone taking better care of that place."

"She deserves a chance to at least try," Billie added.

The chorus of protests in my favour grew so impassioned that my mother had to hold up her hands to stop the onslaught. "You're going to have to tell them," she whispered to my dad, but not quietly enough. We all heard it.

"Tell us what?" I demanded.

With a grimace, my dad met my gaze. "The ranch has a lot of debt, Laura. The last few years have been tough, even before my heart attack, and it only got worse after, at least till Jesse came. I didn't want to saddle you with all of that. He agreed to take it all on when he bought it. It's his problem now, not yours. You've got your degree and your life here in the city, and you're going to find a great job that you love rather than spending years trying to undo the mess I made. It's better for everyone."

His hand went to his chest as he mentioned his heart attack and as soon as he finished speaking, my mother got to her feet. "Alright, that's enough for tonight. We're heading on home. I know this came as a shock for all y'all, but when you sleep on it, it won't seem so bad. Everyone gets a fresh start. Congratulations again, Laura."

My daddy mumbled his congratulations too as he got to his feet, looking frailer than I'd seen him in a long time. For a moment, I felt guilty for causing him any distress, but my indignation quickly pushed those feelings aside.

"What are you going to do?" Tonia asked me during the silence that followed my parents' departure, when no one else seemed to know what to say.

I made up my mind on the spot. "I'm going to Sandy Creek tomorrow. I'm going to convince this Jesse Greenbank to sell the ranch back to me."

Cam gave me a look both sympathetic and a little wary. "Do you really think that's likely, Laura? He just bought the place."

"So, he's not attached to it yet," I pointed out. "No matter what any piece of paper says, that ranch belongs to me, and tomorrow, I'm going home."

~Jesse~

Not many people would be happy with a four o'clock wake-up alarm, but on the first day of officially owning my own ranch, I couldn't wait to jump out of bed. Though it sounded cliché, that day really was the first day of the rest of my life.

The sun wouldn't be up for a couple of hours yet, but when the sun came up, it would get hot, and hot cattle were unhappy cattle. Getting my work with them done while they were still cooled off and settled would make the whole day run smoother, making the early start more than worth it.

I'd been staying at the Callahan ranch, and in the main house, for over a year already, living in one of the guest rooms, so nothing about getting ready in the morning felt all that different. I already knew my way around. Without turning on the light, I grabbed one of my long-sleeved work shirts from the closet and a pair of jeans from the dresser. In the ensuite bathroom, I ran a comb through my hair and brushed my teeth, grabbing my hat and boots on the way out the door. The whole routine took less than 15 minutes.

Stars twinkled above me in the big Texas sky, and I took a deep breath of the fresh air, filling my lungs with the satisfaction of knowing for the first time in my life, the land beneath my feet belonged to me. No one could take it from me, not unless something went terribly wrong, and I had no intention of messing it up.

I couldn't believe it when Jim Callahan asked if I had been serious about wanting to buy the ranch. Over beers one night back in the fall, I told him I'd love to have a place like this of my own, but I only meant it conversationally. I knew he had a family and I assumed he'd want to keep the ranch with them once he couldn't keep up with running it himself.

Then, just a few weeks earlier, he told me he'd decided to sell and he wanted to give me first crack at it. I had some money saved up from my years as a hired man but definitely not as much as I needed for the ranch, especially once I added in the debt he told me about. It took trips to four different banks before I got enough to meet the asking price and enough to run on in the short term, but I didn't hesitate for a second. With hard work, and once I put the changes I had in mind in place, I could get this place earning double what it did at the moment, I had no doubt. Add to that my own minimalist living costs and I'd have it paid off in no more than twenty years. I'd done all the math.

Having no one else to worry about made life a lot easier sometimes.

With all that settled, I just needed to focus on the ranch. Calving season had almost ended but a few stragglers hadn't made an appearance yet. I'd head out to check on the pregnant cows first before visiting the rest of the calves and their moms, making sure nothing had changed since I checked them the day before. When the other hired help arrived, we'd get started on moving the cows and calves to one of the other fields since the one closest to the house could do with a new fence. That project would take at least a week, depending on if the weather held out. As soon as it had finished, I had a long list of other things to get started on.

I definitely wouldn't be getting bored any time soon.

None of that was to say Jim Callahan hadn't done a good job with the ranch, because he had. It had an excellent reputation and good relationships with many buyers and suppliers that I would be able to inherit, making my job a lot easier. However, he'd be the first to admit he'd let things slide with the decline in his health, and he hadn't put any new money into repairs in quite some time. A property as big as this one needed to be kept in a constant cycle of maintenance. If not, things could go downhill shockingly fast.

"Howdy, boss." I'd been so lost in thought that I missed Tyson coming up behind me. He clapped me on the shoulder and gave me a grin. "You ready to start giving orders today?"

"I've been ordering your ass around for a year already," I pointed out, trying not to smile at the reminder that from that day on, I would be my own boss and everyone else's too. Unlike most of the hired help, Tyson lived on the ranch too, in a small house just down the road from the main one. He'd been with Callahan a lot longer than I had but he had no interest in running the place himself. A couple of years older than me and a confirmed bachelor, we had a lot in common. So much, in fact, that we butted heads for the first few months I'd been there, convinced we each knew better than the other. It took a bad lightning storm and a fire, and working together through the night to get the cattle through it safely, to earn each other's trust and respect, but now that we had it, we were more like brothers than co-workers.

I'd never had a brother in that way before. I kind of liked it.

"Let's get started. Busy day."

Those words were all I needed to say as we walked over together to the calving barn. Three heifers were still undelivered, and the first two we checked on still showed no signs of movement. The third one, however, looked like she'd be ready to go that day. Uncomfortable and restless, she must have been up most of the night, and it looked like my plans for the day were about to change.

"I'll stay with her," I told Tyson. "You can check on the calves before the others get here."

Days rarely went exactly as I thought they would, so why not start my first full day as owner by birthing a new calf? It seemed somehow fitting. A lot of new things were starting that day.

Thankfully, aside from disrupting my schedule for the day, the calf's delivery went according to plan. Soon, I had the heifer on her side with two little hooves poking out. Labour for first-time moms often took a bit longer, but after not much more than an hour, the head appeared, and soon, we had a healthy new addition to the ranch. I stayed with the cow until she'd passed the placenta, and once everything looked good, I left the pair in the care of one of the other cowboys while I headed back to the house to get cleaned up.

A truck I didn't recognize sat parked in front of the house, but I didn't give it more than a moment's thought. One of our hired men had promised to bring along a friend that day since we were short-staffed, but with the birthing going on, I hadn't had a chance to meet him yet. The truck probably belonged to him. I'd tell him where the staff trucks got parked once I saw how he worked and whether he'd be coming back again.

My boots were dusty but my clothes were covered in bovine bodily fluids, so I decided to keep the boots on and head straight to the laundry basket once I got inside.

Or at least, that *had* been my plan, until I walked straight into a woman I'd never seen before standing in the middle of my kitchen.

~Laura~

As I told my sisters I would, I got up early the very next morning and made the drive from Houston to the small town of Sandy Creek. While everyone else drank champagne over dinner, I stuck to water, wanting to be clear-headed not only for the drive but for the conversation awaiting me on the other end of it. I would have to be at the top of my game but I had confidence in my abilities. After all, I had just successfully defended my Master's thesis; I could handle a small-town cowboy.

Billie and Tonia both swore they knew nothing about Jesse Green-bank. If our daddy had mentioned him before, we'd all tuned it out. None of us recognized his surname as a local one either, so he must have moved to town to work on the ranch.

The longer I thought about it, the angrier I got. He probably thought he got himself a real good deal, working there for only a year before buying the place out from under its rightful owners. He could have even been some kind of con man. I'd give him a chance to make things right first, but if he wanted to play hardball, I had a few law student friends who could help me look into having the contract voided. Surely, taking advantage of a man in poor health would have to factor into things. Obviously, things with my father were worse than I realized.

By the time I pulled through the familiar gates of the ranch and down the long drive, I had a dozen different plans in my head and different options I could take no matter how the day's meeting went. Still, I tried to keep an open mind. Although I had plenty of reasons to dislike the man without having met him, I would be willing to give him a chance. If he seemed like a decent guy and behaved reasonably by coming around to my point of view, there was no reason we couldn't be friends. In fact, I could always use some help running my ranch. I might even offer him a job.

Driving up to the two-storey house with its wraparound porch, I realized just how long it had been since I'd been there. With the pressures of school and the rest of my family all settled in Houston, visiting hadn't been my top priority. My parents had essentially moved to Houston over a year ago, bringing all their personal belongings from the ranch with them. The last time I'd been down must have been to help them pack, and there had been no Jesse there then. They'd left some of the furniture behind since my daddy still drove down every week to oversee things, but since he'd return to Houston on weekends, there had been no pressing need for me to make the trip.

If I had come sooner, maybe I would have noticed the way the fence on the near field needed to be replaced or the way the main house could use a fresh coat of paint. Obviously, things had gone downhill in my daddy's absence, which just added another arrow to my quiver as to why Jesse Greenbank must not have been the right man to take over the ranch at all.

Some of the ranch hands were out in the field as I parked in front of the house, but having no description to go on, I couldn't tell which one might be Jesse. I wanted to freshen up from the drive anyway before speaking to him. My knock on the door at the house went unanswered, as I expected, so I let myself in just as I'd always done. The house had never been locked during the day in my whole life; people came and went as they liked.

Stepping inside almost felt like walking into a ghost town. The kitchen felt empty without my mom there. She always had something cooking or baking, even if she'd gone to do something else. The slow cooker on the counter had been a staple of my childhood. That day, the counter lay bare, and when I opened the fridge, the meagre contents of it made me wince. Aside from some milk, butter and a bottle of ketchup, the shelves were nearly bare. What did this guy feed himself?

Curiosity getting the better of me, I opened the freezer and found my answer: at least a dozen frozen dinners lay neatly stacked in piles, each one of them a dinner for one. A few burgers and sausages filled in the empty spaces, easy to barbecue. Seemed like someone's mama had never taught him to cook.

Closing the freezer door, I headed down the hall to the main bathroom, a room I'd been in thousands of times before. It looked even emptier than the kitchen. There were no towels, no toiletries, nothing to say it might be used other than a roll of toilet paper propped up on an empty roll on the toilet paper holder.

Men, I sighed to myself, replacing the roll properly. Luckily, I had a comb and some make-up in my purse, so I could touch myself up without needing much else. Needing soap and a towel, I returned to the kitchen to wash my hands and I had just turned the tap off when the front door slammed shut.

My heart beat kicked up as I smoothed out my hair. It looked like I wouldn't have to go in search of him after all; seemed like Jesse Greenbank had come right to me. I headed towards the door to say hello as he took his boots off, but before I could reach the entrance, a tall, broad man came barrelling into the room, running straight into me and nearly knocking me off my feet.

"Whoa there, what the... fuck, are you alright?" He stuttered the words out as we both fought to keep our balance. Somehow, his hands ended up on my waist as my hands went to his chest to steady myself, and I immediately regretted it as they slipped against something slimy on his shirt.

"What is that?"

I looked up for an answer and found myself staring into brown eyes the colour of melted milk chocolate. His hat covered his hair, but the dark stubble on his chin gave me an idea what colour it must be. His skin was tanned like every rancher's, baked to a golden brown by the hot Texas sun. Younger than I'd imagined, he couldn't be much more than thirty.

For a moment, he simply stared back at me, his eyes staying on mine, until he looked down at my slimy hands and his nose wrinkled in regret. "I'm sorry to say that's the remnants of the calving I just finished."

I hoped he meant that as a joke, but it didn't look that way. *Perfect.* I had no trouble getting dirty on the ranch when required, but my whole shirt had gotten covered from pressing against him and I hadn't brought a change of clothes. I'd only planned on being there for the afternoon.

"What are you doing in my kitchen, anyway?" he asked, taking a step back from me and removing his hat. His thick, dark hair looked exactly as I imagined it would, having spent the whole morning beneath his hat. "Who are you?"

Although I'd imagined a rather different introduction, I would have to roll with it. "I'm Laura Callahan. You're Jesse?"

Still looking more confused than anything, he nodded, wiping his hand on his jeans before holding it out to me. "That's me. Nice to meet you, Laura. You're Jim's daughter?"

Tonia and Billie would have turned their noses up at shaking his hand since he'd basically just admitted to having it up a cow earlier today, but I had no such qualms. Determined not to let him intimidate me, I shook his hand firmly. At least he had some manners. "One of them, yes. Guess he didn't mention me to you any more than he told me about you."

"I didn't say he didn't mention you. Jim talked a lot about his girls." That pleased me, but he could just be saying it to flatter me. I had no intention of being distracted by a handsome face or some pretty words. I had to keep my guard up. "What can I do for you, Laura? Did Jim send you?"

Obviously, he wondered why he didn't know I'd be showing up that day, but I didn't really want to have that conversation with the two of us both covered in cow excretions. "Actually, Daddy doesn't know I'm here. I came to talk to you. Why don't you get cleaned up, as you said, and I'll make us something to eat. We can have a talk over lunch."

My proposition clearly took him by surprise. "I've got a lot to do..." he tried to protest, but I wasn't about to be put off.

"I promise it won't take long. You've gotta eat, don't you?"

"I suppose." He looked around the kitchen sheepishly. "There ain't much here to be cooking with though."

I'd already seen that. "I'll find something. Could I trouble you for a shirt, since mine's going to need a wash too?"

He looked down at my shirt in confusion, as if noticing it for the first time. Mostly, he looked bewildered by the whole situation. "Sure, I guess. Gimme a sec."

His manners were a point in his favour so far as he headed down the hall and I followed behind, expecting him to turn in at the master bedroom. He didn't, though, walking straight past it until he reached the last door on the left.

"This is my room." I couldn't stop myself from saying the words out loud and he turned back in confusion.

"Excuse me?"

"This room," I repeated, gesturing to the door. "It belonged to me growing up. I slept here for years."

"Okay?" He looked even more confused, and I shook my head.

"Never mind." Obviously, I found that fact more interesting than he did.

Turning back, he opened the door and let himself in. Although I stopped at the doorway, I couldn't help peeking in out of interest to see how the room had changed, and to say it had changed would be an understatement. If I hadn't known it used to be mine, I'd have never recognized it. The walls were bare, the furniture basic and functional. Not a single photograph graced the space, nothing that looked personal at all.

Jesse moved over to the closet, undoing his shirt as he walked and pulling it off to throw it into the laundry basket inside. From the hanging row, he grabbed a checked blue and white shirt and brought it back to the door to hand to me. "I hope this is okay. I ain't got any women's clothes."

I reached out to take it from him, trying not to notice the broad sweep of his chest and the tattoos decorating it. He obviously had no trouble with the hands-on part of working on a ranch, based on the state of his muscles. "Thanks. I'll have food ready by the time you're done showering."

Before he could protest, I'd already turned around to head back to the kitchen.

Chapter Two

~Jesse~

Stepping into the shower, I tried to wash away my confusion along with the morning's grime. Laura Callahan's sudden appearance in my house had completely thrown me off, especially since she acted like there was nothing unusual about it. At least she didn't seem as upset about having calf afterbirth all over her as most women would be, but I still didn't have any idea why the hell she'd come in the first place.

I hadn't met any of the Callahan kids before. They all had their lives in Houston, Jim had said, which explained why he wanted to sell the ranch outside the family. That matched up with what I'd seen, too; in the year I'd been living there, none of them had ever been for a visit. So, why would one of them be showing up the day after the ranch officially left their hands?

As I towelled off, I tried to remember which one Laura would be. Jim had three daughters, along with his son, and he'd told me about them all, but never having met them or even seen photos, I had trouble keeping them straight. I knew one of them had a husband and a kid, but Laura's finger didn't have a ring on it. I noticed it only because she held up her hands when they got dirty against my shirt. I wouldn't have looked otherwise. That must make her one of the other two, both of whom were in college, if I remembered right.

I'd noticed a few other things too: her soft, dark brown hair, pretty blue eyes and curves that would give any rodeo queen a run for their money, but I pushed all those things to the back of my mind. My number one rule when it came to women was never to get involved with anyone with connections that might get awkward later on. Even if Jim had washed his hands of the ranch, plenty of folks around there still knew and liked the Callahans, which made Laura off-limits for the only kind of relationship I ever got involved in.

Better to stick to business. I just had to figure out exactly what business had brought her there that day. With my hair washed and fresh clothes on, I headed back to the kitchen to find out.

The smell of frying sausages hit me first, making my mouth water. For me, lunch usually consisted of a peanut butter sandwich, something I could make quick and eat on the go. It had been a long time since I'd had a hot meal at midday, or someone to cook it for me.

"You found some food, then?" I asked as I walked into the room. Thankfully, she had her back to me and missed my double take when I caught sight of her standing in front of the stove in her curve-hugging jeans and my shirt, her dark hair hanging down over her shoulders.

Damn. I hadn't been planning on visiting my usual pick-up spot for a couple more weeks, but with that vision in my head, I might need to change my plans.

"I won't say I had an easy time of it, but I rustled up something for us." She gave me a warm smile as she turned around, her eyes widening just a little as she took in the cleaned-up version of me. Seemed I wasn't the only one who liked what I saw. "Have a seat, I'll bring it right over."

She acted like she still owned the place, but I supposed it would be a hard habit to break after growing up there. I'd let it slide, just that once. Heading to the kitchen table, I found she'd already made some iced tea for us, and whatever she'd cooked smelled great. My stomach rumbled as I sat down at the head of the table.

With the practice of experience, she swung the cupboard door open, pulled out two plates and divided up the contents of her frying pan between them. She knew just where to find the cutlery too, and a moment later, my plate appeared in front of me while Laura placed hers down right beside me and took a seat.

"This looks fantastic," I told her honestly, picking up my fork and digging into a chunk of sausage. She'd made a glaze of some kind with berries and some kind of doughy thing that I didn't recognize but it tasted great. We ate in silence for a minute or two while I savoured each bite. "Where'd the berries come from?"

"There's a blackberry bush just out back. The ones on the south side always ripen first. I found just enough there."

Damn, she'd been busy. I didn't think I'd been in the shower all that long. "Guess you know all the ins and outs of this place."

"I reckon so." She smiled at me again, but I caught a glimpse of something else in her eyes, something harder that made me a little uneasy as I finished cleaning my plate. It hadn't taken long for the whole thing to disappear.

"Well, thanks. I appreciate the meal, but I'm guessing you didn't come down here just to make me lunch. What can I do for you, Ms Callahan?"

She squared her shoulders, putting her own fork down though she hadn't finished yet. "I'm here to talk to you about the deal you made with my daddy."

My wariness grew even stronger. "What about it?" She'd come a little late if she wanted to try to add something to the contract. Everything was signed and official.

"Can I be frank with you, Mr Greenbank?"

"I would prefer that." I still didn't have a clue what she wanted, so if she got to the point, I'd appreciate it. Lunch had been a nice treat but I had to get back to work.

"There's been a mistake," she told me bluntly, and my eyebrows raised in surprise as I tried to guess what she meant. "My daddy got this idea in his head that the ranch was in trouble and I wouldn't be able to fix it. He thinks he knows what's best for me, like daddies do, I guess. The thing is, Mr Greenbank, this ranch has always been mine. It's always *supposed* to have been mine. I was born right here in this house, since my mama thought she had plenty of time before she needed to get to the hospital, and honestly, I plan to die right here too. I know you made a deal, but you don't know what this place means to me. This land is in my blood. If I'd had any idea you were in negotiations, I'd have come here sooner, but my daddy didn't say a word about it until last night. That's why I'm here now."

I followed most of that, but I still didn't see her point. "This sounds like a conversation you need to have with Jim. I'm sorry if he didn't let you know in advance but he must have had his reasons."

"I'll deal with him later," she said, rather ominously. "But the problem is, he already sold the ranch to you."

"I'm aware of that. I signed the papers, I was there."

Her lips pursed for just a second, not appreciating my matter-of-factness. "I understand that, but I'm sure you can see now why it should have never happened. There are extenuating circumstances. This is the Callahan ranch, it has been since my great-grandfather started it, and that's how it should stay."

"What exactly do you want from me, Ms Callahan?" She still hadn't got to the damn point.

And then she did: "I want you to sell the ranch back to me."

For a moment, I could only stare at her in disbelief. She couldn't be serious. "I'm not looking to sell."

"I know it's unusual, but..."

"It's not 'unusual', it's insane." Why were the prettiest women always a little bit crazy? All the goodwill she'd earned by making me lunch had evaporated, and I'd just about reached the limits of my hospitality. "Can you even afford to buy it straight out?"

I could tell immediately from the way she dropped her eyes that she couldn't. "I'll have to apply for some assistance, but I'm sure I can..."

"So, let me get this straight: you came down here today to tell me I should sell the ranch that I just bought back to you simply because you want it, even though you can't afford it?"

"It's my family's ranch..."

"No, it *used to be* your family's ranch. As of today, the name on the deed says Greenbank, not Callahan. Whatever miscommunication happened between you and your daddy has nothing to do with me. I've worked damn hard to be here and I bought this place in good faith. If it's all the same to you, I'd rather stay out of your family drama. I've had more than enough of my own in my time."

I got to my feet and grabbed my hat from where I'd left it on the counter earlier as Laura stood up behind me.

"Where's your sense of honour?" Her blue eyes blazed in indignation. "Would you honestly steal my birthright out from under me because of a misunderstanding? Or was that your plan all along?"

My chest tightened as the words hit me, just about the worst words she could have chosen.

"I didn't steal nothing." My voice had gotten dangerously low as I took a step towards her. "If you came here hoping you could sweet talk me with your cooking and your pretty face, you made a serious miscalculation, Ms Callahan. Don't you lecture me about honour when you don't know a thing about me. I'm going back to work, and you can show yourself off *my* land. I assume you know the way out."

With that, I headed for the door, not waiting to hear anything else she had to say.

~**Laura**~

That could have gone better.

As the front door slammed closed behind Jesse, I looked back at the table and his empty plate with a sigh. Perhaps it had been a little naive to think he'd agree simply because it was the right thing to do, but I had been trying to give him the benefit of the doubt. I'd hoped he would hear my story, realize there had been a mistake, and offer to make it right. I didn't want to put him out on the street; far from it, in fact. I could use a good second-in-command around the ranch, and he seemed to like the place and take his job seriously. He had convinced my daddy he would run it well, and recent decisions notwithstanding, I generally trusted my father's judgement.

We could have made a good team.

Instead, he got immediately defensive, basically saying the whole mess was *my* fault when he knew nothing about it. He accused me of expecting him to sell simply because I wanted the ranch, but what right did he have to it other than that he wanted it too? If my daddy had just talked to me about it like he should have, this never would have happened, but Jesse didn't take that into consideration. Men liked to assume they knew everything even when they'd only seen half the picture.

I probably should have broached the subject a little more gradually or delicately, but that had never been my style. Obviously, I'd need to do a little more convincing, but if he thought his surly attitude would scare me off, he had the wrong woman. A Callahan never backed down once she'd made up her mind, at least not without a damn good reason.

So, rather than going back to Houston as he might expect, after I'd cleaned up the remains of lunch, I headed into Sandy Creek to start asking around and get all the dirt I could on the new owner of the Callahan ranch. I still had plenty of ideas about how to proceed but I needed to focus my plans on the strategies most likely to bring me success. I needed to know more about what made Jesse tick.

My first stop, naturally, had to be the hair salon. The town's epicentre of gossip, it also had the advantage of being co-owned by my best friend from high school, Mary-Beth Parker. Our lives had taken different directions after graduation, since she never took a step outside Sandy Creek, married her high school sweetheart and now had four young kids, but whenever we got together, it felt like nothing had changed. Mary-Beth knew everyone in Sandy Creek and all the latest news, thanks to the steady stream of clients in her chair. If anyone could tell me how to win over Jesse Greenbank, or take him down if that worked better, it would be her.

"Laura Callahan!" Mary-Beth called out my name as soon as I walked in the door, making every head in the place turn my way. "I thought you'd forgotten all about us."

Although she said it in a teasing tone, she had reason to complain. I hadn't been to town for way too long, obviously. That helped to explain how everything got so out of hand in the first place.

"I can take you next," she announced, making the other women waiting their turn groan. Mary-Beth didn't do appointments; she said chatting with the other customers while they waited sat at the heart of the whole salon experience, so she'd make them wait. The fact that everyone did was a testament to her talent with a pair of scissors.

A few minutes later, I sat in her chair, watching in the mirror as she looked over my hair. Her own cut looked as stylish as always, her hair dyed blonde, her figure still remarkably slim after her near-constant pregnancies over the past few years. In the six years since we'd graduated, I got my Master's, but she'd created four human beings, ran her business and stayed head-over-heels in love with the man she'd been dating since they were both fifteen. I had no idea how she did it.

"I didn't expect to see you back here anytime soon," she admitted once she'd decided what to do to my hair that day. I didn't tell her I'd just had it cut two weeks earlier in Houston. "With the ranch selling, I figured Sandy Creek had seen the last of the Callahans."

"How long have you known about the ranch?" She said it so casually that it couldn't have been recent news, and I couldn't believe she wouldn't have told me. She knew how much it had always meant to me. We used to sit on the fence together and dream about our futures, her with Wayne, the boy she eventually married, and me with a yet-to-be-discovered cowboy who would help me run the ranch and raise our family.

Her life had followed that blueprint pretty precisely, but mine had taken a small detour. However, with school finished, I was ready to get it back on track. Maybe not the cowboy part, but at least the ranch.

"I found out a couple of weeks ago. Kyle down at the bank told me that Jesse went in to apply for a loan." Mary-Beth caught sight of my reaction in the mirror and frowned. "Why are you looking like you swallowed a lemon?"

"I only found out yesterday. Daddy didn't tell any of us until the paperwork had all been signed."

She let out a low whistle. "He's a brave man, keeping you all out of the loop. I assumed you knew, Laura. I would have told you otherwise."

"I know you would have." I couldn't blame Mary-Beth. My father bore the blame for it and no one else, other than perhaps Jesse himself. "I can't believe he did it though. He knew how much it meant to me. He knew I wanted to take it over."

"Did you, though?" Mary-Beth's question sounded curious rather than accusatory. "We ain't hardly seen you here for years. Everyone assumed you got swept up in city life. That's what always happens. People say they'll come back and they never do."

"Not me. I only went there in the first place to learn how to run the ranch better. Studying kept me there, but if anyone had told me the ranch had any kind of trouble, I'd've been back here in a second."

"Alright, alright, you're not on trial here."

I hadn't realized how forcefully I'd spoken until she laughed about it, and I took a deep breath, trying to calm myself. "Sorry. It just feels like everyone's assuming they know what I want and what's best for me. Maybe I didn't make a big deal each and every day about how much taking over the ranch meant to me, but I didn't think I had to. I thought everyone knew."

"Sounds like you and your daddy need to communicate better," she surmised, which pretty much mirrored what Jesse had said.

As soon as he crossed my mind again, I got back to the reason I had come to see her in the first place. "How well do you know Jesse? Who are his friends? Is he seeing anyone?"

There had been no ring on his finger, I'd happened to notice, but that didn't mean much. He could have just taken it off for work. After all, he'd just had his hands inside a cow that morning.

Mary-Beth shrugged as she cut the ends of my hair. "I know him about as well as most folks around here, which is to say not very well at all. He stays out on the ranch most of the time, keeps himself to himself."

"Antisocial?" That might explain his brusque dismissal earlier, but Mary-Beth disagreed.

"I wouldn't say that. He can be charming when he needs to be and he's always polite and friendly. Just doesn't seem to get too close to people. Wayne doesn't ever see him over at the bar."

Sandy Creek had exactly one bar, so if the town's residents were going to socialize, that would be the only option most nights. Mary-Beth's husband had been frequenting it since long before he turned 21.

"And Jesse's single?" I pressed, wanting as much information as I could get.

"Free as a bird," she confirmed before giving me a knowing smile in the mirror. "Are you interested?"

"No!" Nothing could be further from my mind. "I'm just wondering what kind of man he is, that's all. I can't believe Daddy sold the ranch to a stranger."

Mary-Beth shrugged again, less concerned about the sale than about Jesse's love life. "It's a good thing you're not hoping to start something there because no one's had any luck. I don't know if you've seen him yet, but the man is *fine*. All the ladies in town made excuses to go and welcome him when he first arrived, but he didn't bite. Like I said, very polite, no one could fault him, but didn't take any hints that got dropped, and even when people like Suzanne Stempfle asked him out point-blank, he let her down gently. Consensus around town right now is that he might be gay, but no one's ever seen him with a man either."

So much for flirting my way into his good graces. Good thing I hadn't been relying on that. "What about the people who work with him on the ranch? What do they think of him?"

"Everyone says he's a hard worker and expects a lot, but he's fair too. Never heard anyone say a bad word about him, to be honest."

I sighed in frustration. None of that helped me. I wanted to be told he was a con man, a charlatan, someone who didn't deserve anything good, not a decent, friendly guy who didn't cause anyone any trouble.

"In fact, there's at least five guys I know that have applied for his new job posting," Mary-Beth continued. "People who want to move off other ranches to work with him. That's the best sign he's doing something right."

"Job posting?" My ears perked up with that piece of news. "What job?"

"A full-time, live-in ranch hand to help run the place. Apparently, he's got some big plans and wants some extra help."

That might be the break I'd been waiting for. "Where did he make this posting?"

She named the town's local online marketplace, and I filed it away in the back of my head before asking about Wayne and her kids and catching up on her life. By the time she finished, my hair had lost a few inches but I'd gained a new plan for exactly how to get a new conversation going with Jesse Greenbank.

~Jesse~

By the late afternoon, nearly all my muscles ached but we'd made some good progress on the fence. Tyson commented that I seemed to have some extra aggression to work out that day as I threw myself into the work and he wasn't wrong; every time I thought back to my conversation with Laura Callahan, my adrenaline would spike all over again. She knew absolutely nothing about me but had no problem blaming me for not getting her way.

What did she even want the ranch for? Her dad never told me what she studied at college, but someone who spent years with her nose buried in books up in the city couldn't understand the primal call of the land the way she claimed to. If she could, she wouldn't have been able to stay away.

Her comments about me stealing her birthright got under my skin in a way she probably hadn't meant them to, and in a way that Tyson wouldn't understand either, so when he asked me where my energy came from, I laughed it off. I had no intention of telling him about Laura or what she'd said, and definitely not why it bothered me so much. I'd never been the kind of guy who talked about his past, or his feelings for that matter, and I didn't plan to start.

When I got back to the house after saying goodbye to the hired hands, I found myself opening the door almost tentatively, as if Laura might still be there, asserting squatter's rights over the house or some other kind of bullshit. A quick look around reassured me she'd gone, and although I sighed in relief, I almost felt a small twinge of disappointment too. How strange. I told myself it must be because I wouldn't have a chance to put her in her place properly. She might not be a woman I'd be likely to forget in a hurry, but in the long run, it would be far easier that she'd gone without a fight.

After throwing one of my frozen dinners into the oven, I went to take off my shirt, the new one I'd put on at lunch, now sweat-stained after the day's work, and I grabbed my laptop to take back to the kitchen with me. Unlike just about everyone else on the planet, I didn't have a phone permanently attached to me. I liked being able to control when and how people could reach me, not to mention that I didn't have that many people looking for me anyway. That night, I simply wanted to see if I had any new applicants for the job posting I'd put up.

I already had a few applicants who would be perfect for general work around the ranch, hard workers with plenty of experience, but when I advertised the new position, I really wanted someone who could take on the role I had been playing before I became the owner. I needed a second-in-command, someone I could trust to handle things if I got sick or needed to go away on business, and someone I could bounce ideas off of and plan strategy with. Someone actually interested in running the place with me, not just working there, and so far, I hadn't found the right fit.

One new application sat in my inbox, and I opened the resume first before looking at the accompanying cover letter. The guy didn't have a lot of practical experience besides growing up on a ranch himself; no paid employment in the industry, but his Master's degree in agriculture caught my eye. That suggested someone who cared about the planning and long-term side of things, not just the day-to-day work. Even without the hands-on experience, at least he'd have an idea of what kind of work went on if he'd grown up around it.

That actually looked pretty promising.

Flipping back to the cover letter, I read through it carefully. Polite and professional, it set just the right tone as he explained the focus of his studies and what kind of ideas he'd like to talk to me about. The whole thing almost sounded too good to be true. The only thing I could fault was that he hadn't included his name; both the letter and the resume itself were simply signed L.M. The email address didn't give me any further clues either: l.m.sandycreek@gmail.com

The letter also said he would be in town that night but would be leaving in the morning to look for work elsewhere. He'd be happy to speak to me over the phone anytime, but if I wanted to talk to him in person, it would have to be that evening.

Truth be told, I would much prefer to meet him in person. Talking over the phone had never been comfortable for me and it didn't give a full sense of the person anyway. I needed to look a man in the eye to know if we were going to get along.

I sent a quick email back. *Thanks for your application. I'm available to discuss the job in more detail tonight if you'd like to come to the ranch. Let me know if you need directions.*

Jesse

The reply came back so quickly, I had to guess he *did* keep his phone close to hand.

I know where it is. I can be there in an hour if that works for you.

L.

He still didn't want to give me his name, apparently. It seemed a little silly since he'd have to share it once he arrived, but I didn't make a big deal of it.

Sounds good. The doorbell isn't working right now, just knock when you get here.

With that taken care of, I put the computer away and sat down with my dinner. Nothing about it differed from the dinners I ate just about every other night of the week, but after my fresh-cooked lunch, it tasted a little less appealing than usual. No sign of that lunch remained in the kitchen; Laura must have cleaned it all up before she left. If it weren't for the very real feelings our meeting still stirred up, I might have thought I imagined it all.

When I'd finished eating, I quickly washed my dishes and went to throw a load of laundry in. Working on the ranch could be a messy business so I had to keep on top of it. With that done and nothing else that needed any urgent attention, I sat down in the living room with a book to wait for my interviewee to arrive.

When it came, the knock on the door sounded firm and confident; another good sign. Placing my book down on the end table, I made my way to the door, but when I opened it, the face on the other side took me by surprise.

"Laura Callahan."

Somehow, she looked even better than I remembered her. Not that I'd been thinking about her, I quickly reminded myself. If anything, the fact that I thought she looked better now just showed how little attention I'd paid to her in the first place. She'd changed back into her own shirt, I noticed, and held the one I'd given her in her arms, neatly folded. Maybe that explained why she'd turned up on my front step again?

She gave me a confident smile that felt entirely out of place considering how our first conversation had ended. "Nice to see you again, Mr Greenbank."

If she honestly meant that, she must have taken away a completely different memory than I did of our lunch together. "I'm actually expecting someone any minute, but thank you for bringing my shirt back." I took it from her arms even though she hadn't offered it to me yet, and moved forward just a touch to block the doorway with my body, just in case she tried to push her way in. I wouldn't put it past her. In retrospect, it actually surprised me that she'd knocked.

"You're waiting for the applicant for your job." She stated it like a well-known fact, making my brow furrow in confusion.

"How do you know about that?"

She held out her hand to shake mine. "Because I'm L.M. L is for Laura, M for Montgomery, my mother's maiden name."

I stared at her outstretched hand in disbelief. She had to be kidding. "If this is some kind of joke, I really don't have time for it. Why on earth would you think I'd want to hire you?"

Saying I didn't have time might have been a stretch. I had no other plans for the night, but she didn't need to know that.

"I don't think you're going to hire me," she countered, which came as a relief, at least until she continued her thought. "I *know* you are. Now, invite me in so I can tell you why."

Chapter Three

~Laura~

The way Jesse's mouth dropped open when he realized he'd actually invited me there for an interview made it really difficult to keep from smiling. I managed it, though, maintaining the professional air of detachment I'd been working on all afternoon.

Mary-Beth had let me use her house after my haircut while her kids were still at school or with their grandparents, so I had time to wash my shirt and put together a resume to send to Jesse for the job posting. I also reviewed the conversation Jesse and I had in my head several times along with what Mary-Beth had told me about him, and I put together an entirely new approach, something I hadn't considered before. It would be a shift in my thinking, but I had to accept that circumstances had changed, so I would need to adapt. I could be flexible when it mattered.

Mary-Beth invited me to stay for dinner with the whole family once she and Wayne got home from work, and to stay there overnight so I didn't have to make the drive back to Houston that night. Wrapping my arms around her, I gave her a big hug in thanks for letting me crash into her life at such short-notice.

"You always have been and always will be welcome," she promised me. "I feel sorry for Jesse, though. He's got no idea what's coming his way."

That didn't quite sound like a compliment. "I'm not *that* bad."

"You're not that good either." She gave me a wink as I headed out the door. "Good luck!"

It looked like I would need it as he stood gaping at me after I told him to invite me in, and I raised my eyebrows impatiently. "Are you planning on doing the whole interview out here on the porch?"

"Interview?" he repeated in confusion before shaking his head. "Look, Ms Callahan..."

"Laura." If we were going to be working together, we needn't stand on ceremony. "And yes: my interview. You invited me here to talk about the job. You also said you've got other things to do tonight and I don't intend on keeping you longer than necessary, so let's stop wasting time and get down to business."

Still looking more bewildered than anything else, he stared at me a moment longer, but I held his gaze calmly until he finally stepped aside. "Alright. Come in and let's get this over with."

Just what every woman wanted to hear. Brushing his rudeness off, I walked past him and kicked my shoes off as I'd done in that hall thousands of times before. "Kitchen or living room?"

When I turned back to him, his expression had turned almost bemused, as though he'd made a conscious decision to simply let this happen and enjoy the ride. "The living room, I suppose."

A worn copy of an old Zane Grey western on the side table caught my eye as I led the way into the room. I hadn't really pegged him as the reading type. Aside from the table, TV and sofas, all of which my parents had left behind, the room looked almost barren. Combined with what I'd seen in his bedroom and the kitchen, he didn't seem to have very many personal belongings at all.

"Did you do something different with your hair?" he asked as we both took a seat, me perched on the edge of the armchair to keep a professional posture while he leaned back, one arm slung over the back of the sofa.

Maybe he really was gay. I'd had boyfriends who saw me every day and never would have noticed such a small change in my appearance. In any case, the question gave me the perfect opportunity to bring up one of the points in my favour as a candidate for his job. "Yes, I stopped in at the Main Street salon this afternoon. I know the owners. I know most people in Sandy Creek. If you want someone with local connections, you'll be hard pressed to find someone better suited than a Callahan."

For the first time, he almost smiled. "You really came prepared to give me the hard sell, didn't you?"

"I understand why you might be hesitant or doubt my motives, but I promise you, Mr Greenbank, all I want to do is make this ranch the best it can be. That's what I've always wanted. That's why I went to Houston and studied for *six years* on the best way to do that."

He leaned forward, almost as if he couldn't help it. "You really got your Master's in Agriculture?"

"Are you suggesting I would lie on my resume?" I couldn't help asking, and his lips pressed together again, almost as if he were trying not to smile.

"I didn't say that."

"But you implied it."

"I thought I was the one asking the questions here, Laura." The way his lips curled around my name distracted me for just a moment. If I ignored the fact that he stole my ranch and the fact that he probably preferred the company of men, I could see why the single women of Sandy Creek would have been falling over themselves when he moved to town. "What made you want to get your Master's?"

I hated repeating myself. "I already said: I wanted to run this ranch the best I could. This would go faster if you pay attention to me."

"It's hard not to." That time, he couldn't hold the smile back. "Let me ask it a different way, then: why did you go to college rather than just staying here and learning on the job?"

That, at least, was a reasonable question. "I wanted to stay, but my daddy thought I should go and learn about all the latest advancements and theories about the best way to do things. He never studied, he just took over from his daddy, same as his daddy did, and he thought we could use some fresh ideas."

Jesse frowned as I finished my explanation, the smile having vanished from both his lips and his eyes. "If you did what he suggested, why did he want to sell?"

"If you figure out the answer to that, please let me know." I gave him a grim smile of my own. "I suppose it had to do with his heart attack and me extending my studying for an extra two years. He seems to think circumstances changed, but he never talked to me about it. He did, however, mention the debt."

Jesse's eyes quickly scanned the room, as if we might be overheard though there wasn't another soul around. "I'd appreciate if people didn't know about that. People hear a place is struggling and they start getting funny about wanting to do business with you. It becomes a downward spiral."

He made a valid point. Not all people would behave that way, but some would, not wanting to climb onboard a ship that was going down. "I haven't said a word, and I won't. Just how bad is the debt?"

His eyebrows raised in disapproval. "You really don't know? You came down here wanting to buy the place from me without even knowing what you'd be taking on?"

He really seemed determined to make me feel naive, and I knew I hadn't done myself any favours over lunch that day. Rather than responding sharply, though, I took a breath before answering. "I know the ranch can make money. I know how I can make it better. The debt doesn't matter because it can be overcome. Any bank that listened to my business plan would agree and lend me the money."

"Is that so?" A flicker of amusement returned to his eyes. "Well, let's hear it, then. What's your plan?"

"I'm not going to give you my whole plan so you can go ahead and implement it without me. You can hire me first, and then I'll tell you."

Jesse's eyebrows shot up again. "And I'm just supposed to take you on your word that you have this amazing plan in the first place?"

"Yes, because a Callahan never goes back on their word. You ask anyone in town and they'll tell you the same." He'd lived there for a year, he had to know that.

"Seems like your daddy went back on his word to you."

His words knocked the air out of me for a moment, and I let out an involuntary gasp as I struggled to get it back.

Jesse's expression immediately softened. "Shit. I shouldn't have said that, I'm sorry."

He shouldn't have, but I couldn't deny the truth of it either, so I pushed down my indignation to get to the point I'd come there to make. "I'm going to make you an offer, Mr Greenbank."

He grimaced as I used his full name again. "If I'm calling you Laura, you can call me Jesse. And can I remind you that I'm the one making the offers here? You're the one applying for *my* job."

I ignored that. "Here's the deal: you hire me on a one-year contract and you show me the projections you've made for the year. I assume you have some. Afterwards, I'll show you my plans, and if we agree to implement them *and* the ranch outperforms what you were projecting over the course of the year, you agree to sell 50% of the ranch to me. I'll pay you the fair market value."

Jesse sat in silence for a moment as he reviewed it all in his head. "And if we don't improve on my projections?"

I spread my hands in resignation. "Then I leave you in peace, never to bother you again."

One corner of his mouth began to curl upwards. "And you're not worried that I'd try to sabotage your plans?"

"You'd be sabotaging your own success. If you care about this ranch as you claim to, you'll follow them to the letter."

Both sides of his mouth twitched. "And you'd be happy to share ownership with me?"

"It's not what I'd always envisioned," I admitted. "But I understand that things have changed. From a practical standpoint, the ranch is big enough for two families. We could build another house just down the drive, one for me and my family, one for you and yours. We'd be neighbours and colleagues, which is a good deal for you. I'm a delightful neighbour."

He laughed out loud before he could stop himself. "I'll reserve judgement on that last point for now. And where are you planning on living during this one-year trial?"

I looked around the room we were in and its sparse furnishings. "The job posting is for a live-in hand, isn't it? Where was the accommodation going to be?"

A grimace preceded his words. "In the house with me, but I expected to hire a man, I have to be honest."

He said that as if women were a completely foreign species. Mary-Beth's gay theory looked more likely all the time. "Would it make you uncomfortable to have me here?"

"No. It's just... it used to be your house. Wouldn't it be strange for you?"

That was almost thoughtful of him, but unnecessary. "I don't see why it would have to be. You can move into the master bedroom and I can take my old room."

He leaned back again, exhaling like he'd just done something particularly difficult. "I assume you've got this proposal of yours in writing?"

"Of course. I can email it to you right now." I pulled my phone out of my pocket to demonstrate my willingness.

Once again, his lips twitched. "Alright. Send it to me and I'll have a look. Your email earlier said you'd be leaving town tomorrow. Is that true?"

I nodded. "One thing you'll need to learn about me is I always tell the truth, for better or worse. I'm heading back to Houston first thing. I have to pack up my dorm room, but I can be back tomorrow evening, ready to start work first thing the next day."

"Let's see what your plan looks like first." He shook his head, like he couldn't quite believe the words coming out of his mouth. "Does anyone ever say no to you, Laura?"

"They can try." I gave him a smug smile that made him laugh again.

"You won't regret giving this a chance, Jesse."

"I'm not at all convinced about that, but I'll take a look at it, like I said. Have a safe trip, and I'll let you know when I've made a decision."

With that, we shook hands and I went back to my truck, sending him my proposal as soon as I sat down inside. Tucking my phone back in my pocket, I headed for Mary-Beth's and perhaps the last night I would spend away from the ranch for a long time to come.

~Jesse~

What in the world had I gotten myself into? Sitting on the sofa with my laptop, reading over Laura's proposal, I found myself simultaneously impressed with her nerve and taken aback by her audacity.

At first glance, I had no reason to agree to her offer. I already owned the ranch in full, so why would I want to give half of it away? My own plans were strong and I honestly couldn't see how hers could be that much better.

But therein lay the appeal: she only got her 50% if we did better than my projections, which she hadn't even seen yet. My projections were realistic, but on the optimistic side. They assumed good weather, good health among the cattle, and no major unexpected costs or setbacks. She might have some good ideas, and that was the whole reason I'd advertised the job in the first place, but I still didn't think they would make *that* much of a difference in just one year. The risk to me seemed relatively low, especially considering I would gain a hard worker and a smart, strategic thinker with a local name and connections.

She'd already proven she wasn't afraid to push the boundaries to achieve her goals.

People would see the presence of a Callahan on the ranch as a good sign, a symbol of continuity and an endorsement from a family that the whole area knew and liked. Those things went a long way in a small town. And as she'd already pointed out herself, I wouldn't have to worry about her sabotaging my efforts, not when the whole success of her plan hinged on the ranch doing well.

Closing the laptop, I set it down on the couch next to me and took a deep breath, looking around the rather spartan living room. The Callahans had left their furniture here, telling me they had no use for it in Houston, but they'd taken everything personal and decorative with them. It worked fine for me, just like the frozen dinners did, but I had a feeling Laura was used to things being a little different. Aside from the whole question of working together, could we really live together for a whole year?

For almost as long as I could remember, I'd made it my goal not to get too close to people. People couldn't hurt you as much if you didn't let them in. You wouldn't feel their loss as much if they had never been a big part of your life in the first place. Some people might consider it lonely, but I'd never had a problem with my own company. My problems had always come from other people.

Men like me and Tyson were friendly on the job but wouldn't expect any kind of socializing afterwards. That was the kind of person I'd imagined as my live-in hand, someone who would take care of themself once the working day was done without expecting anything more of me.

What would Laura expect? Would she want to have dinner together? Watch TV together? Talk? Or would she be happy to go out and spend her evenings with her friends in Sandy Creek? It seemed like she already had a lot of them, and the thought sent an unexpected and completely unreasonable spike of jealousy through me.

I would have to set some ground rules if we went ahead with this, and God help me, I was actually considering it. A good night's sleep would be needed before I made up my mind, so I headed for my bed at nine o'clock, as usual, ready for my four a.m. alarm.

Half-formed dreams filled my head all night, images of a curvy, sexy body wearing my shirt, dark hair tangled in my hands, and a plate filled with sausages. I woke up both utterly confused and sporting a significant erection.

By the time I got dressed and ready for the day, I'd made up my mind and sent Laura a quick email before heading out to the fields.

I'll accept your offer on two conditions:

1. *The details of the contract remain between us, including the ranch's financial situation and the possibility of shared owner-ship.*

2. *We agree on a set of rules for our shared accommodation.*

I'll be finished work around dinner time today so if you're back in town, you can come over to review the paperwork.

Jesse

~Laura~

I was already awake when Jesse's email came in, partly in anticipation for what the day might bring, and partly because Mary-Beth's pull-out couch was not the comfiest bed I'd ever had. As soon as I skimmed the short note, I knew I wouldn't be going back to sleep.

His first condition sounded perfectly reasonable to me. There should be no question of outside factors interfering in our wager, so keeping quiet about the details of it seemed fair to me.

The second condition struck me as a little stranger. What kind of rules did he have in mind? How difficult would he be to live with?

Whatever his rules might be, he said we could agree on them, not that he would impose anything on me, so I would simply have to wait and see what they were. Otherwise, I considered his message a complete victory, and I couldn't wait to get started on a new phase of my life, bringing me closer to where I'd always imagined being. Leaving a message of thanks for Mary-Beth, I headed out the door and back to Houston before the sun came up.

The college campus that had been my home for the last six years already felt foreign to me as I packed up the last of my belongings. I'd shared one of the apartments for Masters' students with another woman, so living with someone else didn't worry me in the least. As I told Jesse, I was a delight to live with, happy to cook and clean and do my share. He had nothing to worry about.

With my truck full of boxes, I headed over to my parents' house. We hadn't spoken again after my daddy's announcement at my celebration dinner, but I wanted to deliver my latest news to them in person.

"You're not going to yell at him, are you?" my mom asked me warily as I walked in to find them both having breakfast at the kitchen table.

"You're only asking that because I have every reason to," I pointed out. "But no, I'm not here to yell. I just wanted to let you know that I have a job offer. I'm hoping to start tomorrow."

My dad's face lit up with that news and my mom told me to sit down while she grabbed me a plate of eggs and fruit.

"Is it here in Houston?" my dad asked curiously.

"No, but you don't have to worry about the family dinners. I'll still make time to come up for them."

My family had a barbecue every other week at my parent's house. It had become tradition since they moved to Houston, and although it would be a lengthy drive to and from Sandy Creek just for dinner, I had no plans to miss it. My family meant the world to me so I would make the time.

"Where is it, then?" my mom asked from the counter. "Don't keep us in suspense, Laura."

I had no intention of it. I couldn't wait to see their reaction when I told them. "It's in Sandy Creek."

They both froze in surprise, my mom part way through chopping up an apple, my dad with his fork halfway to his mouth. "Why would you take a job there?" he asked in confusion.

"Because it's my home and because it's where I've always wanted to live. Is that really so hard for you to understand?"

He blinked a few times, still looking uncertain. "What's the job?"

"Assistant manager on Jesse Greenbank's ranch."

The knife in my mom's hand skittered across the counter as it fell from her grip. "This must be a joke."

That wasn't quite the reaction I'd been hoping for. "Why 'must' it be? I want to run the ranch. I always have. Just because you sold it from under me doesn't mean that dream has changed. Jesse took a little bit of time to warm up to the idea, but he's coming around."

"A little bit of time?" my dad repeated. "What time? You only found out about him 36 hours ago."

"It might seem fast but I've had six years to prepare for this. I'm meeting with him later today to sign everything, but I wanted to let you know so you don't hear it from someone else. You know how news travels."

"Are you sure about this?" My mom set my plate down in front of me, taking my dad's hand as she sat next to him. "You're not doing this just to make a point?"

They still didn't get it. "I'm a grown woman. I'm not going to take a job just to spite you. I'm beginning to think you really don't believe that I know my own mind at all."

"It's not that, Laura," my dad tried to assure me. "I know you could do a good job at it. I just didn't want you to have to give up your whole life to it. The world is a lot bigger than Sandy Creek and you could do anything you want. With your degree and your personality, companies all over the city would be lining up to hire you."

"I don't want to work for a company in the city. I want *this*, Daddy. I always have."

I held his gaze firmly, neither of us willing to look away, and finally, he blinked first. "Well, if it's really what you want, I hope it works out. Greenbank's a brave man to take you on."

"Daddy!" Why did people keep saying it like that? First Mary-Beth, now my parents.

He shrugged unapologetically. "I mean it. He's a reserved kind of fella who's just invited a hurricane into his life. I hope he's ready for it."

"I haven't met him myself," my mom admitted. "Though now I'm wishing I had. He's a brave man, knowing the situation."

After finishing breakfast, I dropped by Tonia and Cam's house to tell them about my plans, made a phone call to Billie who was at work at her summer job, and stopped in at the hospital to see Dex and Shawna. Shawna smiled at me from her hospital bed when I told them my plans.

"You've got to do what makes you happy, Laura. Enjoy it all, even the tough parts."

I knew it would be tough, but I also knew it was exactly where I wanted to be. Finally, I was heading home.

Chapter Four

~Jesse~

"I'm starting to think buying the ranch is going to your head," Tyson commented as we finished putting away all the materials for the fence. We'd made good progress on it that day and should be finished in three or four more days, a little ahead of schedule.

"What are you talking about?" I could tell he was teasing me, but I missed the joke.

"Usually, you've got just one mood, but yesterday, you were in a funk all day. Now today, I keep expecting to see rainbows flying out of your ass, you're looking so pleased with yourself."

"Rainbows? Really?" I shook my head at his crass turn of phrase. "Ain't I allowed to be in a good mood?"

"Sure, if there's a reason for it. Can I guess it had something to do with that pretty pair of legs I saw leaving your house last night?"

Damn it. He must have been outside when Laura left and caught sight of her. Luckily, I knew just how to shut down this line of speculation. "I think you might need glasses, Ty. That was Laura Callahan."

His eyes bugged out in surprise. "Shit, seriously? I was too far away to get a good look at her. What was she doing here?"

Since he'd been at the ranch longer than I had, I guessed he had probably met Laura before, and it looked like I was right.

"Don't tell Jim I said that, alright?" He looked genuinely nervous, but personally, I would be more afraid of Laura overhearing it.

"I won't say a word," I promised. "She came to discuss business. I can't say too much more yet, but she'll be back again tonight. Just letting you know now so you don't get any more ideas."

Curiosity was written all over his face, but he knew me well enough to know if I wanted him to know something, I'd tell him. "Well, shoot. I thought you'd actually gotten some action last night. A man's got to have some distraction every now and then."

Tyson had a 'friends with benefits' situation with a woman in town for his own 'distraction'. He had no interest in being in a relationship and she seemed to accept that, but everyone thought of them as a couple anyway. He had tried many times to get me to go into town with them for a drink at the bar, but I always found an excuse not to. Though I wasn't celibate, he seemed to think I was simply because he never saw me with anyone.

"My love life is even less of your business than my business is," I said, laughing it off. "I'll see you tomorrow."

We said good night and he headed down the road to his own house while I walked back over to the main house, which I still didn't quite think of as mine yet. Even though I'd already claimed the land, the house was a different matter. It couldn't be more obviously a family home. Two storeys high with a wrap-around porch, there were five bedrooms inside, one for the previous owners and each of their kids. I didn't know if that was intentional or simply a lucky coincidence. Three of the bedrooms were on the upper floor, along with the large family bathroom and a living room, but I never went up there. The master suite and the guest suite, which each had their own bathroom and shower, were on the main floor, along with the kitchen, a smaller living room and another bathroom. It seemed like a lot of bathrooms, but the house was usually left open for the hands to use when they needed it.

Laura had suggested I could move into the master suite and she'd take the room I'd been using, but that seemed unnecessary to me. My current arrangement suited me perfectly fine. In fact, if she actually did end up getting part ownership of the ranch, she could have this house and I'd build myself a new, smaller one. She talked about us both having families but that wasn't in the cards for me. I only needed room for myself.

After changing into clean clothes and throwing the ones from that day in the wash, I had just sat down with my reheated dinner when Laura's knock echoed through the house. It had to be her; no one else could make a knock sound that impatient.

"Did I interrupt your dinner?" Those were the first words out of her mouth as I answered the door. She had her hair pulled back into a ponytail and wore a soft t-shirt with a scooped neck and a fitted pair of jeans. She looked fresh and down-to-earth and ridiculously good. Tyson hadn't been kidding about her legs.

"Uh, yeah, but it's alright," I managed to say, trying to pull my mind out of the gutter. It really had been too long since I'd had a night away, apparently. "Come on in."

She let me go first that time, following me back to the kitchen where my dinner sat on the table, still in the container I'd cooked it in. Laura's lips pursed as she caught sight of it, but she didn't say anything. Instead, she took a seat and pulled out a folder full of printed documents as I sat back down and shovelled another forkful into my mouth.

"What's all that?"

When she looked up, a smile pulled at the corners of her mouth. "I've got everything here to show you my plan, once we get the contract signed. And you've got some gravy on your chin."

Fuck. I quickly wiped it away with my hand and then realized I probably should have used a napkin or something. I didn't usually have to worry about that kind of thing, which brought me back to what I wanted to talk about before we got onto the contract.

"You said you accepted my conditions, so I guess the first thing we need to do is settle on the house rules."

She crossed her arms on the table, leaning forward. "I'm all ears."

I didn't have it all written down like she seemed to, but I knew the basic points I wanted to agree on. "Even though we'll be sharing the house, we each stay responsible for ourselves. Cooking, laundry, cleaning, everything like that, I'll do my own and you can take care of yours."

"Fair enough," she agreed, her lips twitching again as I took another bite of my food. "We wouldn't want any of my panties ending up in your laundry."

My throat closed around the food I'd just swallowed, making me cough, which only made her laugh. Was she actually trying to kill me? The last thing I needed to be thinking about was her underwear.

"What else?" she asked, her eyes sparkling with amusement as I tried to regain some control over the situation.

"You can take the master bedroom, or even the whole of the upstairs if you prefer. That might be better."

"Is the idea of running into me really that intolerable?" She said it as a joke, but I could see the curiosity in her eyes.

It might just be intolerable, but not in the way she meant it. "I'm just trying to make you comfortable. You don't actually know anything about me. I thought some distance might be a good thing."

"I didn't know anything about my college roommate either and I had to live in a lot closer quarters with her." She shrugged as if it really wouldn't be a big deal. "I'm sure we'll figure it out, and the downstairs room is fine with me. You're sure you don't want to trade?"

"I'm sure." I tried to remember the rest of the conditions I'd come up with, but she wasn't making it easy. "If you want to have people over, that's fine, just let me know and I'll make myself scarce."

"Or you could just join us," she suggested, an eyebrow raised. "Do you expect me to leave if you have guests?"

"I don't. I won't."

Her expression shifted to something closer to confusion. "What, never?"

"Never." I didn't want to get into the reasons why. We were almost at the end of my list. "If you plan to have anyone stay overnight, I'd appreciate if you could let me know in advance, though I understand it might not always be possible."

"I could always leave a sock on the doorknob," she suggested, teasing me again. "And you'll give me the same courtesy, I suppose?"

"You don't have to worry about that. I live a pretty simple life here, Laura, but it's my life and I'm happy with it. So, when we're not working, you can live your life and I'll live mine. If you can agree to that, then we'll have a look at the contract."

~Laura~

The picture Jesse painted of himself confused me. As Mary-Beth had pointed out, nothing about him suggested a man who was ill at ease around other people. Charming, well-spoken, well-mannered and, to be fair, very good-looking; on the surface, he appeared to be the kind of guy people usually flocked to. His social isolation seemed to be entirely self-inflicted, and I couldn't figure out why.

He told me he wouldn't have people over, not socially and not sexually either. He stated it with such certainty that I had to believe he meant it, but why he should be so certain, I could only guess. Assuming he *was* gay, which I had pretty much accepted must be true, maybe he thought his sexual orientation would have a negative impact on people's perception of him, so he kept it hidden?

That made me rather sad. Texas might not be the most forward-thinking place on the planet, but even in Sandy Creek, most people would accept it. There would be talk for a little while, sure, but people would get used to it. More scandalous things went on all the time than one handsome rancher preferring the company of men.

Maybe I could help him to see that. He said we'd live our own lives, but surely, living in the same space, we'd get to know each other pretty well anyway. He couldn't expect to never talk to me. I'd give him space, if he wanted it, but hopefully, he'd soon learn that he didn't have to hide who he was from me.

"That all sounds reasonable to me," I agreed. "Though I assume if I occasionally cook too much, you won't be offended if I offer you some?"

"You don't need to cook for me, Laura," he replied quickly. "I don't expect you to. I don't subscribe to any kind of traditional male/female domestic roles."

Of course he didn't, but that wasn't what I meant anyway. "I like to cook. My momma taught me, right here in this kitchen, but cooking for one isn't a lot of fun. I promise it won't come with any obligations to sit and talk with me if you don't want to. You could use some vegetables though."

He glanced down at his frozen dinner with a touch of embarrassment. "There are peas in here." I simply raised my eyebrows at him and he sighed. "Fine. I won't be offended if you want to cook something extra for me. Occasionally."

I could live with that. "Alright, then. Let's see the contract."

We spent the next half-hour reviewing the contract and the amendments I'd made to include my proposal into it. When we'd agreed that everything looked satisfactory to both of us, we both signed the document, making it official. For the next year, Jesse Greenbank would be my boss and this ranch would be my home again. Hopefully, it would be just the beginning.

With that settled, he went to his room and brought back his financial projections for the next year. He'd put it together when he applied for the loans to buy the place, he explained, and I had to admit he'd done a good job. The plans were well explained and well supported, and optimistic while still being achievable. He even included a few of the improvements I had in my plan too.

His eyes held a hint of smugness as he leaned back in his chair once we'd finished going over it. "With your help, I'm sure we can do all of that, but I'm not sure how much we can improve on it."

I'd been counting on that fact. "Well, let me show you what I've got."

Jesse listened carefully, asking a lot of good questions as I ran through my ideas for diversifying the land use and partnering with neighbouring ranches to cut down on equipment costs. Some of it duplicated what he'd planned, but a lot of it was new, and I could tell he was impressed. And I still hadn't got to the best part yet.

"Labour is a key expense, but you've got to pay people well if you want them to feel valued and be invested in the success of the ranch. My daddy always paid well, and I can see from your numbers that you take it seriously too."

He nodded firmly. "I won't skimp on that, Laura. It's a hard job and when you find the right people, you need to treat them right."

"I completely agree. But what if you could get some additional labour for the more routine parts of the work, at a negative expense, freeing up your experienced hands to do the jobs they're best suited for?"

His brow furrowed in suspicion. "Negative expense? How? What do you mean?"

This was the part I was really excited about. "We open the ranch up for working holidays. People pay *us* to come and work here."

"No." His response was instant as he shook his head emphatically, not even considering the idea. "No way. This ain't some kind of cushy retreat. It's a working ranch."

"Of course it is." I'd anticipated a bit of resistance given his earlier stipulations about not spending time around other people, but I'd done all the research and all the math. It made complete sense. "That's *why* people will come. They don't want to be babied, they want something authentic. They want to go away feeling like they achieved something."

"They'd have to be babied, whether they want it or not. They'd have to be watched at all times. We can't have totally green folks running wild. Someone loses a hand in the thresher and we'd be sued into bankruptcy."

"No one's running wild." He was being provocative on purpose, but he wouldn't scare me off. "I'll oversee the whole thing. We'll need to hire additional staff to cook and clean for them, but the program will pay for itself and more besides, not to mention the free labour."

His lips pursed as soon as I said I'd oversee it. "I thought you were going to be working for me?"

"I will be, just in a different way. Look at these numbers, Jesse. You can have me out there building fences with the rest of the men, or you can have me overseeing a whole group of people doing the same thing. Which is the better return on my time?"

He couldn't argue with that. The numbers spoke for themselves.

"Where are you finding these people?" he tried next. "I don't see advertising built into your budget here."

"We'll rely mostly on word-of-mouth. My sister, Tonia, runs a business dedicated to helping other businesses improve their productivity. Part of that involves team building, and she'd love to start sending oil executives out here to get their hands dirty for a while."

"And where are they going to stay while they're here? Not in here." He looked around the kitchen as if he could already picture it overrun with strangers.

I wouldn't dream of it, especially now that I knew how much he valued his privacy. "We'll build a small bunkhouse down the road. It'll be basic, but that's what they want. That'll be part of the experience. I've already costed it out and it can be ready to go in a month. We'd need that much time to get the first bookings set up and hire some staff anyway."

He was running out of excuses and he knew it, so he stuck to basics instead. "This isn't the plan I had in mind, Laura. This isn't how I pictured my ranch."

"I know. It's *my* plan, and *our* ranch, and it will blow your projections out of the water. I guarantee it."

~Jesse~

I really hadn't expected anything like this. When Laura first started laying out her plans, they were intelligent and innovative, but roughly in line with what I expected. With concrete suggestions and a bit of lateral thinking, this was exactly what I'd wanted from the person I hired for this position. Also, in the back of my head, I couldn't help thinking that although her plans would definitely be productive in the long run, they wouldn't show much return within a year. My ownership of the ranch looked pretty secure.

Then, she pulled out this working holiday idea and turned my expectations completely upside down.

I could see the business sense of it. She'd laid it out so clearly, it would be impossible not to. It would make money, and it would get the ranch's debt paid down faster, which we both wanted. It just wasn't what I'd always envisioned when I imagined owning my own place. It felt like a completely different business, something not about the cattle and the land, something about *people* instead, and that had never been my strong suit.

Laura's triumphant expression began to soften when I didn't say anything in response to her declaration, and she surprised me by leaning forward and placing her hand on mine. "Look, Jesse, we both have to agree to implement my plan, right? We're partners in this, at least for the next year, though hopefully longer than that too. I'm not going to force you to do anything you're not comfortable with. I *want* you to be excited about it with me, so tell me why you're not. I know I can come across a little strong sometimes, but I promise I'm a good listener too if you give me a chance."

Her warm hand felt both foreign against mine and also unexpectedly natural.

"Someone told you that you come on too strong?" I joked, trying to lighten the mood with a bit of sarcasm. "I can't imagine."

It worked. She laughed, lifting her hand to swat my arm playfully before pulling her arm back onto the table in front of her. I actually kind of missed her touch when it had gone. "I know, hard to believe, right? But don't change the subject. Tell me: what are you worried about?"

I tried to put my concerns into words that might make sense to her. "Being on a ranch is something special to me. You've got to earn your way here through hard work. I want to be able to trust the people I'm working with and I want to know they have the same respect for the land I do. I don't want to be surrounded by a bunch of wannabe cowboys who think they can put on a hat and call themselves a ranch hand."

To her credit, Laura considered my words carefully, not responding with a knee-jerk response. "I think this place is incredibly special," she agreed after a moment's consideration. "When you've put in a hard day's work and you watch the sun go down, knowing both that you've done your best and that at any moment, everything could go wrong, you realize both how small you are and also how connected to the land we all are. It's powerful."

That was a good way of putting it. I couldn't disagree.

Her eyes sparkled mischievously. "Now, imagine someone who's never had that feeling before, feeling it for the first time after breaking their back working for you for free."

I groaned, but she hadn't finished yet.

"I'm serious. This place *is* special and that's what I want to share with the world. I want people to come here and be able to feel it for themselves, but I hear what you're saying too. You don't want them working beside you and that's fine. We've got acres of land that need tending. You give me a list of projects you want them working on, far away from whatever you and the rest of the hands are doing. You wouldn't even have to see them. We put the bunkhouse behind the row of trees down at the end of the back drive and you'll never even know they're here. They'll make you money without you lifting a finger, and you get projects checked off your to-do list at the same time. Not to mention that I'll be out of your hair during the day too. You can run the ranch just like you always have, just like you want, without anything really having to change other than the new income you're creating."

Her logic was frustratingly sound. I had a never-ending list of things to work on, things that didn't require any specialized skill other than a willingness to work hard. Tyson and I had gone weeks without seeing each other when we worked on different projects over the winter. With a little effort, Laura and I could work out a schedule that kept any paying guests out of my way.

And on a personal level, it might actually be good if we didn't end up working too closely together. Just the thought of her in a cowboy hat and boots did things to me that no other ranch hand had ever done, so if she kept herself occupied with this whole side project, leaving me and the others to get on with the more traditional parts of her plan, it could be a win-win.

"You don't have to decide right now," she said, misinterpreting my silence for reticence. "I'm not going anywhere, so think it over and we can talk about it again when you're ready. In the meantime, I'll help out wherever you need me. It's been a few years since I got up at five, but I think I remember how."

"Four."

Her brows furrowed. "Excuse me?"

"We get up at four. Work starts at 4:30."

I expected at least a token protest, but she simply nodded. "Alright, then I better get myself unpacked so I can get some sleep."

I should have been a gentleman and offered to help her get settled, but the thought of being in a bedroom with her in my present state of mind would be a dangerous road to walk down. I'd stayed focused on business through our whole talk, but as soon as I let myself think about how good she looked, I couldn't think of anything else. As Tyson had put it, I was in need of a little 'distraction', and I couldn't find it there.

"I've actually got plans for tonight. Are you okay if I leave you to get moved in on your own?"

Surprise flashed in her eyes, but she quickly covered it up. "Of course. I won't even ask where you're going. That's what we agreed, right? You've got your life, I've got mine."

"Right." It relieved me to know she took that agreement seriously. "In that case, I'll see you in the morning."

"Four thirty," she repeated, giving me a salute. "Got it, boss."

"Don't... don't do that."

She laughed, but I wasn't kidding. I had never found it sexy when anyone called me 'boss' before, but I'd also never had an employee quite like Laura Callahan. Just another reason I needed to clear my head, and I had one foolproof way of doing that.

Two hours later, I pulled into the familiar hotel parking lot and checked into a room for the night, making sure everything about the bill was settled in advance. I never stayed the night since I needed to be at work early in the morning, but I always gave my companion the option to stay if she wanted to. I didn't allow myself very many unnecessary expenses, but this was an exception.

The hotel sat on the outskirts of the city of Austin and attracted a lot of business travellers as well as locals. Its bar had a reputation for being a good place to go if you wanted a casual, anonymous hook-up, which was how I'd heard about it in the first place. A fellow ranch hand took me there several years ago when I worked closer to the city and it had never failed me yet. I didn't go often; once every few months, or even less, whenever I craved a moment of connection with none of the accompanying entanglements.

It worked perfectly for me. The woman and I both got exactly what we wanted from the encounter, never even exchanging names. Far enough from Sandy Creek that the odds of seeing anyone I recognized were next to none, I also didn't have to worry about awkwardly running into my hook-up in line at the grocery store a few days later. I never saw any of the women again. That made the drive more than worth it.

On a Saturday night, the place practically pulsed with pent-up energy and anticipation. Eyes were on me as soon as I walked through the door and I'd barely taken a spot at the bar when a woman walked up to me.

"Can I get you a drink?"

A little older than me, well-dressed and pretty, she was obviously used to taking charge, which would normally be right up my alley. Unfortunately, she also reminded me of my step-mother, a fact that definitely acted as a turn-off. "No, thanks. You have a good night though."

Her eyebrows raised in surprise and she turned away without another word.

The two women waiting to be served beside me struck up a conversation next. They were a lot younger than the first one; too young for me. We chatted for a few minutes before I excused myself politely.

Over the next half hour, women approached me a dozen more times, and each time, I had a reason why I didn't feel any interest. The heat that had been running through my veins earlier had been replaced by a cool indifference that I didn't fully understand. The bottle in my hand had been empty for a while and I wouldn't have more than one since I had to drive back to the ranch that night. The whole thing started to look like a bust, the first time I had ever struck out at that particular bar.

Finally, I headed back to reception and handed in my key, never even having visited the room. Taking a seat back behind the wheel of my truck, I glanced at the clock. Normally, I'd be in bed by then, but I still had the two-hour drive home. Would Laura already be asleep? A fleeting thought crossed my mind, wondering what she wore to bed, and immediately, the arousal that had been missing the whole time in the bar came rushing back.

Fuck. This was worse than I thought. My usual distraction hadn't worked, so I only had one option left that I could see: focus on the job. Work always helped me drown out anything else, and I hoped to hell it would do the trick that time too. If not, I might have just made a very big mistake.

Chapter Five

~Laura~

It took two days before Jesse brought up the working holiday idea again. Somehow, I resisted the urge to ask him about it before then, even though I was dying to know what might be going on in his head.

My first morning on the ranch, I was up and ready by 4:15, just to be sure, with my hair back into a low ponytail and just a touch of foundation on. I still had to go grocery shopping and fill the fridge properly, but I'd brought some yogurt, fruit and eggs with me the day before so I'd be able to have some breakfast before we got to work. Jesse walked into the kitchen just as I finished poaching the eggs.

"Good morning," I greeted him cheerfully. He looked tired, I couldn't help noticing, like he hadn't slept very well. Whenever he got back the night before from wherever he'd gone, I had already been asleep. Once I lay down in my parents' old bedroom, it didn't take long before the familiar nighttime noises of the ranch lulled me to sleep. In Houston, I'd missed the lowing of the cattle and the whinny of the horses. Once summer came, the chirping of the crickets would take over, but in the spring, the night was quieter and the sky full of stars that I could see out the window from my bed.

It felt like home.

The stars were still there in the morning if we looked out the kitchen window, but Jesse didn't look, his attention focused on getting ready for the day as he pulled out a loaf of bread from the bread bin and a jar of peanut butter from the cupboard. In his jeans, wide belt and long-sleeved navy work shirt, his hair still a little tousled from his bed and the shadowy stubble along his jaw, he looked damn good. I'd never really understood women moaning about all the hot men being gay, but now, I could understand the sense of loss. From my perspective, it seemed a damn shame for womankind.

"'Morning," he mumbled back before shoving a piece of bread with a thick smear of peanut butter into his mouth. His eyes quickly scanned me, as if checking I knew how to dress for the kind of work we'd be doing that day, but he wouldn't find any fault there. My clothes mirrored his with my checked shirt tucked into my work jeans and my buckled belt. I had a hat and boots too, ready to go by the door, my hat hanging next to his, my boots looking rather delicate beside his much larger ones.

"Do you want some eggs?" I gestured down to the pan as I slid my own onto a plate. "Banana? Blueberries?"

A hint of a smile appeared in the corner of his lips, but he shook his head. "I'm good, thanks."

"Coffee?" He didn't have a coffee maker, I'd realized, so I had brought instant coffee with me. I could go shopping for any other appliances I needed later this week. I'd have to make a list.

As I poured the boiling water from the kettle into my cup and the scent made my mouth water, Jesse immediately took a step back. "No. I don't like... actually, the smell kind of bothers me."

He hadn't mentioned that before, and I quickly grabbed a plate to put over the cup, trapping most of the scent inside. "Sorry. I didn't know. I need a cup to get going in the morning, but I can keep it in my room if it makes you feel unwell."

"It's not a physical thing, it just... never mind." He shook his head, like he hadn't fully woken up himself yet. "I can get used to it."

He shouldn't have to if it bothered him. "Don't be silly. You should be comfortable in your own house, and it's not a big deal for me. I was going to buy myself a coffee maker anyway, so I'll just keep it in my room. Maybe I'll put it on my bedside table so I can get a cup in the morning before I even get out of bed."

I was kidding, and he got that, smiling for just a second before clearing his throat. "Alright, I'm going to head out. Take your time, you've still got ten minutes."

Stuffing one more piece of bread in his mouth, he left the kitchen without another word.

Sipping on my coffee thoughtfully, I sat down to eat my breakfast. What did Jesse mean that his aversion to coffee wasn't physical? Mental, then? Emotional? He didn't say he didn't like it, only that it bothered him. A bad association, maybe? It felt like he had almost been about to share something with me but changed his mind at the last minute. What made him close himself off that way?

The more of those little glimpses of him that I got, the more intrigued I became.

With my hat and boots on, I stepped out the door at 4:30 on the nose, and found Jesse talking to Tyson Keller, one of my dad's longtime ranch hands. Tyson tipped his hat to me as I came down the front porch steps.

"Good morning, Ms Callahan. Jesse was just letting me know about you joining us."

He shot Jesse a disapproving look that I hoped was only because Jesse hadn't given him a heads up, not because Tyson didn't want to work with me.

"It's Laura," I quickly corrected him. Though I might have been the boss' daughter before, we were on more equal footing this time around. Tyson had seen me working out there as a teenager, so he should know I'd always do my fair share. "It's good to see you, Tyson."

"Alright, let's get started," Jesse cut in, looking uncomfortable with even a small amount of pleasantries. "I'll give you a rundown of the current situation before the others get here."

We spent the next half hour reviewing the herd and, when the other hands showed up, Jesse made a proper introduction. The reactions from the men seemed mixed: curiosity, wariness, some blatant looks of appreciation and maybe a touch of resentment. They were probably worried they'd have to watch themselves more with a woman around, but I could deal with men being men. They'd learn soon enough they didn't have to censor themselves around me.

Only one cow still hadn't had her baby, but it didn't look like it would be happening that day. I stayed close to Jesse as we herded the rest of the mothers and their calves into a nearby field for grazing, taking mental notes as he pointed out different animals. He knew the herd very well, that couldn't be clearer, and he was a skilled rider, looking natural and in command on his horse. I felt awkward and ungainly by comparison since it had been a while since I'd done any riding. I'd have to do some practice on my own time until it became second nature again.

With the animals taken care of, we spent the rest of the day working on a fence that they'd already started on. I worked with Tyson and another of the hands, Mark, quickly falling into an easy banter with them both.

As first days went, it couldn't have been a lot smoother. We took a break for lunch, but Jesse only had another peanut butter sandwich, refusing any of the salad and grilled chicken I made. Most of the hands clocked out before three, but Jesse, Tyson and I stayed out in the field until five as Jesse continued to give me an overview of the ongoing work and what still needed to be done.

When we got back to the house, I had a shower, and by the time I got out, Jesse was already pulling his frozen dinner out of the oven, making it clear he didn't intend to eat with me. After the conditions he'd made, I should have expected it, but it disappointed me anyway. He seemed very determined not to spend any time with me.

"I'll be having an early night tonight," he announced as he put his food on a plate and headed to his room. "Do you mind taking a look at the pregnant heifer once more before bed?"

"Of course."

I spent the night video chatting with Shawna and Dex in the hospital and making my shopping list for the house before checking the barn one more time. The expectant mother seemed comfortable enough, so I gave her a small pep talk before leaving her for the night.

The next day started out much the same except that I drank my coffee in my room as I got ready. As soon as Jesse and I got out to the barn, however, we could tell the day wouldn't be as routine as the previous one. Things had clearly progressed with our pregnant cow, and she should be giving birth that morning.

"You want to stay or go with the others?" Jesse asked me as he rolled up his sleeves, reminding me of our first meeting with him covered with afterbirth. He definitely had no problem getting hands on in these situations.

"I'll stay, if you don't mind. It's been a while since I've helped out at a birth, and since it's the last one of the season, it'll be good to get the practice in."

He nodded in agreement, passing on his instructions for the other men to Tyson while I got down on my hands and knees to examine the calf's presentation.

"Any sighting?" Jesse asked, but I shook my head.

"Nothing yet."

"Do you want to check?"

After scrubbing up, I reached up as gently as possible into the birth canal, looking for a foot or a head, but what I felt made me grimace. "Shit. It's breech." What I felt could only be the rear of the calf, which meant it would have to be turned prior to delivery. I had assisted in births before but I'd never turned a calf on my own. "Should we get the vet?"

Jesse shook his head. "Not yet. Let's see if we can't give him or her a little assistance on our own."

I stepped back to let him get to work and he talked me through the whole process as he pushed the calf back into the uterus where it would have room to turn around. His arm was in well past his elbow as he felt his way along the body to find a hoof and gently worked the calf into its proper position. I did my best to keep the cow calm and steady. "I'm a woman too," I whispered next to her ear. "True, I've never been pregnant, but I can imagine that doesn't feel too good."

Once he had the calf in proper position, we got the cow down onto her side and Jesse stepped back to see if labour would proceed on its own, but it soon became clear it wouldn't be that easy. "Better get the chains."

The obstetrical chains would help us to aid the birth, pulling gently as the mother pushed, and he efficiently got them into place along the calf's leg.

"Alright, we're almost there," I assured the cow. "Let's get that little one out now."

We had some long, tense moments as the cow strained and Jesse pulled, firmly but not too hard. Finally, the calf came loose and Jesse immediately cleaned its nostrils and mouth, clearing its airways. It took some shaky breaths, but it didn't look very strong and we both knew it.

"Damn it." Jesse got back to his feet as the mother started to lick the calf clean. "I don't think she's going to make it."

Despite the calf's weakness, we went through the necessary steps, cutting the umbilical cord and attempting to hand feed the calf to make sure it got the nutrition to give it the best start possible. It didn't seem strong enough to feed, though, and soon, the writing was on the wall.

Jesse kept glancing over at me, as if to make sure I was okay, but he didn't have to worry. Although sad, calf loss was part of ranch life. With hundreds of cows calving each season, it was bound to happen. I kept the calf as comfortable as possible until it took its last breath.

The mood felt somber as we made our way back to the ranch house at the end of the day. There had been no time to break for lunch, and we both needed to shower and change, so I suggested we order some pizza for the night. I knew a place in town that would deliver out to the ranch, and to my surprise, Jesse agreed without argument.

An hour later, we sat down in the living room together in our clean clothes with a large pepperoni pizza between us, and Jesse looked over at me with what almost looked like a new kind of appreciation in his eyes. "So, you want to talk about your business plan again?"

~Jesse~

Laura looked surprised when I brought up her plan, but at that moment, it felt like the safest thing for us to talk about.

After my frustrating evening in Austin, I walked into the kitchen at 4:15 in the morning the next day ready to focus on work. Then, Laura turned around and smiled at me, her face mostly free of makeup, her hair pulled back and her fitted shirt tucked into her jeans, and I couldn't honestly remember ever seeing anything more enticing.

Clearly, jacking myself off in the shower that morning wasn't going to cut it in order to get her out of my head.

Once we got outside and got to work, things went smoother, but that evening, I hid from her in my bedroom. No matter how I tried to dress it up, it came down to that: I cowered behind my closed door because I couldn't be around her without thinking about just how much she turned me on.

For both our sakes, I needed to get a grip.

The next day had been better in one way, and even more dangerous in another. She took her coffee in her room that morning, and I appreciated the thoughtfulness of it even though it frustrated me that the smell still had the power to affect me. The day passed quickly as we worked together to help birth the calf, and Laura impressed me with both what she knew and how willing she was to learn the things she didn't. She had no problem getting her hands dirty and she handled the loss of the calf well.

Better than I did, to be honest.

Most of the time, I could separate the loss of one of our animals from my own personal issues with death. Sometimes, when we lost the cow rather than the calf, it would hit me. I'd find excuses to work on another part of the ranch so I didn't have to hear the newborn calf calling for its mother. But usually, I could deal with losing a calf without letting it get to me. That day felt different though, for reasons I couldn't quite put my finger on, and as we sat down together on the couch, me in my fresh t-shirt and jeans, Laura in yoga pants and an oversized sweater, I almost wanted to tell her about it.

That was the most dangerous thought I'd had about her yet.

Instead, I brought up her business plan, knowing she'd be eager to talk about it, and she didn't let me down.

"I'm definitely ready. What are you thinking?" she asked, her blue eyes fixed on me curiously. Her feet rested on the coffee table as she took a large bite of her pizza. I'd brought us a couple of beers to go with it, and I took a drink before I got started.

"It took me by surprise, as you know, but I've been thinking about why I put up that job posting in the first place. I wasn't just looking for another hand. I wanted someone to help me elevate this ranch to a new level and someone I could trust to have the ranch's best interests at heart. That's the whole reason I agreed to hire you, even though we didn't get off to the best start. I trust your heart is in the right place, Laura."

"Well, thanks." She seemed amused by my assessment, though I had been trying to be complimentary. "My heart's in the right place but I come across wrong, is that it?"

I supposed I did kind of say it like that, which wasn't exactly what I meant, but rather than apologizing, I teased her right back. "You're kind of proving my point here, aren't you? Would you just let me finish?"

Her eyes sparkled, letting me know that she took no offense. Rather, she liked a bit of pushback. "I'm all ears, I promise."

I had it on the tip of my tongue to tell her from where I was sitting, she seemed to be all mouth, but that could easily be misinterpreted. I didn't need to be talking about or even thinking about her mouth.

"So, I'm willing to give it a try..."

She squealed in delight before I could finish and I held up my hands, one of which still held my beer, to try to temper her excitement.

"... so long as you can do it with the conditions you promised me. I don't have anything to do with it and no one gets in the way of the real work of the ranch. If I feel like it's not working, we shut it down. My word is final, no complaints."

I did my best to sound stern and no-nonsense, but she looked so thrilled that I couldn't stop the smile that tugged at my lips.

"I promise you won't regret it, Jesse." She pulled her phone from her pocket in excitement. "Look, I already started getting quotes on liability insurance policies, since you seemed concerned someone would hurt themselves. We'll be fully protected against any kind of accident."

The word 'accident' sent a pang of pain through me, making me grimace, but luckily, Laura was still looking down at her phone and she missed it.

"I think this one will work best, it also includes cancellation insurance if we ever need to cancel a booking and the price is pretty reasonable."

She continued to go through details as we demolished the pizza and emptied our bottles of beer.

"This is your baby," I reminded her. "You can keep me updated on the big things, but I'll leave the day-to-day details up to you. I've set aside a small budget to get you going, but it'll need to get profitable pretty quickly to sustain itself. You're going to have to work hard, Laura."

"I've never been afraid of a little hard work," she assured me, finally putting her phone away and turning back to me. "Neither are you, apparently. How long have you been working on a ranch? You were pretty impressive out there today."

It made me happier than it should have that she'd been impressed. "I got a job in high school as a live-in hand. Been on a ranch ever since."

"Live-in during high school?" she repeated in surprise. "You couldn't work from home?"

"Didn't have a home. Not one I wanted to live in, anyway." Though I kept my answer short, it was still more than I'd told most people, and I didn't know why I said it. One beer wouldn't usually loosen my tongue so much.

"That sounds rough." I could see the blatant interest in her eyes, wanting to know more, but she held herself back, perhaps sensing that I didn't want to talk about. She asked a more general question instead. "Where did you grow up?"

I didn't want to talk about that either. "A little town, a lot like this one."

Laura's lips pursed at my vague response. "Did it have a name?"

"Does it matter?" I shot back, hoping she'd take the hint. "You've seen one, you've seen them all."

"Is that why you don't want to make friends here? Because you think the people are just like the ones you grew up with?"

"Who said I don't want to make friends?" That seemed pretty presumptuous, no matter how accurate it might be.

"You did. You don't want to be around if I have people over, you never have people over yourself, and you don't want to have anything to do with the people who might come and stay here. Am I crazy, or does that sound like someone who doesn't want friends?"

She thought she had it all figured out, apparently, though she didn't know why I felt that way, so she had no right to judge me for it. "Maybe I just don't want people to stick their noses into my life, even when I've specifically asked them not to."

My reply came out sharper than I intended, and she flinched beneath the words before backing down. "I'm sorry. Obviously, I don't know what you've been through."

She didn't, but a little voice in the back of my head reminded me that there was no way she could so long as I refused to tell her. But that would be crossing a line I had specifically drawn to keep us from getting too close. The fact that I was tempted to step over it after just two days together scared me even more than the fact that I found her so attractive.

The sooner she got started on her new project, far away from me, the better.

~Laura~

Two nights later, Mary-Beth and I stood at the kitchen window, washing and drying the dishes from dinner as we watched Wayne and the kids playing outside. I had gone into town the night before to get everything on my shopping list and to invite Mary-Beth and her family over that evening. When I told Jesse I'd have company, he made good on his promise to disappear.

"Is anyone... spending the night?" he asked almost hesitantly, not looking thrilled about the prospect.

"It's my best friend and her husband coming over, and last I checked, they weren't looking for a threesome, so no. I think they'll probably go home after dinner."

He nearly choked on the air, making me laugh. We hadn't talked about anything personal at all since he shut down my questions over pizza, but I knew he had a sense of humour from our time out in the field. He just liked to keep it hidden when we were alone.

"This must be what they mean by the circle of life," Mary-Beth pointed out with a laugh, her gaze warm with affection as her husband chased her kids around the huge yard, their shrieks of excitement filtering through the open window. "I'm pretty sure fifteen years ago, that was us out there while your mom was here at the sink."

She was right, and that was exactly what I'd always wanted: passing the ranch experience on to a new generation, raising my own family here just as I'd been raised. Being there gave me a sense of peace and completeness that I had never found in Houston, even if the family part of my future remained theoretical for the time being.

Fully on board my train of thought, my friend gave me a searching look when I didn't say anything. "There really wasn't a single guy in Houston good enough for you?"

She handed me a plate from the sink which I caught in a towel. She'd insisted on washing, even though she'd just had her nails done. It amazed me how she always looked completely put together with everything she had going on.

"I dated," I assured her. "Plenty. It just never turned into anything serious. I don't really know why."

"Because they didn't measure up to your standards?" she teased.

I gave her a smack with the towel in my hands. "You make it sound like it's all my fault. I'm not that picky."

Her snort of disbelief said otherwise. "Am I or am I not talking to the same Laura Callahan who went to senior prom alone because none of the guys at our school could hogtie a calf quicker than her?"

"That was meant to be a joke and you know it!"

I had let it be known, just for fun, that anyone who wanted to take me to prom would have to beat me in a basic calf roping exercise. That eliminated some of the town kids, but there should have been *someone* capable of it. It really wasn't my fault that no one managed to do it.

The Callahan girls seemed to be cursed when it came to prom. It wasn't just me who hadn't had the best experience.

Jesse probably could have done it, I couldn't help thinking. Over the past two days, I'd had the opportunity to see him working with the cattle and his strong, sure hands had caught my attention more than once. No matter how much I told myself he was off limits, both because of his position as my boss and, obviously, his own preferences in the matter, I couldn't stop my mind from wandering every now and then to what it might feel like to have those hands on me. The memory of seeing him shirtless on my first day here had crossed my mind once or twice too, especially when I lay alone in my bed. Since it would never happen, I considered it a bit of harmless daydreaming.

"Laura?"

Mary-Beth looked at me curiously as she said my name and I quickly shook my head to get rid of the thoughts inside it. "Sorry. What?"

"Where'd you go there?" she teased as we put the last of the dishes away. "Or are you just trying to get out of answering the question?"

"I'm sorry, I got thinking about the calves when you brought them up." That wasn't *entirely* a lie. "What's the question?"

"About whether you want me to set you up with anyone."

That time, I was the one who nearly choked on nothing. "I don't think I'm that desperate just yet."

I grabbed the bottle of wine from the counter that Mary-Beth had brought with her and poured us two glasses, using the new glassware I'd just bought. Jesse didn't have any wine glasses, which didn't really surprise me. He seemed like more of a beer drinker.

With drinks in hand, we headed into the living room to continue our conversation.

"I only just got back to town," I reminded her as I took a seat, glancing over in satisfaction at the artwork I'd hung on the wall earlier that day. The beautiful landscape painting of the ranch was by my brother, Dex. He made it for me when I got my first degree, and I'd bought a few framed prints that complemented it, black and white shots of the Texas landscape. When I asked Jesse if he would mind if I hung them up, he told me to knock myself out, which, while not particularly enthusiastic, was at least a green light. "I'd rather see if anything happens naturally before trying to force it."

"I get that, but you've got to understand your options are limited. This ain't Houston." Mary-Beth took a long sip of her wine, obviously savouring the child-free moment. "Most of the men our age are either settled down or there's a good reason why they're not."

"Like being gay?" I couldn't help asking and Mary-Beth's eyes lit up in curiosity.

"Do you know something I don't? Have you seen Jesse with some-one?"

I quickly shook my head, not wanting to feed any rumours without proof. "I haven't seen him with anyone, male or female. Nothing to prove or disprove your theory, but it seems possible, at least. He definitely hasn't shown any interest in me."

"How is it going, living here with him?" The way she leaned forward made it clear she'd been wanting to ask me all night, she had just been waiting until I brought it up.

"He's..." I trailed off, realizing I didn't have the first idea how to describe him. I finally decided on Mary-Beth's own words back when I'd first asked her about him. "Just like you said: polite, friendly, but guarded at the same time. Keeps himself to himself. He wouldn't even tell me where he grew up. If I try to ask him anything personal, he clamps up tighter than a virgin's daughter."

She nearly spit out her wine at my phrasing, making us both giggle. "Do you want me to do some digging?" she offered. "I'm sure I could at least find out where he's from if I tried."

As curious as I was, I knew that snooping around in his past would be the last thing Jesse would appreciate. "No, thanks, but I wouldn't mind some advice."

Her eyebrows raised. "From me? About what?"

"You're so good at getting people to talk to you," I pointed out, completely truthfully. "How can I get him to open up a bit more? I think we could be friends, but I know I come on a bit too strong sometimes. How do I get him to trust me without forcing the issue?"

Being aware of my flaws was one thing; knowing how to fix them, I hadn't quite figured out yet. I was great at getting animals to trust me, but I couldn't just bribe Jesse with food. I'd already tried that and it hadn't worked.

Mary-Beth took my question seriously, which I appreciated. "I'm afraid there's no secret shortcut, especially with someone who's used to staying private. You've just got to show that you're trustworthy, and maybe share some things about yourself too. If he thinks you trust him, he'll be more likely to trust you too."

"I do share things," I protested. "He knows all about me already. We're living in the house I grew up in, for crying out loud."

"He might know *about* you, but does he really know you? I think you two actually have something in common, you know. You're great with people on a friendly, surface level. That's why you dated 'plenty' of men in Houston, and that's why you're going to absolutely knock this ranch holiday idea out of the park."

I'd told her and Wayne all about my plans for the ranch over dinner. They were both complimentary and enthusiastic about it, and Mary-Beth couldn't wait to start spreading the word as soon as I gave her permission to do so.

"But when it comes to emotions and sharing who you actually *are*, on a deeper level, that's not your strong suit, Laura. I'd be willing to bet it's at least part of the reason why you haven't found the right guy yet. And I know you don't want to hear this, but I think it might be why your daddy didn't realize just how much you wanted the ranch. He didn't know how you felt because you assumed he knew and didn't actually tell him."

My knee-jerk reaction was to try to defend myself, to protest that she had it wrong, but this was my best friend who wouldn't say anything to try to offend or hurt me. A little voice in the back of my head whispered that she might even have a point, at least when it came to the guys I'd dated. I'd never let myself be vulnerable in the way that Dex and Shawna were with each, for example. Maybe I just wasn't built that way.

It had never bothered me as much as it did now that I was faced with a man I really did want to get to know, someone who interested and intrigued me and whose life looked set to be linked to mine for a while, but who kept his feelings locked up even tighter than I did. When he said the other night, almost casually, that he hadn't had a place to call home growing up, I could almost feel his hurt. I wanted to know more, but I knew if I simply asked, he'd find a way not to answer.

Maybe Mary-Beth had it right that if I wanted Jesse to open up to me, I'd have to go first, but I didn't know quite how to do that.

Once again, my friend seemed to read my mind. "You guys must have something in common, right? You both care about this place. Maybe you can find some common ground there and build on that."

We did have the ranch in common, and I had been feeling self-conscious about my rusty riding skills next to him. It wouldn't be easy to admit I could use some help, but maybe if I did, he'd start to see there was more to me than just the brash, overconfident woman who'd talked her way into his house and his life.

Maybe he would even see that talking to me wouldn't be the worst thing in the world.

Chapter Six

~Jesse~

As I reached the end of the drive, I caught sight of the minivan sitting in front of the house, meaning Laura's guests must still be there. I could head over to the barn until they'd gone, but fate had other plans. As I pulled up to park, the front door of the house opened and a flurry of kids tumbled out, almost literally tumbling as they raced each other down the porch. The father carried the smallest one while their mother gave Laura a hug.

Pretending I hadn't seen them would be useless. I would have to go and say hello.

"Hey, Jesse." Laura waved as I got out of the truck. "This is my friend, Mary-Beth Parker, and her husband, Wayne."

"Howdy." I tipped my hat to them both with a polite smile. "Hope y'all had a nice visit."

The woman looked vaguely familiar. I must have seen her in town but I never knew her name before.

She smiled over at me as the kids all piled into the van, chattering the whole time. "We sure did, but we'll leave you in peace now. Though I don't imagine you get a lot of that since this one moved in."

She raised her eyebrows in Laura's direction, who narrowed her eyes back at her. "Y'all talk like I'm some kind of terror. Jesse, back me up here. Am I really that bad?"

Her blue eyes turned to me with a pleading look that had not only my lips twitching. No, she definitely wasn't that bad, but letting her know what I really thought could be dangerous.

When she first told me she intended to have company over, I immediately thought she meant a date. She hadn't mentioned being involved with anyone, and it seemed like the kind of thing she would have mentioned, but I didn't want to make any assumptions. When I asked if the person would be staying the night and she informed me the company was simply a friend, the relief I felt was far stronger than it should have been, considering the whole situation had nothing to do with me.

"I'm getting used to it," I decided on as my reply.

Laura threw up her hands in exasperation as Mary-Beth laughed, and after a couple more minutes, the van headed back down the drive, leaving a vacuum of silence in its place. Laura and I hadn't talked much since I'd snapped at her for asking me questions, and though I felt just a tiny bit bad about that, I knew it was for the best. Reaching into the truck's passenger side, I grabbed the groceries I'd gone to get that night, driving to a nearby town instead of using the local store so it would take up more time.

"You know, I'd be happy to pick up whatever you need when I go to the store," Laura offered as we both headed into the kitchen. "It makes no sense for us both to go."

"That ain't part of your job." I put the bags on the counter before opening the freezer to restock my supply of frozen meals while Laura leaned back against the table, keeping her distance.

"It's not, but my roommate and I used to pick things up for each other all the time. It's more efficient."

She wasn't wrong, but things were never that simple. Favours created obligations. "I wouldn't want it to be one-sided, and I wouldn't feel comfortable picking out things for you. I don't even know what half the vegetables you have in the fridge are called."

Her pretty smile felt like a beam of sunshine, so warm and comforting that I had to look away. "I could teach you. In fact, I've got a proposal for you, a two-sided one."

"Another proposal?" I couldn't hide the wariness in my voice, making her laugh.

"A simple one," she promised. "I've been feeling a little out of practice on the horses this week after all my time away from the ranch. I hoped you might be able to go for a ride with me tomorrow after dinner and help me figure out what I'm doing wrong."

To be honest, I had noticed she didn't look entirely comfortable while riding, but I tried not to pay too much attention to her body astride the horse.

"I'm not asking for a favour, though," she quickly assured me. "It's a quid pro quo. I'll make you dinner first, and I can teach you the names of the vegetables I use while I'm at it."

In another circumstance, it could almost sound like a date, but I quickly pushed that thought aside. One of my employees was asking for help with something that would make them better at their job, nothing more.

"Sure, we can do that." We didn't need to talk while riding, and we could check on things around the ranch as we went. It would just be an extension of the work day, and if I got a home-cooked meal out of it, no strings attached, all the better. "I'll see you in the morning."

Grabbing my empty grocery bags, I headed back to the safety and solitude of my room.

The next evening, the sun hung low in the sky as we chose the horses for the evening's ride. Our dinner of sweet chilli steak and stir-fried noodles hadn't been what I expected, but I had to admit it tasted incredible.

"Your mom cooked meals like this?" I asked curiously as I cleaned my plate. Every ranch I'd ever worked on, the food was good and hearty but much more traditional.

"She's more of a meat and potatoes kind of woman," Laura admitted, which confirmed my suspicions. "But she taught me all the basics, and then once I got to the city, I could use those skills to try out some new recipes. That's the thing about venturing outside our comfort zones once in a while: you might find something great."

In the stable, I chose one of our more challenging horses for Laura to use. She had grown up riding so she didn't need to be babied. She'd just been out of the saddle for too long and needed to get her confidence back.

"Buddy likes to think he's the boss," I warned Laura once she'd mounted. "If he senses you're even a little bit unsure, he'll try to get away with taking over."

"Great," Laura deadpanned. "No pressure, then."

"That's exactly why I chose him for you: you need the pressure. You need a challenge."

She couldn't argue with me there. "How's my position?" she asked instead.

I circled around her on my own horse, checking her posture and alignment. "Stand up in the stirrups and hold it," I instructed.

Buddy immediately took a step forward when she did, which meant she was too far forward. I didn't need to tell her that, though. She corrected it herself right away, while I tried not to stare too much at her rather perfect ass in her jeans.

Once it felt right to her, we set off at an easy trot towards the farthest fields. I rode behind her to keep an eye on her form, and once she felt more confident, we broke into a gallop with me in front, taking some tight corners that she had to follow. She struggled the first couple of times to keep her momentum, but it soon got better.

We kept going until the sun touched the horizon, at which point I headed back towards the barn. Laura fell into place beside me as we resumed a steady trot. "It's not perfect," she acknowledged, "but it does feel better. I wouldn't mind doing it again if you have the time. Not every night, but maybe a couple of times a week for the first month or so?"

"Sure." I'd actually quite enjoyed it. It had been kind of nice to have her quiet company, enjoying the solitude of riding without being fully alone.

"Can I tell you a secret?" she asked with a rather cute grimace after a couple of more minutes of comfortable silence.

"I guess?" I had no idea where she might be going with this, but she had me curious anyway.

"My first year at college, we went to a bar in Houston with a mechanical bull. I bragged all night about how I'd been riding since I was five. Everyone else in the group had never even been on a farm before, so I figured I would have no trouble showing everyone up, but when my turn came, I went to dig my heels in, and the heel of my shoe broke off. I got thrown in two seconds and landed flat on my face. My so-called friends never let me live it down."

I could picture her frustrated outrage so clearly, I had to laugh. "It doesn't seem to have damaged your self-esteem too badly," I pointed out. I'd rarely met anyone so sure of themselves.

"That's what you think. You didn't know me before."

Her grin made it clear she was joking, and I found myself smiling not only the rest of the way back to the barn but later that night too while I got ready for bed. Even worse, I found myself looking forward to teasing her about it later on when an opportunity arose.

The memory of her smile competed with the picture of her body on the horse as I slipped beneath my covers, and I honestly didn't know what to make of it. I'd made it so many years without forming any kind of attachment to anyone. How, in less than ten days, had Laura Callahan lodged herself so firmly in my thoughts?

~Laura~

Life on the ranch quickly fell into a routine, as if I'd never been away at all. Each day was different yet the rhythms were all the same.

As I'd predicted, the men soon relaxed around me, realizing I hadn't come to police their conversation or make their lives difficult, and they loosened up to the point that they sometimes forget I was there. Occasionally, Jesse would clear his throat if he thought they stepped over the line and said something they shouldn't have in front of me, and that would be enough for the others to mumble a quick, "Sorry, Laura," accompanied by a sheepish smile.

Jesse never seemed to forget I was there.

We started eating lunch together since it made sense in the limited time we had off. For the first little while, he stuck to his peanut butter sandwiches, but after several days of eyeing my turkey sandwich with provolone, tomato and lettuce, he asked if I could show him exactly how I made it. I picked up some extra ingredients for him the next time I went to the store and put them on his shelf, and although he insisted on paying me for them to the exact penny, he did, at least, use them. When he bit into the first one he made, I thought his eyes would roll right out of his head.

"Shit, that's good. And it's so easy."

"Things don't have to be complicated to be worthwhile," I teased him. "Whoever told you they did was probably selling something."

We still ate our dinners separately, other than the nights we went out riding. If I hung out in the living room, he'd go to his room or go out for a walk, but if I went out, I'd usually come back to find him in the living room. Each Friday, I went into town and had dinner with Mary-Beth, and then we'd leave Wayne at home once the kids had gone to bed and head to the bar. There were faces from high school that I'd missed and some I definitely hadn't, but they all came over to say hi and ask me questions about the ranch and about Jesse. I saw the clear appreciation in the women's eyes when they talked about him, and they hadn't even seen him shirtless as I had on several occasions now. If he got too hot or dirty during the day's work, his shirt would often come off, as would some of the other hands', but Jesse's was the only chest I found myself sneaking glances at, completely against my will.

It also made me laugh how the single women at the bar all found excuses about why he hadn't shown any interest in them, usually coming back to the idea of him being gay. They dropped hints, trying to get me to offer my opinion, but although I did secretly think they might be right, I kept my mouth shut.

Jesse didn't spend any evenings away from the ranch. Wherever he'd gone on the night I moved in, it seemed to be a one-off.

On the nights when we did go out riding, Jesse allowed me to cook in exchange for his time. Cooking for him hardly felt like a chore since he always emptied his plate and complimented my efforts. When it came to my riding, the feedback was more limited, but when he did make a suggestion, it always helped. After a couple of weeks, I felt much more confident and the lessons became almost unnecessary, but neither of us suggested that we stop them. It gave us an excuse to hang out together without any pressure, and though we mostly rode in silence or talked about the ranch and what needed to be done, I tried to throw in the occasional personal thought or story from my past, without any pressure or expectation that he'd do the same.

For a long time, he didn't, until one night about three weeks after our first ride when we went out to the back fields after taking a look at the construction on the guest bunkhouse at the end of the drive. Construction should be finished the following week, and I'd already hired a cook-housekeeper to help look after the guests. We had our first booking in a month, from one of Tonia's corporate clients in the city, and several more lined up after that. The advance payments were covering the operation costs and part of the construction outlay as well. Everything was falling into place.

"I never rode a horse until I was thirteen," he told me, out of the blue, after leading me through a series of exercises to test my control and we had stopped for a minute to let the horses catch their breath. "I lied and said I had, though. I thought I fooled them, but looking back, they probably knew. They were just too polite to say anything."

That was by far the most he had ever told me about his childhood, even though it still didn't tell me very much. It did, however, open the door for a lot more questions, and I tried to step through it as gently as possible. "Who's 'they'?"

"The Buchanans. They were my first employer. If they hadn't hired me, I might have never been a rancher at all."

He kept his eyes in the distance as he spoke, not looking at me, and every word only made me more curious. I did my best to keep my questions casual, as if he could answer them or not as he pleased. "They hired a thirteen-year-old? I thought there were laws against that."

He grinned, just for a second, making my stomach flip. He really was damn good-looking. Just when I thought I'd gotten used to it, he'd go and smile like that, sitting on his horse beneath the evening sky, his jeans stretched across his firm thigh muscles, and it would hit me all over again. "I lied about that too. Told them I was fourteen and they took my word for it. Or they pretended to. But they took a chance on me anyway and I made it up to them. I worked damn hard."

I had no doubt he would have. I'd never seen him give less than his full effort yet.

"They didn't have any more experienced applicants for the job?" I tried to keep my questions open and not specifically about him. He seemed to respond better to that.

It worked that time too. "There was no job to apply for," he explained. "I was just walking down the highway past their farm, trying to hitch a ride, when I saw some of the cowboys at work. I'd never seen them actually working before, I'd only seen the fancy riding at the rodeo, you know? But they were herding the cattle and I just walked right onto the farm to get a closer look. Mr Buchanan was coming back from somewhere and found me there on his land, uninvited, but instead of kicking me out, he started asking me questions. Next thing I knew, he offered me a job."

So many details were missing, but I didn't want to push too hard. Instead, I tried to connect it to one of the only other things he'd told me before. "Is that the ranch you ended up living on, then?"

For the first time since he'd started talking, he glanced over at me, looking almost surprised that I'd remembered. "Yeah, that's right. Stayed there until I was seventeen. I woulda stayed longer, but things got awkward with his daughter. She tried to tell everyone I came onto her and wouldn't take no for an answer."

I gasped so loud that my horse startled beneath me and I had to take a moment to calm him again. "She said you assaulted her?"

He grimaced, understandably. "Not fully. She just said I got rough with her and she had to run away. Nothing could be further from the truth. *She* came onto *me*, and when I told her I wasn't interested, she cooked up this story to make herself feel better, I guess."

"What did you do?" I was so caught up in the story that I forgot about not asking direct questions. Luckily, Jesse didn't seem to notice either.

"I told Mr Buchanan the truth and, thankfully, he believed me. He knew what she could be like, but her mother believed her and wanted me gone, which, if it had been true, I could completely understand. I considered myself lucky to walk away with a good reference. He even put in a good word for me at another ranch the next town over, so I ended up going there next. At least by then, I knew how to ride."

He gave a self-deprecating shrug as he brought the story back to where it had started, but I could imagine he'd glossed over the hardest parts. Why would a rancher offer a thirteen-year-old kid a job on the spot in the first place? Why had he been trying to hitch a ride on the highway? Where was his family in all of this?

I still had a million questions, but more than anything, I wanted him to feel comfortable talking to me about who he was now, not just the things that had happened in the past. I tried to approach the subject as delicately as I could.

"Did you tell the girl the reason you weren't interested? That might have softened the blow if she felt rejected."

Jesse glanced over at me again with a slightly confused expression. "What do you mean?"

I hadn't meant to imply he did anything wrong, and I quickly tried to clarify my comment. "I'm not saying you should have had to, or that what she did was your fault in any way. I just mean that she might have taken it less personally if she knew it wasn't just her."

In my own slightly heavy-handed way, I was trying to show him that I didn't care about him being gay, that he could tell me and it wouldn't change anything between us, but Jesse still continued to look utterly baffled by my words. "You've lost me, Laura. I don't follow."

Subtlety had never been my strong suit. Maybe I should just rip the Band-Aid off and get it out in the open, once and for all. It might make things awkward for a day or two, but then, hopefully, we could move on with a better understanding between us.

Taking a deep breath, I blurted it out plainly. "I just mean that if she knew you didn't like women in general in that way, she might have been less offended."

His chocolate-brown eyes continued to bore into me, uncomprehending, until finally, something seemed to click and he let out a small, strangled sort of laugh, his hands tightening on the reins. "Hang on. You... you think I'm gay?"

He sounded so surprised that guilt immediately rushed through me. He must have thought he had done a better job of hiding it.

"It doesn't matter to me," I quickly assured him. "And for the record, I probably wouldn't have immediately jumped to that conclusion if the others hadn't mentioned it first."

"The *others?*" He looked almost equally bewildered and horrified at the idea that anyone else would know.

"Some of the women in town," I admitted. "But it's honestly not as big a deal as you think. No one thinks any less of you for it. So, if that's the reason you don't want to have people over, if you think I'll judge you for it, you really don't have to worry. It makes no difference to me."

His eyes stayed on me but the expression on his face had turned completely inscrutable. I couldn't have guessed what he was thinking if my life depended on it.

"It makes no difference to you," he repeated back to me, speaking each word slowly and clearly before shaking his head. "Alright, fine. If that's what you want to think, then we'll go with that."

Not giving me a chance to say anything else, he dug his heels in and his horse took off, heading back towards the ranch at a gallop and not once looking back.

~Jesse~

With the horse's hooves thundering beneath me, I didn't know whether to laugh or scream my frustration into the evening air.

Laura thought I was gay. The whole damn town did, apparently, but that part didn't matter to me. They could think whatever they wanted. Laura, however, was another matter. For nearly a month, I'd been torturing myself, reading so many things into the way I sometimes caught her looking at me, the way she laughed when we spent time together, the way she asked what I thought and felt about things and I thought... damn it, I thought she felt the same as I did. I knew all the reasons why nothing could come of it, why I wouldn't *let* anything happen, but it had given me some small amount of comfort to think she might be feeling it too, as ridiculous as that sounded.

Apparently, it had all been in my head. She saw me as nothing more than a boss and a housemate. Sexually, physically, emotionally, she obviously felt nothing at all. She told me so herself: it didn't make any difference.

Which was exactly what I wanted. In fact, it had to be that way: no attachments, no getting close to anyone, so why the hell did it upset me so much?

Although I would have liked to keep galloping, the wind against my face and my muscles tense until my feelings started to make a lick of sense to me, I had to think about the horse too. He'd already had a workout that night even before my escape, so I slowed down to a walk as the barn came into view, letting him cool down, and I made sure to run through the full after-care routine with him once I'd dismounted, not letting my emotion take over. The horses, the ranch, and the work had to come first, always.

Even so, my nerves were on edge as I waited for Laura to arrive, anticipating at any second that I'd see her riding up, asking for an explanation for my behaviour, asking me more questions in that way of hers that made me feel like it might not be the end of the world if I answered them. I'd finally given into that urge and opened up with her, just a little, and look where it got me.

She didn't show up, though. I finished getting the horse ready for the night and she still hadn't arrived. That must mean she had decided to give me space, which really wasn't like her. Even when she tried, which I knew she had been, Laura didn't really get the idea of keeping out of each other's way. We'd been spending more and more time together over the last few weeks, gradually, almost without me noticing it, until I began to look forward to it. Until I missed it when it didn't happen, exactly as I hadn't wanted to.

What was I supposed to do? With my mind still racing, I headed back to the house and to my room, looking around at the empty walls and austere surroundings which wouldn't be out of place for a monk or a hermit, someone who had chosen to cut themselves off from the rest of the world. I *had* chosen this life, or at least I'd tried, and I'd been doing a damn good job of it too until Laura Callahan turned up at my door.

It all started with my mother. Sitting down on the bed, my thoughts still in turmoil and my defenses down, I let myself think back on the reasons I'd chosen this life in the first place. Usually, I avoided thinking about it, for obvious reasons. Though I'd only met Mrs Callahan once or twice, from the way Laura described her, I thought she and my mom probably had a lot in common. They were both warm and kind and loving. My memories of my mom were fuzzy around the edges, more like memories of memories than actual recollections, but I remembered the feeling of safety and security when she was around. I had never doubted that I mattered.

I'd only been seven when she died but the moment had seared itself into my brain. Nothing about that day was fuzzy; all the edges were sharp and painful, even after all this time. She'd called upstairs to tell me to hurry up and get dressed so I could have breakfast before school. My two-year-old sister was following me around, as she liked to do, and I took my time helping her down the stairs, making sure she didn't fall. At some point, I heard something break downstairs, but I didn't think much of it. Mom would fix it. She always did.

The smell of coffee hit me first when we walked into the kitchen. My mom always had a cup of coffee while I ate my breakfast, but it smelled stronger than usual that day and I soon realized why: little rivers of it flowed along the kitchen floor, the mug that had been holding it shattered in pieces, lying next to my mother's body.

What happened after that did get a little fuzzier. When she didn't answer me as I shouted her name, I called 911, like she'd taught me to do. I could remember the numb, cold feeling that spread through my body as I waited for someone to come and help, and the way my sister lay on the floor next to her for a while, thinking they were playing some kind of game. The coffee soaked into my socks when I ran across the floor, and I could smell it for days afterwards, no matter how many times I washed my feet.

The paramedics called my dad when they got there but there was nothing they could do for my mom. A ruptured brain aneurysm, the autopsy said. Apparently, she complained of a headache when she woke up, but she told my dad to go to work anyway. She thought she could deal with it. We had no more warning than that.

The closing of the front door as Laura came back into the house pulled me out of the past and back into my present dilemma. Shaking my head to put all those memories back where they belonged, I stood back up and pulled off my shirt, tossing it into the laundry basket.

People might think of my life as empty or lonely, but I knew the truth: a bit of loneliness beat the deep pain of loss any day of the week. If I didn't get close to anyone, I couldn't be hurt that deeply ever again, and I had definitely been getting too close to Laura Callahan, whether she knew it or not.

"Jesse?" Her voice followed a soft knock on my door. "Can I talk to you for a second?"

Taking a deep breath, I tried to let go of all the conflicting thoughts in my head. None of the way I felt was her fault and I didn't want to take it out on her. I needed to be calm and detached. It didn't matter to her if I was gay, after all, so none of it should matter to me either.

"I can give you *two* seconds, tops." I kept my tone light and my expression neutral as I opened the door, trying to ignore her wind-swept hair and those sweet blue eyes that looked up at me.

Her gaze dropped to my bare chest for just a moment before she brought it back to my face. "Listen, I'm sorry if I crossed a line out there. Sometimes my mouth just runs away with itself before it checks with my head and things come out wrong. If it helps, it's not just me, it runs in my family, but... that probably doesn't help."

Her apology was actually rather adorable. I hadn't seen this humbled side of her before.

"What I was trying to say out there, badly, is that I like you. I know I'm not supposed to, we're supposed to 'live our own lives' and all that, but you're a good guy, Jesse. I like you a hell of a lot more than I expected to when I first showed up here, and I just wanted you to know that you don't have to hide things about yourself from me. I'm annoying and inappropriate, I get it, but I'm also a good friend. I'd have your back if anyone tries to give you trouble."

I could believe that; I just didn't need her help in the way she thought

I did, and I really didn't know if I should tell her that or let her continue to think what she thought.

Turning around, I took a step back into my room as I thought it over and Laura stepped to the side, leaning back against the open door. "I could even set you up if you're interested," she offered before I could come up with a response, and I looked back at her in disbelief.

The idea of her bringing another man into the house made my stomach twist, against all my logical reasoning and all my better instincts, but she would have no problem seeing me with someone else? I didn't believe that. It couldn't have *all* been in my head. Maybe she was overcompensating?

She immediately crossed her arms defensively against the look I gave her. "Well, why not? I can't imagine you have many options here in Sandy Creek, but I know some folks in Houston who would jump at the chance to date a hot cowboy..."

That did it. My patience snapped as I stepped up to her, placing my hands on the door on either side of her, boxing her in with my body. We weren't touching, but we'd never been quite so close to each other before either.

"Let me see if I've got this straight. You like me?"

My eyes were fixed on hers in challenge, and she nodded up at me mutely, holding my gaze.

"And you think I'm hot?"

Her lips pursed together as she realized she had, in fact, just said that. She blinked a couple of times but didn't look away as she nodded again.

I leaned just a little bit closer. "But it wouldn't make any difference to you if I'm attracted to women or not?"

Her blinking got more rapid, her breath seeming to catch. "But... you're not?"

I didn't answer that. I just left the question hanging between us as I took a step back.

Laura's brow furrowed as she watched me, the wheels turning in her head so fast that I could practically see them moving. It felt way too good to turn the tables on her and put her on the back foot for once. "You're not," she repeated, more firmly this time, but that certainty faltered when I still didn't answer. "Are you?"

"Goodnight, Laura." Grabbing the edge of the door, I swung it gently closed, pushing her out of my room at the same time.

Chapter Seven

~Laura~

No matter what I did, I couldn't get comfortable in my bed. My body refused to relax and my mind wouldn't turn off.

That moment with Jesse at his door had been one of the most electrifyingly sexy experiences of my life and he hadn't even touched me. I still didn't even know for sure if he was gay or not. But when he leaned close to me, those warm brown eyes piercing into mine, his masculine, musky scent filling my nose, a mix of his cologne and leather and horses, and his naked torso so close to me I could feel the heat he gave off and see the tension in his muscles, I had never been more attracted to anyone in my entire life. For once, I found myself completely lost for words.

And then he just backed off, like the moment hadn't happened, like he hadn't felt anything, leaving me guessing about whether I had misjudged the whole situation. Did he suggest he wasn't gay to confuse me, or had I got it all wrong? Did he like women or not? Did he like *me* or not?

Maybe I had jumped to conclusions. Mary-Beth told me the rumours and I picked out things in his behaviour that I thought would fit that theory, but if I looked at each piece of evidence on its own, the sum total was hardly conclusive. I thought he left me out in the field because I'd crossed a line in trying to out him, but maybe I'd offended him if what I said hadn't been the truth at all. But in that case, why wouldn't he just tell me so? Why did he have to be so secretive? Why couldn't he just say what he meant?

He frustrated and intrigued me, and got me more worked up than I'd been over a man since... well, ever, I supposed. Even the possibility that he might be interested in me on a physical level had my body buzzing with excitement, little pangs of lust hitting me as I thought back to that strong, firm body and what he might be able to do with it. And he hadn't even given me the least bit of encouragement! What the hell was wrong with me? I rolled over again, pressing my legs together as I tried to wish away my arousal.

The last time I remembered checking the clock, it said 1:43, and I must have fallen asleep after that because the next thing I knew, I opened my eyes to the sun streaming in the window and the clock reading 7:16. Panic raced through me as I sat bolt upright. How could I have slept through my alarm? Why didn't anyone wake me? What was Jesse going to think of me?

I made it halfway across the room to the bathroom before I remembered that I had the day off and I hadn't set my alarm because I didn't have to. I didn't expect to sleep quite so long, but the late night had obviously taken its toll. I still did need to get up and get going, but at least I hadn't let Jesse down.

His opinion meant a lot to me, and I didn't want to disappoint him.

An hour later, showered, dressed and determined to put Jesse Green-bank out of my mind for the rest of the day, I headed out on the road to Houston. I had missed the last couple of family barbecues, with my family's blessing, wanting to stay on hand in case any of the construction work on the ranch needed my help, but now that things were wrapping up, I wanted to make up for it. It sounded like the gatherings I'd missed had been rather sombre anyway since Dex's wife, Shawna, had been in the hospital for weeks, ever since my graduation. The hospital would be my first stop that day.

The scene when I walked into the hospital room had grown far too familiar: bouquets of fresh flowers, some of Dex's sketches and drawings scattered around the room to give it some colour, Shawna lying in her bed looking paler and thinner than I'd ever seen her, and my brother sitting at her bedside, his face drawn and tired.

"I don't know if there's even room for these," I announced as I walked in, holding up the vase full of daisies I'd picked up from the florist next door. "It's a good thing you don't have any allergies."

Shawna smiled over at me, her eyes still bright even if her face didn't quite match, but Dex struggled to even give me a nod, his lips pressed tightly together.

"Am I interrupting something? I can come back later…"

"No, stay, please." Shawna shot Dex an affectionate warning look. "Dex was just leaving to get something to eat, weren't you?"

"You don't want me to stay?" She shook her head and he let out a long breath before nodding. "Alright. I'll be back soon, baby."

He leaned down to place a kiss on her forehead before getting unsteadily to his feet. On his way past me, he squeezed my hand but didn't say anything, and an uneasy feeling settled in the pit of my stomach. I'd never seen him looking quite so hopeless before.

Shawna didn't seem to be in the same mood, though, so I pasted a bright smile on my face as I walked over and took Dex's seat at the side of the bed, squeezing my vase of flowers between the ones already there.

"What's got his panties in a twist this morning?" I asked, trying to make light of what could only be called an awful situation, and Shawna gave another quick smile.

"Don't mind him. He's just upset because I'm dying."

"What?" The bottom of my stomach seemed to give way as I gripped onto the arms of the chair for support. Shawna had a dry sense of humour at times, making her a perfect foil for my rather sunny brother, but as much as I hoped she was joking now, she didn't seem to be.

She reached her hand out and I immediately took it. "The doctors told us two days ago there's nothing more they can do. The cancer has spread too much. We stopped the chemo, so it's really just a matter of time."

My hand trembled around hers as the words sank in, but she looked remarkably serene for someone who had just announced her impending death. How could she be so calm? "How much time?" I managed to ask.

She tried to shrug, but her shoulders barely moved. "A couple of weeks at most."

My shock was too strong for tears to come. I just stared at her in disbelief. "That can't be right."

"It is." She gave my hand a gentle squeeze. "My body's had enough, and I don't blame it for that. It did its best. We all did."

The haunted look in my brother's eyes made a lot more sense to me now. "Dex..." I started to say, but I didn't even know where to start. This would crush my brother. He loved her so much. I could barely even remember a time they weren't together.

Shawna took a shaky breath, fighting for control as much as I was. "I know. He's still in denial, I think. I tried to talk to him this morning about moving on after me and he didn't want to hear it. That's why he's pouting now."

She forced another smile, but I couldn't imagine how that conversation would have gone. "You want him to meet someone else?"

Her nod was as firm as she could make it. "I don't want him shutting himself off and missing the rest of his life. I need your help with that too, Laura. I want you to promise me that when he does meet someone special, y'all will make her feel welcome. Make it as easy on him as you can, okay?"

Finally, the tears started to gather in my eyes as the reality of it all began to sink in, and Shawna shook her head.

"Don't go getting all sad on me now. You were doing so well."

I choked back a laugh, trying to blink the tears away. Shawna had always understood how to be blunt when necessary, fitting into our outspoken family just like a glove. "I promise I won't give anyone he brings home a hard time," I assured her. The thought of Dex with anyone else seemed impossible, but I didn't say that. I could, on occasion, hold my tongue. "What else can I do? What do you need?"

"Nothing," she said, shaking her head when I tried to protest. "Honestly, I mean it. Everyone wants to help, but all you can do now is be there for Dex. That's the most important thing. And please, for the love of God, talk to me about something else. I'm so tired of everyone crying."

She'd never been one for self-pity, so her words didn't surprise me, and I did my best to comply. "What do you want to talk about?"

"Tell me about the ranch," she requested, the brightness returning to her eyes once more. "How are things going?"

I filled her in on all my plans and how they were coming along, about working with the other hands and needing to practice my riding again. She paid careful attention, asking lots of questions, and when I'd finished my rundown, she gave me a shrewd look. "And what's the deal with Jesse?"

"The deal?" I repeated, pretending I didn't know what she meant, but Shawna had always seen right through me.

"You smile every time you say his name."

"I do not!" I protested, but she had no intention of letting me off the hook.

"Come on now, Laura, you can't leave out the juiciest bits. Is there something between you two?"

Reluctantly, I filled her in on the development of my friendship with Jesse so far, such as it was, leading up to the previous night's encounter in his room. Her eyes were sparkling in delight by the time I'd finished.

"You Callahans never do anything the easy way," she said with a laugh. "So let me tell you what I told Tonia not that long ago: if you feel something for him, don't waste time. Love doesn't come around every day, so when there's something special there, don't let it pass you by."

"Love?" I repeated, almost choking on the word. "Whatever drugs you're on are making you delusional. I barely even know him. He still might be gay, for all I know."

She laughed so hard that she started coughing, and I quickly got her a drink from the water bottle next to her bed. When she'd caught her breath again, she gave me an indulgent smile. "First of all, that man is not gay, I'd bet my life on it."

"That isn't saying much right about now." The words slipped out before I'd fully thought them out, and my eyes widened in horror as I realized exactly what I'd said, but Shawna simply laughed again.

"Fair enough. I'd bet Dex's life then, that's how sure I am. He sounds like he's been hurt before, bad enough that it's made him skittish about letting anyone close. Maybe you just gotta push him out of his comfort zone a bit. Lay a kiss on him and see what happens."

The idea of kissing Jesse made my whole body flare with heat as I remembered how it felt when he had me pinned against the door the night before, but it could so easily backfire. "He told me flat out that he doesn't want any kind of relationship with me. We're supposed to 'live our own lives'. That's pretty clear, isn't it? I don't want to lose the small amount of trust I've managed to earn from him so far."

Shawna thought that over and, in the end, she had to agree with me. "Alright, maybe go a little less direct. Get all dolled up, looking your absolute best. Tell him you're going on a date and see how he reacts."

"Isn't that a little manipulative?" Games had never been my style. I preferred to be open and honest, sometimes to a fault.

"It sure is, but no more manipulative than him refusing to answer your question last night. He started it."

I still wasn't sure, but she looked so excited, I couldn't say no. "I'll think about it," I offered instead.

"Call me and let me know how it goes," she begged. "Lord knows I could use something to look forward to."

How could I refuse a dying woman's request?

Dex walked back in a minute later and he gave me a grateful look when he took in Shawna's good mood. I visited with them both a while longer until Shawna's eyelids began to droop. I gave her a long hug, knowing this could very well be the last time I saw her. I offered to ask for another day off this week, but she told me next week would be fine. "I've got a few people I need to see, and it takes a lot out of me," she told me honestly. "Come up again next week when you were planning to. I'll see you then."

I didn't say goodbye since I knew she wouldn't appreciate it, but when Dex walked me to the door, I couldn't stop the tears that filled my eyes. Out in the hallway with the door closed behind us so Shawna wouldn't hear, I sobbed in my brother's arms, feeling his body shuddering against mine.

"It's not fair, Dex," I sniffled.

"No, it sure ain't." His voice was raw and sore. "But thanks for helping her forget about it for a little while."

He took a deep breath as he pulled back from me, wiping his eyes dry before he went back into the room.

"She wanted to tell you in person, but I'll keep you updated by text now."

I nodded and with a forced, sad smile, he went back into the room while I headed to Tonia's house. Billie was already there and the three of us spent the rest of the day laughing and crying and trying to come to terms with the fact that even when love was true, it didn't mean it would last forever.

~Jesse~

I couldn't believe how much I noticed Laura's absence while she was away. Somehow, in the month she'd been there, I'd grown accustomed to the sound of her in the kitchen in the morning, the way she hummed along to whatever song was in her head without even realizing she was doing it, and the smile she gave me when I walked in.

I'd gotten used to talking about ranch business with her over lunch, to seeing her joking around with the other hands out in the field, and to her giving me a hard time about my frozen dinners. Even in the evenings, when I did my best to keep my distance, I always remained aware of her, listening out for her to get home when she'd gone out so I knew she was safe before I went to bed.

I tried to tell myself I did it the same way a brother might watch out for a sister, but the thoughts I had about her at other times were far from brotherly.

And now, she'd been gone the whole day without any kind of contact, and no clue as to what she might be thinking after the way we'd left things the day before, and I couldn't help watching the clock hands as they ticked closer to 10. I knew she'd gone up to the city but she also knew she had to get up early in the morning, so it worried me that she hadn't returned yet.

Finally, I couldn't take it anymore and I sent her a quick text, knowing she had her phone connected in her truck. She had her phone everywhere.

You on your way back?

Straight to the point, nobody could accuse me of coming on too strong, and I wouldn't admit to anyone how relieved I felt when her reply came in.

Just left the city so I'll be late. Don't wait up. See you in the morning.

Taking her advice, I headed to bed, but I left my bedroom door open a crack and I didn't fall into a deep sleep until I had heard her come in.

The next morning, she was in the kitchen as usual when I came in, but the smile she gave me seemed a little more forced than usual. Her eyes looked tired and a little sad, but I hoped that came from the late night and early morning combo. I could have asked, but it felt dangerous to go down that road. I had to follow my own rules: separate lives and all that.

Out on the ranch, she worked hard as always and laughed with the other hands, but I couldn't shake the feeling that something was bothering her. I brought it up to Tyson as casually as I could. "Does Laura seem okay to you today?"

He gave me a funny look. "Same as always. Why?"

I had no answer to that, just a gut feeling that something had changed.

We had no plans to ride that night so I made my own dinner, eating at the table while Laura cooked herself something, still uncharacteristically quiet. My ego wasn't big enough that I thought her mood had anything to do with me. Something must have happened in Houston, but I didn't know how to ask her about it. I had avoided getting involved with people for so long that I had no idea where to begin.

Maybe humour was the way to go? She liked to laugh and tease me, and she seemed to like it when I repaid her in kind. I could also reference our conversation from the other night in an oblique way and see how she reacted. At least it would confirm if her general discomfort had anything to do with me.

"If you don't have any plans tonight, I'm thinking about watching a movie. You could join me if you want. I think Brokeback Mountain's on TV."

I knew she wouldn't miss the reference to gay cowboys, and she didn't let me down, giving me exactly the response I expected. Choking on a surprised laugh, she turned to me with her usual fire back in her eyes. "Really?"

I shrugged, trying not to smile. "I'm sure it's streaming somewhere."

Her lips twitched as her eyes searched my face, looking for any clue about how serious I might be. Finally, she seemed to give up, shaking her head. "Another time, maybe. I do have plans for tonight, actually."

That shouldn't have disappointed me nearly as much as I did, so I did my best to appear uninterested. "No problem."

After I finished eating, I made my way into the living room and Laura went to her room to get ready. Nothing seemed to catch my interest as I flipped through the channels, and I was about to give up and head to my room instead when Laura appeared in the doorway. "Alright, I'm off. See you later."

Out of instinct, I turned my head to say goodnight, but when I got a proper look at her, I couldn't stop myself from doing a double take.

Gone were the jeans, checked shirt and cowboy boots that acted as her uniform on the ranch. A deep green dress wrapped around her body instead, hugging her hips and drawing attention to her breasts in a subtle yet undeniable way. The high-heeled shoes she wore showed off her toned legs perfectly and her dark hair curled down over her shoulders. During the work day, she hardly wore any makeup, but now, her cheeks were pink, her eyes highlighted and her lips a deep, enticing red.

"Where... uh, where are you going?" I stuttered, both fire and ice racing through my body at the sight of her. She looked absolutely incredible and I couldn't stop the flare of desire that ran through me, nor the uncomfortable tightness in my chest at the thought of anyone else seeing her that way and thinking they had a shot with her.

"Out with Mary-Beth," she told me, looking down at her phone, completely oblivious to my reaction. I tugged one of the pillows closer to my lap anyway, just in case she happened to notice what she'd done to me. "She's promised to introduce me to the eligible men of Sandy Creek. It shouldn't take long."

She laughed as though there was anything funny about it. Her words only made it worse, knowing that she actually meant to advertise the fact that she was single, looking like that. If the men in town had any sense, they'd be lining up for a chance with her.

"Have a good night, Jesse," she added before giving me a sweet wave and heading to the door, leaving me in a state of confused arousal and jealousy that I barely knew how to process.

What the hell did I expect? I'd done my best to keep my distance, done such a good job that she decided I couldn't possibly like women at all, and yet I didn't want her to be with anyone else either? That made no sense and I knew it, but it didn't change the fact that I felt that way anyway.

No matter how hard I tried to focus back on the TV, I couldn't get rid of the slightly nauseous feeling that had settled in my stomach. The idea of someone else's hands on Laura in that dress frustrated me, but if I was being totally honest with myself, that wasn't even the worst part.

The idea of her sitting down to breakfast with someone else, laughing and teasing him, going out for rides around the ranch with him, those things all bothered me even more.

Fuck. I hadn't realized just how far I'd let things get out of hand already. I'd told her I didn't want any kind of relationship between us and now, Laura was calling my bluff. I'd tried to turn the tables on her the other night, giving her a hint of the electricity I felt between us, but she'd upped the ante. Now, she'd left me with a decision to make: did I stick to my guns and insist she meant nothing more to me than any of the other hands, or did I show my hand and make her aware of my interest?

It would mean opening the door to the kind of connection I'd avoided for so long, the kind that could break me if it went wrong. But seeing her in that dress, and seeing the sadness in her eyes that morning that I wanted to be able to help her deal with, I had to wonder, perhaps for the first time, if it might not be worth taking the risk.

"Damn you, Laura Callahan." With a frustrated sigh, I turned the TV off and grabbed my car keys instead. Sandy Creek only had one bar, so I had to guess she'd gone there. Maybe if I left right away, I could still get there before it was too late.

~Laura~

The Sandy Creek bar hadn't changed much in the six years I'd been away. The bar itself took up one wall of the large rectangular room, a few booths lined the opposite wall, and the space in between was filled with a few tall tables set wide apart and a pool table in the back. Sneaking into the bar during senior year was considered a rite of passage, and I'd been lucky to have an older brother who understood that. When he turned 21, Dex brought me and Mary-Beth with him one night so we could say we'd been, but I'd found the whole experience pretty underwhelming. Aside from a few ranch hands from out of town, it had just been the same people I saw every day while doing their groceries, or those who had graduated a few years before me; just regular, everyday folks having a drink with their friends.

No drama, no love-at-first-sight, no jealous rivals fighting over their lovers, nothing like TV shows and movies made it seem.

In Houston, I went to a lot more bars where there were a lot more strangers, the scene a little closer to what I had always imagined, but with a lot more men just looking for a casual hook-up too. One-night-stands were trickier in a place like Sandy Creek where everyone knew everything about everyone else.

Maybe that had something to do with what kept Jesse away, I mused while Mary-Beth went up to the bar to get us some non-alcoholic beers since we both had to get up early in the morning. He didn't want to get involved with anyone, but casual was hard to do in a place like this. Maybe that explained why he turned all the local women down, rather than it having anything to do with his sexual orientation.

Maybe Shawna was right about him not being gay at all.

I'd only gone out that night because of her. The whole day, my emotions cycled between sadness and anger and helplessness, wishing there was something I could do for her or my brother that would make any bit of difference. She'd asked me not to spread the news about her prognosis around town since she knew there'd be people who would insist on going up to see her whether she wanted them to or not, and she'd rather spend her final days with the people who truly mattered to her. So, I hadn't said a word about my motives to Mary-Beth when I called her up and asked what she thought about getting dressed up and having a night out. She'd agreed with excitement and I did my best to play along, although the part I cared the most about had already happened: the expression on Jesse's face when he got a look at me in my outfit for the night.

He definitely noticed that I'd made an effort, that was for sure, but he didn't tell me I looked good or anything along those lines; he simply stared, looking rather shell shocked, and asked what my plans were. That was it. It wouldn't be much to report back to Shawna, but at least I could tell her I'd tried.

"Don't think I've ever seen you wearing anything but jeans before," a voice said in my ear, shaking me out of my thoughts as the owner of it perched himself on Mary-Beth's empty seat, giving me an appreciative look that bordered on a leer. "Heard you were back in town, Laura. Or hiding over at the ranch, anyways."

"I'm not hiding, and you're one to talk, Dale. Aren't those the exact same jeans you wore in high school? They look dirty enough."

The former football player and all-round creep from my class simply chuckled at my words. "I'm flattered you were paying that much attention. Maybe you'd like to see them around my ankles later."

"Oh, hell, no." Mary-Beth had returned to catch the last part of the conversation and, after placing our beers on the table, she physically pulled Dale away from her seat. "I'm trying to convince her to stay here rather than go back to the city, and you ain't doing Sandy Creek any favours, Dale. Why don't you go find someone with a lot more liquor in her and a lot less common sense?"

He simply laughed, tipping his hat to me before walking away. "I know you'll be thinking about it now."

"Any time I need to make myself sick," I retorted, shaking my head as he wandered off, completely unfazed. It was impossible to shame someone that shameless. He actually wasn't even bad-looking but his personality was as completely off-putting as it always had been.

"Like I said before: the single guys our age usually have a good reason why they're still single." Mary-Beth rolled her eyes as she climbed back up into her tall chair. "Good news is he's all talk. If you actually took him up on it, he'd probably have a heart attack."

"So do you actually have anyone in mind you *would* set me up with?"

When her eyes lit up, I quickly added a qualifier. "I'm not asking you to, I'm just curious. Who are the decent single guys left in Sandy Creek?"

She ran me through the short list, which was very short indeed. "Then there's Wade Johnson," she added after a minute. "Not exactly single, though."

"Not *exactly* single?" I repeated with a laugh. "He's married to Barbara, isn't he?"

They were the power couple in our class at school: the football quarterback and the homecoming queen, every small town's royalty, though their relationship had always been volatile.

"They're still married, but it's touch-and-go," Mary-Beth told me, leaning closer. "Barbara's been spending a lot of time out at the Swancoat ranch. Apparently, one of the new hands there caught her eye and a whole lot more."

"Does Wade know?" Though we'd never been friends, I hated the thought of the whole town talking about it behind his back.

"I don't know how he couldn't. Rumour is he wants to work through it, but she might not be interested. So, if she calls it quits, he might be back on the market before long."

"With an awful lot of baggage," I couldn't help pointing out, making Mary-Beth laugh.

"Oh, honey, we've all got baggage. Even you. But speaking of single men, would you look at what the cat just dragged in?"

She gestured towards the door behind me, and I twisted around in my seat just in time to see a man ducking into one of the empty booths, his hat pulled down over his eyes as if he didn't want to be recognized. It didn't work, though: I'd know that body anywhere.

Heat flushed through me as I quickly turned back, not wanting Jesse to catch me staring. Did he come to the bar because of me? Mary-Beth said he never hung out at the bar, and it seemed an awfully big coincidence that he'd choose that night to start. Could Shawna's plan really have been that effective after just one try?

Never one to miss anything, Mary-Beth picked up on my flushed cheeks immediately. "Are you holding out on me, Laura? Is something going on between you two?"

"No!" I protested, a little too quickly. "I'm just surprised he's here, that's all. He usually hangs out at home."

"Let's go say hi." She started to get to her feet, but I quickly pushed her back down.

"He'll come over if he wants to come over. He's made it clear he doesn't want us being too friendly."

Looking unconvinced, she leaned back, thinking things over. As she reached for her beer, her hand missed, knocking it over instead, the liquid pouring over the side of the table as we both leapt to our feet. "Oh, shoot!"

"I'll get some paper towels from the bar," I offered, grabbing the bottle so no more of it could spill.

"Don't worry about that, I've got some wipes in my bag. Kids, remember? But could you grab me another beer?"

She smiled over at me so sweetly that I had a feeling she must be up to something. "Sure," I agreed warily, looking over to the bar where Dale stood, chatting to the bartender who had no escape. As she cleaned off the table with the wipes from her bag, I headed over and caught the bartender's eye. "Can I get Mary-Beth a refill, please?"

Looking grateful for the interruption, the bartender turned away while Dale sidled over closer to me though I'd made no invitation or even acknowledged his presence. "It must get pretty lonely out on the ranch. If you ever need some company, I'd be willing to make the drive."

"That's awfully generous of you. You'd sacrifice a whole $4 worth of gas, would you?"

"For you, I would." He looked so pleased with himself, as if I would actually be impressed, that I had to laugh.

"What makes you think I'm lonely? There are plenty of men working out on the ranch."

"Plenty of men who see you as one of the guys," he corrected. "Just like in high school, Laura. If you dressed up like this a little more, maybe you'd have a few more of them interested." His hand drifted over to my hip as he stepped even closer.

"Maybe what she chooses to wear ain't any of your business."

Jesse's growled voice behind us took us both by surprise, but rather than pull his hand away, which would have been the smart thing to do, Dale dug in deeper, letting it drift closer to my ass.

"Don't see how it's any business of yours either," he replied with a smugness that was completely unjustified. "Laura and I are having a private conversation here."

From the tick in Jesse's jaw, I knew Dale was on thin ice. I hadn't seen Jesse lose his temper yet, and though I had to admit I was curious what it might look like, it didn't seem the smartest move for anyone involved. I grabbed Dale's arm instead, pulling his hand off of me.

"No, we are not having a conversation. Laura is here to get a drink and that's all. You're excused, Dale."

"But what about..." he started to protest, but Jesse stepped in front of him before he could even finish whatever cringeworthy thing he'd been about to say next.

"Are you deaf? She said you can go."

Though Dale still had his linebacker's width, Jesse had the advantage on height and sheer muscle too. After sizing him up for a minute and weighing his chances, Dale finally backed off. "You can always find me here, Laura," he said by way of parting. "Think about it."

When he finally left to go join the group of men at the pool table, I let out a laugh. "It shouldn't be possible to be that clueless."

Jesse turned to me with no hint of humour in his expression. "Are you alright?"

I raised my eyebrows back at him. "Of course. You think I can't handle a guy like him?"

"I think you shouldn't have to." His jaw still hadn't unclenched and his usually warm brown eyes were conflicted.

"What are you doing here, Jesse? I thought we were staying out of each other's way."

"That's what I said," he muttered in agreement.

"So?" I prompted, wanting him to get to the point. He was still standing awfully close to me, the tension between us almost as strong as it had been in his room the other night, but that time, I didn't intend to let him get away without answering me.

"So... maybe we could be a little more in each other's way. If you want to."

Oh, no. He was not putting this back on me. He'd followed me into town, he could damn well tell me why. "What do *you* want, Jesse?"

His eyes searched mine for a long minute, looking for something I didn't understand, but at long last, he spoke again. "I want you to come back home."

Not good enough. "Why?"

His nostrils flared, the muscles working in his cheeks even harder than before. "Because if I do what I want to do to you right here, I'm liable to get charged with public indecency."

Oh. That was a good answer, one that had every nerve in my body on edge in an instant, heat flooding through me stronger than ever before, but I wanted to make sure I understood him completely. No more crossed wires. "So... you're not attracted to men?"

He gave a short, pained bark of a laugh. "No, I damn well ain't. Now, are you coming or not?"

Chapter Eight

~**Jesse**~

When I walked into the bar, I still hadn't entirely decided what I planned to do. I figured there was no point in deciding for certain until I got there and saw the situation for myself. Maybe I'd completely overreacted and she'd merely be with a group of friends. Maybe she and Mary-Beth would be having a quiet drink between them. Going in guns blazing seemed like overkill, so I did my best to sneak in instead, slipping into the first empty booth I saw, hoping no one would notice me.

It didn't entirely work. My eyes were drawn immediately to Laura, shining like a beacon in the middle of the room, putting everyone else around her to shame without even trying, and I saw the moment she looked over at me. Even in the dim lighting, designed to hide all kinds of imperfections, I felt certain she would have recognized me, but she turned around as though she hadn't. Like she didn't know me at all, keeping our lives separate exactly as I'd asked her to.

My eyes remained fixed on her when she went over to the bar, and when I saw the way the man standing there looked her up and down, not even bothering to hide it, a strong, possessive streak I never knew I had flared up inside me. I knew how ridiculous that feeling was since Laura had never even been mine in the first place, but it didn't stop me from getting to my feet and heading to the bar myself. I simply wanted to get a drink, I tried to tell myself. People drank in a bar.

But when I heard the way he spoke to her, the overly familiar tone and the audacity of his words, not to mention his hand on her hip, I couldn't help myself. I wanted him to know that no one spoke to Laura that way, even if she *could* handle it, as she herself pointed out to me.

She didn't ignore me once I stood right in front of her, but she called me out on my presence, asking why I'd followed her since it was pretty obvious I had. I surprised us both by telling her the truth: that I didn't want to stay out of her way anymore.

Laura's pretty blue eyes looked up at me with her beguiling mix of confidence and uncertainty, surprise and interest as I confirmed for her that she had completely grasped the wrong end of the stick when deciding that my choosing to stay away from her in the first place had anything to do with not finding her attractive.

"Are you coming or not?" I asked after laying it all on the line for her. My heart pounded as I waited for her response, afraid she'd say no but almost equally scared she'd say yes. I'd broken all my rules that night and I planned to go on breaking them, as long as she came along for the ride, and that possibility both exhilarated and terrified me.

"I... I drove my own truck here," she replied, and it took me a second to realize what that had to do with anything. Her truck was the least of my worries right now.

"So, you can drive it back home again. I'll be right behind you."

Her cheeks began to colour as she realized just how completely serious I was, but thankfully, she didn't make me wait any longer for her answer. "Alright. Let me just say goodbye to Mary-Beth."

I could do that, barely. Every muscle in my body felt tense as I watched her walk back to her table, leaning down to whisper something in her friend's ear. Mary-Beth looked over to me with an entirely-too-knowing smile, but at that point, I couldn't bring myself to care about the gossip either. The only thing that mattered to me was getting Laura alone.

The drive back to the ranch from town had never felt so long before. I stayed behind Laura's truck the whole way as promised, and when we pulled up to the house, I ran ahead to unlock the door and hold it open for her.

As soon as we were inside, I had her back against the wall, pinned there between my arms just as she'd been in my room two nights earlier, but this time, I wasn't playing any games.

"I've told you what I want, Laura. It's your turn now."

"You really haven't told me much," she retorted. The surprise had gone from her expression and I could see the excitement that had taken its place, the way her pupils dilated and her breathing had turned shallower, but her stubbornness remained on display too. She'd obviously been thinking about it on the drive. "You want to 'be in my way'. What does that mean? Sex? Roommates with benefits? A relationship? What exactly are you proposing, Jesse?"

That was a damn good question, and one I didn't know how to answer. All I really knew was the way my body pulled itself towards her, attracted by some kind of magnetic force, and the comfortable way she'd worked herself into both my personal and professional life. I wanted what we already had and I wanted more, but exactly what that 'more' looked like, I couldn't define. I'd never had to before.

I never wanted to before.

"Right now, I want to get you out of that dress and show you exactly how attracted to you I am. After that, I think it's equally up to you, but I'm open to suggestions."

Her eyes sparked with both arousal and amusement. "That's a very clever way of not answering my question at all."

A groan of frustration, nearly a growl, echoed from deep in my throat. "It's a lot more than you've told me. You've got to meet me halfway here, Laura. What do you want?"

Her hand went to my chest, nearly making me jump with the current of excitement it sent through me, a shot of adrenaline that went straight to my groin. "I think we can take it one day at a time. For tonight, I want to know if you feel just as good as you look."

Fuck. She couldn't turn me on any more if she tried, and the fact that she barely even tried drove me completely crazy. Any self-control or resistance I'd been holding onto broke with those words and my hand wrapped around the back of her neck, lifting her face to mine as I brought my lips down to hers, her body still pressed against the wall.

All the times I'd imagined that moment, and there had been more than a few of them, didn't begin to compare to the real thing. Her warm, soft lips molded to mine perfectly and the slightly bittersweet taste of the beer she'd been drinking lingered there, which couldn't be a more perfect analogy for Laura herself: feminine and sexy but down to earth at the same time. She didn't hold back either, kissing me back with just as much fervour as I felt, her lips and tongue moving against mine in a way that sent wave after wave of need and desire through me. My body, already on edge, flooded with pleasure as blood pumped to my cock in anticipation.

Laura let out a moan as she felt it hardening against her, my hips flush with hers as I leaned into her, and the sound was almost more than I could take. Never had I been so turned on so quickly, not wanting it to be over too fast but not willing to wait either.

My hands ran down her body, gripping the back of her thighs as I hoisted her up, her back still against the wall so her legs could wrap around me, her dress riding up her thighs. My cock pressed against the junction between her legs and even through our layers of clothing, it felt absolutely incredible. As tempted as I was to take her just like this, right here against the wall in the entrance hall, I wanted to please her too. Like I said, I planned to show her exactly what she did to me, and that involved making her feel good too. With that in mind, I pushed us back off the wall, her body still wrapped around mine, my lips still on hers, and walked blindly down the hall until I reached my bedroom.

"Door," I managed to mutter against her lips, and with a breathy laugh, Laura reached down to open the handle.

I walked forward until my shins hit the mattress before lowering her down gently onto her back, her legs still wrapped around me. She felt incredible beneath me, soft and supple, her perfume filling my nose and the heels of her shoes digging into my ass. I didn't want to disconnect from her for even a minute, but I'd have to if I wanted to make good on my promise to get her out of her dress, which I definitely intended to do.

Pushing myself back onto my knees, I started with her shoes, untying the straps while Laura watched, a smile playing on her lips. "I've noticed how good you are with your hands on the ranch. I've been wondering if it carried over to other activities too."

My cock twitched again within my painfully tight jeans as my fingers slipped. "You're trying to throw me off my game. It won't work."

She laughed as she wiggled her toes. "Why would I want to do that?"

"I don't know why you do half the things you do." The first shoe came off and I grabbed hold of her other foot. "You should let me concentrate."

She gave a hum that didn't entirely sound like agreement, and as I worked on the second strap, she looked around the room curiously. "It's strange to be back in this room. This bed is where I had my first orgasm."

"Fucking hell." I got the second shoe loose and tossed it over my shoulder before glaring down at her. "You're going to talk to me about other men right now?"

Her eyes sparkled mischievously. "Oh, there was no man. Just me and my fingers and too much time on my hands."

I had never talked to a woman about masturbation before. Why would I have? But for some reason, the idea of her touching herself and knowing exactly how to make herself come made my body even hotter. This was a woman who knew how to get what she wanted, if I hadn't already known that by the way she talked herself into my job in the first place, and the fact that she wanted me flattered and excited me more than I would have thought possible.

Reaching up to spread her legs, I got my first glimpse of the thin, lacy panties she'd worn that night, and I couldn't stop my groan. If I'd known she was wearing those beneath her dress, I'd have been even more crazy at the idea of her going out. Running my hand up her thigh, as I got closer to the piece of fabric that stood between me and my ultimate reward, I could feel the heat of her arousal which only turned me on more.

"Are you planning on giving me some pointers, then?" I asked as I brushed my fingers over the narrow strip of material covering her pussy. "You gonna let me in on your secrets?"

Laura's hands clenched against the sheets, bunching them up as she squirmed beneath my teasing touch. "Isn't figuring them out for yourself half the fun?"

She had me there. "I'm always open for feedback, though. Just because I'm the boss doesn't mean you don't have any good ideas."

As I expected, that got her attention, her eyes opening wide. "Who said you're the boss right now..."

Pushing her panties aside, I slipped one finger through her wetness, sliding it up to her clit and cutting off her words mid-sentence. "You were saying?"

I didn't give her a chance to come up with a response to that, letting my index finger slide back down until it reached her warm, wet entrance. As I gently circled it with my finger, her hips tilted towards me in clear invitation, one I gladly accepted by pressing my finger slowly inside her, as deep as it would go as Laura gasped out my name. "Fuck, Jesse."

With that encouragement, I really went to work. As she rightly pointed out, my hands weren't just good for roping cattle. My fingers pumped and swirled inside her, my thumb teasing her clit until I replaced it with my mouth instead, licking and sucking her while my fingers continued to fuck her. Every sound she made brought me satisfaction, every inhale of breath, every time she tried to speak but couldn't form the words. Having Laura Callahan lost for words was a rare occasion indeed, and the fact that I'd done it to her, that the pleasure I gave her left her speechless, might have just been the best thing of all.

It only held that title for a short time, though, until she completely lost control, calling out my name one more time as her body contracted, her pussy gripping my fingers tightly as her back arched off the bed, and my tongue slowed, giving her clit one last, lingering kiss before I raised my head to grin at her.

"Any suggestions for improvement?"

Laura laughed shakily before looking down at me. "Just one. I think this whole thing would be a lot better if you were wearing a whole lot less."

~Laura~

Jesse grinned up at me from between my legs when I suggested he get naked, a self-satisfied smile that had my stomach doing cartwheels in anticipation despite the orgasm he'd just given me. He'd said he wanted to get me out of my dress, but so far, all he'd done was take off my shoes. I still had my dress and even my underwear on and he was still fully clothed, but I took it as a compliment. He couldn't even wait long enough to pull my panties off before he had his face buried in my pussy, and I had absolutely no complaints.

He had definitively put the rumours of his homosexuality to rest.

And best of all, I suspected he was just getting warmed up. Anything he did on the ranch, he did it fully and completely, never cutting corners, and I knew instinctively that his work ethic would carry over to the bedroom too. All of that had my stomach fluttering again as he pushed himself up off the bed and pulled his shirt over his head.

Firm abs contracted in the overhead light, the tattoos on his chest flexing as he reached down to unzip his jeans. I quickly shimmied out of my panties too, not wanting to waste any time, but when I started to pull my dress up, Jesse's hand reached out and stopped me. "I said I'd take it off, didn't I? I always keep my word, Laura."

The low heat of his voice sent a shiver through me as I slowly dropped my arms. "There's nothing wrong with accepting some help now and then. You don't have to do everything all by..."

The words dried out in my throat as he pulled his jeans down, revealing his hard cock to me for the first time and definitely living up to any expectation I might have had of it. I still couldn't quite believe this was happening, but seeing him fully naked as he finished pulling off the rest of his clothes made it feel a lot more real.

I hadn't asked him what he wanted out of that night because I expected him to offer me any kind of commitment at that point. We'd only known each other a month and we didn't even know how compatible we'd be on a sexual level. When I asked the question, I just wanted to know if this was *only* physical for him or if it might be something more. If he had told me he only wanted sex, I would have said yes anyway, I wanted him so badly. I just wanted to make sure I didn't set my own expectations at a different level from his. That was the quickest path to heartbreak.

So, it didn't offend me at all when he said he'd like to wait and see where things went after that night. I felt just the same. We were on the same page, and I knew he wasn't going anywhere, not when we lived in the same damn house. And it meant that, if nothing else, we'd have one night, and as I stared - yes, stared - at his erect cock, I was more grateful for that fact than ever.

"You were saying?" he asked, his eyes full of amusement as he threw his clothes aside and noticed my distraction.

Had I been saying something? I honestly didn't recall.

"On your feet," he instructed, holding his hand out to help me up. "Now, we can take your dress off."

Ah, that was it. We'd been talking about my dress.

My heart beating quickly, my body already pulsing with need again, I let him pull me up, pulling me straight into his arms and into another deep kiss that nearly made my knees buckle. His tongue flicked against mine, his firm, naked body pressed against me as his hands slipped beneath my dress, caressing my bare ass.

"It's almost a shame to take it off," he murmured. "You look so damn good in it."

"You don't think I'll look just as good out of it?" I teased, trying to catch my breath.

I loved the way his laugh rumbled in his chest. "I'll bet you do." With that encouragement, he finally grabbed the bottom of the dress and pulled it up over my head. I had gone without a bra that night since the dress held my breasts firmly in place, and as they came free, Jesse groaned again. "Fuck, Laura."

His rough hands felt surprisingly soft as they brushed over my firm nipples in admiration, his eyes devouring me just as mine had done to him earlier.

"There are so many things I want to do to you, I don't know where to start," he admitted, his voice thick as he trailed one hand lower, over my stomach and back down to my sensitive clit. "Do you have any requests?"

Men didn't usually ask me that. Some of the ones I'd been with before even got a little insulted if I made suggestions, but Jesse seemed very open to my input, even if he liked to tease me for offering it too freely sometimes.

"I haven't been able to stop thinking about the way you had me against the wall the other night," I told him honestly. "I've imagined what it would have been like if you'd touched me then."

He gave another groan, this one of appreciation. "You and me both. We can definitely make that a reality."

Lifting me up by my thighs, his strong arms holding me steady like I weighed nothing, he walked back over to the door, his stiff cock pressed against my stomach, my breasts against his chest. When my back hit the wall, he reached down to rub my clit again, as if I needed any further stimulation.

"Shit," he muttered unhappily a moment later, to my surprise. I didn't see what the problem could be. Everything felt amazing.

"What's wrong?"

"My condoms are all the way over there." He gestured towards the bathroom as if it were miles away, making me giggle.

"If it's just for me, we don't need one. But if you want one, I can wait."

He understood my meaning without me needing to spell it out any further. I was as disciplined with my birth control as with everything else in my life, and I had no concerns about my past partners. The last one had been quite a few months ago, to be honest, but Jesse didn't need to know that.

"I don't usually..." he trailed off, his fingers still teasing my clit as my hips rocked against him.

I understood him perfectly too. He normally wore one, which seemed like a pretty good reason he didn't need to that night if he didn't want to.

"It's up to you, Jesse, but I'd love to feel you."

As I expected it might, that seemed to make up his mind. His fingers disappeared from my clit, replaced a moment later by the head of his cock as he rubbed it across my aching slit. I couldn't help whimpering in anticipation and that seemed to break any control he had left as his cock began to slide into me: firm, thick, and absolutely perfect. When he'd filled me completely, he paused there a second, letting the moment sink in for both of us. Things had definitely shifted between us that night, but I couldn't see a downside to that. I only wanted more.

My arms wrapped around him for leverage with my back pressed against the wall as he began to thrust into me, slowly at first, controlled and measured.

"I've imagined this for so long," he admitted, his breath coming hot and heavy. "How the hell do you feel better than I thought you would?"

Pleasure flooded my body, brought on by both his actions and his words. I'd honestly had no clue he'd been thinking about me that way, mostly because I'd been so convinced he didn't like women. Why did he wait so long to tell me?

"You had to go and show off your chest the first day we met," I reminded him breathlessly, the words broken up as his cock filled me over and over again. "And remember, I thought I had no chance with you on account of my gender. I think I've had it worse."

His whole body shook in laughter, shaking me along with him since we were still connected. "It ain't a competition, Laura."

"Everything is," I countered. "And I think I'm about to win."

Another orgasm had been building inside me with every movement of his hips, and when he realized I meant I was close, he began pumping harder, all our words forgotten as he pushed me over the edge yet again.

My arms loosened around him as my whole body went weak with pleasure, and Jesse immediately pulled me away from the wall, returning to the bed, still not finished yet. Buried deep inside me, he lay me down on my back and rotated his hips, grinding against my swollen clit until I wanted to cry out at the exquisite painful pleasure of it.

"I don't think I can wait any longer," he groaned as my hands clawed at his back.

Did he think I expected him to? "I'm good, Jesse. So good. Fuck me until you come. I want to feel it."

"Fucking hell," he muttered back as his hips began to thrust against me again, harder and faster. My eyes closed and my head fell back as I lost myself in the sensation and soon, his breathing grew more erratic. Whispering my name as he climaxed, I felt him contracting, the base of his shaft flush against my skin as he let go deep inside me, and I came again too, the orgasm taking me completely by surprise as his pleasure fed my own.

It had never been that good for me before. The combination of the month of repressed longing and the sudden breaking of the dam of restraint that night, the mixture of his dominance and his respect for me, and the absolute perfection of his body, all of it resulted in a feeling of deep satisfaction that lingered even as my orgasm faded.

When we'd both recovered, Jesse kissed me gently before lifting himself off me. We took turns getting cleaned up in the bathroom, but when I went to grab my clothes off the floor, he took my hand again.

"Stay here tonight, if you want to."

I did want to, I just hadn't wanted to assume anything. We didn't say much as we climbed into bed, both still naked, and he held me until he fell asleep. All those teenage nights I spent in my room dreaming about what it would be like when I had my own cowboy had undersold it. That night exceeded all my expectations, and I couldn't wait to see what came next.

Chapter Nine

~Jesse~

For once, I appreciated waking up a few minutes before my alarm since it gave me a chance to gather my thoughts before the world came crashing back in. Though the dim pre-morning light obscured my view, I could make out Laura's dark hair on the pillow, the pretty slope of her nose and those sweet lips of hers that I had done my best to brand the night before. I hadn't planned to ask her to stay the night; hell, I hadn't planned any of it, but it felt like the right thing to do at the time. The situation was completely different from the women I hooked up with at the bar. There, I had the excuse of needing to drive home, but Laura lived literally ten feet away from me. Sending her down the hall to her own room felt almost childish. We had sex and we couldn't pretend we hadn't by sleeping in separate beds afterwards. We were going to have to deal with it like adults in the morning light.

I'd tried to draw out the experience the night before for the same reason I savoured those quiet moments before she woke up. In the heat of the moment, there had been no expectations beyond simply enjoying ourselves. We'd agreed to that. In the light of day, we'd have to figure out what came next and everything that came with it, but before it could be diluted or changed in any way, I could simply appreciate how damn near perfect it had been.

I'd never really seen so clearly the difference between anonymous sex and sex with someone I knew and liked. At the hotel in Austin, things were always focused entirely on the physical, which I had always thought was ideal. But Laura knew me better than any of those women ever had. She made me laugh, knowing how to push my buttons even when I was inside her. It made the whole experience feel more complete somehow, in a way I hadn't known I even wanted.

Had she felt it too? She seemed to enjoy herself, but maybe it had been a far more typical experience for her than for me. Did I want to know? What would I do if she said it had been special for her too?

My clock radio turned on as the clock turned to four, halfway through an old George Strait song, and Laura immediately stirred, her eyes blinking open in disorientation.

"Oh. Hey. Good morning." Her mumbled, sleepy greeting felt casual and just right for the situation.

"Morning. I'm going to hop in the shower, we've got a busy day today."

"Sure." She pulled herself up, the covers falling from her chest to reveal her breasts that even in the moonlight woke my cock up in no time at all. "Do you want anything for breakfast?"

She didn't usually make me breakfast and I didn't want that to change. I didn't want anything to change, not until we'd had a chance to figure out what happened next. "No, thanks. I'll see you out there."

I got out of bed before I could get any harder, heading to the bathroom and shutting the door behind me without a backwards glance.

By the time I'd showered, taking the opportunity to rub one out quickly to deal with my unhelpful state of arousal, gotten dressed and made it to the kitchen, Laura was already there with an omelette and some fruit on her plate. She'd had her coffee in her room, as usual, and she looked just as good as ever. Maybe better, now that I knew exactly what she looked like beneath her jeans and work shirt.

"Forecast is for rain starting tomorrow and lasting for a few days," I told her, peering out the window at the sky before grabbing my bread and peanut butter. It looked clear so far. "We'll have to make the most of today."

She seemed happy to stick to talking about work. "I've got to meet with the construction team around noon to sign off on the bunkhouse. They're just doing a final clean up today, and then I can start furnishing and decorating it. I've got a few errands to run in town too around advertising and insurance later this week. That'll keep me occupied unless you need a hand."

"Sounds good." She'd done a great job with her side project so far while still contributing to the main work of the ranch. Once guests started arriving in a few weeks, we'd see less of each other during the day, and the thought actually disappointed me.

Neither of us said a word about the previous night as we finished eating and headed outside to meet Tyson to talk over the day. In fact, everything went completely normally until Laura headed off for her meeting with the construction crew, leaving me and Tyson alone while the other hands took their lunch break.

"So, you and Laura, huh? I suppose it was bound to happen with two single folks living together."

"Excuse me?" I did my best to look like I had no idea what he was talking about even though my heart had started to race. How could he possibly know? She'd acted no different that day and I didn't think I had either. If the memory weren't so firmly imprinted in my mind, I'd have to wonder if I'd imagined the whole thing.

He just grinned back at me, looking entirely too smug. "Kayla was at the bar last night. She saw you come in, talk to Laura for two minutes, and the two of you left together. You didn't think that particular piece of news would fly around town faster than a load of monkeys in a space rocket?"

Damn it. I'd forgotten about that part, the memory lost in the wake of everything that came after it.

"I had to talk to her about something to do with the ranch," I tried, knowing he wouldn't believe me no matter what I said. "Her phone was off."

"Uh huh. Listen, you're both adults, you can do whatever the hell you want, but don't break her heart, all right? We all like Laura and we like having her around."

She *had* fit in with the other hands remarkably well, but that was beside the point. Nobody's heart would be getting broken. It had just been one night. "How long are people going to be talking about this?"

"Until something juicier happens." He gave me a grin. "If it makes you feel any better, you're both doing a great job of pretending nothing happened."

"Yeah, that makes me feel much better." I shook my head as he laughed. "Let's get back to work."

Laura and I were meant to go riding that night so she cooked supper for the both of us, same as always. Her cooking was incredible; I had yet to find anything this woman didn't excel at. The previous night certainly hadn't disappointed either. She still didn't say anything about that and I had to assume she was waiting for me to bring it up, so I used Tyson's comments as a way to ease into it after we'd finished catching up on the day's work.

"Apparently, my appearance at the bar last night set some tongues wagging, just so you know."

Laura shrugged philosophically, looking unsurprised. "We should have expected that. It is Sandy Creek, after all."

"It doesn't bother you?"

Her blue eyes sparkled with amusement as she took a drink. "That people might think I'm hooking up with the hottest cowboy this town has ever seen? I think I can live with it."

That assessment of our situation had my body standing to attention almost immediately. "Is that what we're doing?"

She put the ball firmly back in my court, not letting me put the decision on her. "Isn't it?"

That was what we needed to figure out. "I suppose we need to talk about that."

She looked about as excited by that idea as I did. Neither of us wanted to mess things up. "Maybe we'll be in a more talkative mood after a ride."

I had to laugh. "Are you telling me you've ever been in a non-talkative mood in your life?"

She narrowed her eyes at me playfully. "I was being polite by suggesting that applied to both of us."

"So, you still want to go for a ride?" My eyes drifted over to the window where the sky had started to cloud over. Rain was definitely on the way, but we should probably still have time to take the horses out before the storm hit.

However, when I looked back at Laura, her eyes twinkled more than ever. "That wasn't exactly the kind of ride I had in mind."

My fork hit the plate with a clang as I tried not to choke. How did she keep catching me off guard? I honestly never knew what would come out of her mouth next. "Don't tease me, Laura. I've only got so much restraint."

"Who said I'm teasing?" she challenged back, and along with the amusement in her expression, I could see desire lurking there too. "I've been thinking about it all day: every time you bent over, every time you lifted something heavy, watching you handle your horse. You're damn near irresistible."

I couldn't help but be flattered by that, but I still didn't know if she was entirely serious about skipping the conversation we still needed to have. "Most women would want to talk first."

Laura grinned as she pushed her plate away, leaning forward on the table, closer to me. "Do I strike you as 'most women'?"

"No, you definitely do not." She was one of a kind, that was for damn sure. "And if you're sure..."

She was on her feet before I could even finish my sentence, heading down the hall towards my bedroom while I scrambled to catch up, knocking my chair over in my haste. I reached her just before the door, wrapping my hand around her waist and lifting her up so her feet dangled uselessly in the air.

"Put me down," she tried to order me, giggling as she struggled against my grip.

"Gladly." In just a few steps, we were at the bed and I tossed her down onto it so that her back hit the mattress. Before she could recover her balance, I followed after her, covering her body with mine as our lips found each other like two starving people who hadn't seen food in days. No matter how good her cooking was, Laura herself tasted far better.

Longing and need already flowed through my veins, my cock straining against my jeans as her hips pushed against mine, obviously just as eager as I was. What she'd said in the kitchen had been how I felt all day too, trying not to see something seductive in every move she made. Knowing that she'd been thinking about it too had me growing harder by the second.

Taking advantage of my distraction, Laura pushed me over, rolling onto my back with her on top of me as she smiled down in satisfaction. "That's better."

I didn't know about better, but I certainly wasn't about to complain. Her thighs straddling me as she rocked her hips against my aching cock, Laura began to unbutton her shirt just as I'd been imagining all day long. Not wanting to waste time, I undid mine too, keeping my eyes fixed on her at all times. She had a bra on that day, a pink one with lace trim that she filled out perfectly, and my cock twitched beneath her once again. Whatever I did to have this woman turn up at my door uninvited, it must have been very good.

She had to climb off me in order to get her jeans off, and I took advantage of the chance to pull mine off too, sighing in relief as I freed my cock. No sooner had I pulled my socks off than Laura pushed me back down, taking charge once again as she bent over to press her lips against my shaft while I inhaled sharply, the pleasure almost too intense.

"Fuck, that feels amazing," I told her, half as praise and half in warning. If she wanted a ride, as she said, she better not spend too long down there.

Laura grinned up at me, her tongue sliding up to the tip of my cock and teasing the edge. "Just make sure you're ready for me."

My eyebrows shot up, making her giggle. "How hard do you need me to get?"

Her fingers wrapped around my cock, giving it a squeeze that sent another rush of blood pumping through it. "This ought to do nicely."

Thankfully, she didn't tease me any longer, swinging her leg back over my hip as she positioned herself over me, and when she sank down onto me, wrapping my cock completely in her warm, perfect wetness, I could have sworn I saw heaven.

Like any skilled cowgirl, Laura knew how to handle her ride. She moved slowly and deliberately at first, her hands tracing lines across my chest before she shifted her angle and began to move faster. While I leaned forward to take one of her nipples into my mouth, she found a perfect rhythm, her body stroking my cock exquisitely, bringing me almost to the edge before backing off and making me wait for it. Nothing could be better than that sweet torture, and it gave me a chance to make her feel good too, sucking and licking her breasts while my fingers found her clit, rubbing it in circles as she continued to rise and fall on top of me.

I meant it when I told her the night before that I didn't usually go bare during sex. I had a couple of times when I was younger and a bit more careless, but for years now, it hadn't even been a question. Knowing Laura, I trusted that she'd been just as careful, so if she didn't insist on it, I wouldn't either, and at that moment, I couldn't be any happier about it, feeling every wet inch of her as she took me deep inside her, over and over again. When she peaked, the feel of her gripping me combined with the sight of her pink, flushed cheeks and the parting of her lips made me groan out loud.

"Fuck, you're perfect when you come."

She must have heard the tightness in my voice, telling her just how close I was too, since she didn't slow down for a second. Her forehead rested on my shoulder as she rode me harder, hips slamming into mine in frenzied passion, and I couldn't hold back any longer, my fingers digging into her ass as I released deep inside her: quick and dirty and perfectly satisfying.

We stayed that way for a little while, her laying on top of me with my cock still inside her, neither of us wanting the moment to end. We'd managed to delay the inevitable, but we both knew it couldn't last forever.

Finally, I cleared my throat. "Well, that wasn't the ride I'd anticipated tonight, but I ain't complaining."

With a smile, Laura lifted her head. "I aim to please."

My arms tightened around her as my old fears began to creep back in. I had no doubt she'd please me; that had never been my concern. "Do you want to talk here, or should we get dressed?"

Lifting herself the rest of the way, Laura climbed off me. "Why don't we go outside?"

It sounded like she had a plan, so we both freshened up and got redressed, heading out to the near field beneath the sky filled with dark clouds growing thicker all the time. There might even be a thunderstorm that night, the way things were shaping up. When we reached the fence, Laura climbed up and perched herself on top of it.

"I used to sit out here all the time when I wanted to think," she explained. "The sky always made all my problems seem smaller."

I knew just what she meant, so I hauled myself up next to her. "What kind of problems did you have?"

"Nothing big," she quickly assured me. "The usual teenage stuff: my parents not letting me do what I wanted, boys not liking me back, that kind of thing. Nothing like the stuff you went through."

She'd set me up perfectly to tell her more about my past and more about why I'd resisted her as long as I had. If we were going to be honest with each other about what we wanted out of this new phase of our relationship, I owed her some of those answers, even if I'd never told anyone about them before.

I decided to start with part of the story she already knew and work backwards from there, looking out over the field in front of us so I didn't get distracted by those pretty blue eyes. "I told you about getting hired on at the Buchanan ranch at 13. I didn't mention that I only went out of town that way because I was trying to run away from home."

Laura didn't look shocked by that. Maybe she'd already guessed that might be the case. "What were you running from?"

"My stepmother. She was…" I trailed off for a second, trying to figure out how to put her into words. I'd never had to explain this before. In the distance, a low rumble of thunder sounded as I searched for the right words. "Well, let's just say she'd give Cinderella's stepmother a run for her money. She had two boys of her own and they could do no wrong while nothing I did was ever right. She saw me as a burden and a thief."

"A thief?" Laura repeated curiously. I could hear the confusion in her voice without looking at her face. "In what way?"

"She resented the fact that my dad left almost everything to me when he died. She got the house but that was it. She accused me flat out of stealing her boys' inheritance from them, though I was only ten years old at the time and didn't even know what an inheritance was."

"That's ridiculous! That's…" Laura had just started to get worked up when she suddenly went silent. Against my better judgement, I glanced over at her to see her looking back at me in horror, her face drained of colour. "Shit, Jesse. That's what I said to you on the day we met."

I remembered. She accused me of stealing the ranch from her, not knowing just how deep those particular words hit home. "You didn't know."

That didn't seem to make her feel any better as the thunder rolled across the sky again, a little closer this time. "No, but I shouldn't have said it anyway. I let my frustration get the better of me. On the drive down here that day, I'd come up with this whole theory that you scammed my dad into selling to you, though I didn't know a thing about you at the time. That's where that came from, but it wasn't fair to you. I should have given you the benefit of the doubt."

"You were upset and still in shock. I get it, Laura. I assume you've changed your mind on the matter, and that's what's important." I gave her a quick smile to assure her I'd forgiven the careless words before turning my gaze back to the land. "My stepmother, unfortunately, never had a change of heart. She took everything I did as a personal attack, like I existed just to make her life harder. Even when I started working at the ranch, she'd take my pay from me, claiming I owed it to her for feeding and housing me. Mr Buchanan noticed the holes in my jeans one day and asked why I didn't buy myself some new ones with the money he paid me, and I had to confess I didn't have it. That's when he offered to let me move in."

A crack of thunder sounded almost directly above us, followed by a flash of lightning as some of the horses neighed in the nearby barn. We'd already brought them in, anticipating the rain if not the storm, and it seemed like we should head back inside too. I hopped down off the fence and held my hand out to Laura.

"I'll tell you the rest inside."

Her hand slipped into mine and stayed there as we made our way back to the house, but before we arrived, Tyson came driving up the road from his place.

"Just got a call from the Fisher ranch. They had a lightning hit on the barn. It's grounded, so it looks alright, but they need to move all the animals out to be safe."

"Give me just a minute." Ranchers had an unspoken code: though we may be competitors, we had each other's backs too. When someone needed help, we gave it, no questions asked.

Dropping Laura's hand, I ducked into the house to get my hat and the keys to my truck. When I turned around, Laura was pulling her coat on too.

"What are you doing?"

"I'm coming to help." She said it like it was a given. "I know the Fishers too."

"You're not going anywhere. The only reason Tyson and I are both going is because you're here to keep an eye on things. Someone has to stay."

She knew I was right, but she still argued with me. "And that someone has to be me? Why?"

"Because it's dangerous. Because Tyson and I have dealt with this kind of thing more than you have."

Because I can't risk losing you too, I added in my head. That was my biggest fear of all, that someone else I cared about would be taken from me. It terrified me so much that I hadn't let myself care for anyone. Laura had thrown a wrench in that whole plan and I still didn't know what that meant for the both of us, but I did know for sure that I wouldn't put her in harm's way.

"Stay here, Laura. Call Mary-Beth if there are any problems. She'll know how to get the word out. I'll be back later."

I headed out the door before she could get another word in.

~Laura~

If the Fishers didn't need the help as quickly as possible, I would have followed Jesse outside and continued my argument. Where did he get off telling me I didn't have enough experience at moving animals during a storm? Just because he may have done it more recently than I had didn't mean he'd done it more. I'd lived on the ranch for eighteen years growing up and I'd dealt with my fair share of bad weather.

It smacked of sexism, of him thinking I might be too delicate to handle a crisis, which was bullshit. Technically, I sat above Tyson in the ranch hierarchy so he should be the one to stay behind and 'keep an eye on things', not me.

Things had been going so well that evening until he pulled that power trip. I thoroughly enjoyed our return to his bedroom, and he actually started to open up to me about his childhood too. I had guessed that his home life must not have been great and he'd confirmed that, though he still left me with a lot of questions. How did his daddy die? What happened to his mother? Didn't he have any other family who could have helped him out so he didn't have to stay with a stepmother who apparently didn't want him?

He'd obviously been through a lot and I was prepared to take that into account if it affected how ready he felt to move our relationship forward. Shawna had suggested he'd been hurt before and at the time, I thought she meant by a previous romantic relationship, but maybe it went deeper than that. Maybe he'd never had any kind of stable relationship he could rely on at all.

As soon as Shawna crossed my mind, I glanced up at the clock on the wall. With everything going on, I hadn't had a chance yet to fill her in on the results of her excellent advice, but it might be too late to call her that night if she wasn't feeling well. On the other hand, I didn't want to put it off until the next day either, not when the number of tomorrows she had left were so limited.

I decided to send a text instead of calling. That way, she could call me back if she felt like talking, but if she was sleeping, I wouldn't disturb her.

I had to smile as I reread the message before sending it. *Definitely not gay. I have updates when you feel up to it.*

Shoving the phone back in my pocket, I returned to the kitchen where our dishes from dinner were still on the table. We'd been in such a hurry to get to Jesse's room that we hadn't cleared them away. Lightning flashed again outside the window, brightening the sky, and a moment later, the rain started to fall. The sound of it hitting the window made me shiver and I hoped Jesse wouldn't have to be out in it too long.

Just as I finished with the dishes, my phone rang, and a wide smile spread across my face as I saw Shawna's number. I couldn't wait to let her know how helpful she had been. "Hey! I didn't know if…"

"Laura, it's Dex." My brother cut me off before I could say anything else. "I've got Shawna here but I'm going to have to put you on speaker.

She can't hold the phone for very long, alright?"

A lump immediately formed in my throat at the idea that my sister-in-law couldn't even hold her phone but I did my best to remember what she'd said the other day about not being sad. She didn't need to spend her time comforting me about her own illness. I wouldn't bring it up unless she did.

I kept my tone light instead. "That's fine, but are you sure you want to hear this? Things might get a little graphic."

I could hear Shawna chuckling in the background while Dex groaned. "You know, this might be a good time for me to get a little air."

"Good plan," Shawna told him, and I could picture the way he'd be leaning over to kiss her. "Give us at least ten minutes. Maybe more."

"Not too much more. You've got more visitors coming tomorrow." Dex's tone was affectionately concerned and I marvelled again at how well he was holding himself together in front of her. It must be killing him to know how short their remaining time was, but he put her needs first, just like always.

I stayed silent, waiting until I heard the door close, followed by Shawna's eager question. "How graphic are we talking about?"

"Completely x-rated," I admitted, laughing as she gave a quiet squeal of excitement. Her voice might be weak, but her enthusiasm hadn't dimmed.

"Start from the beginning," she commanded. "I want to hear everything."

I did just that, telling her about what happened at the bar the night before. She groaned as I mentioned Dale, remembering him from high school as well as I did, and cheered when I described how Jesse had shown up. I told her about the short conversation we'd had upon our arrival back at the house and how he said he was open to more, we just hadn't defined yet what that might look like.

"It's no grand declaration," she had to admit. "But it sounds like it's still a pretty big deal for him, especially since you said he hasn't seen anyone else the whole time he's been in town, right? He must think you're something special."

I hoped so. It kind of felt that way.

I didn't go into too much detail about exactly how things went in the bedroom, though I knew Tonia would demand that information later. I simply said it had been one of the best nights I'd ever had, if not *the* best.

"I'll take your word for it," she laughed. "I don't really know what it's like when it's bad."

I supposed she wouldn't. She and Dex had only ever been with each other.

"Do you regret not... trying out a few more horses before you bought the farm?" I couldn't help wondering, and Shawna laughed so hard, she started coughing again. I listened uselessly as she tried to get her breath back, wishing I could help.

"That is one thing I don't regret," she finally said once she'd regained her composure. "When you've found perfection, why waste your time on anything else?"

For the first time, I could kind of understand how that felt.

Trying not to keep her too much longer, I explained how things had gone that day, how we'd kept things casual all day and ended up in bed together after dinner, about how he'd started to open up and then how he'd left me behind.

"Laura, it's Dex again." My brother's voice took me by surprise and I winced as I tried to guess how much he had heard.

"How long have you been there?"

"I only came back in when you were sitting on the fence talking. I think I missed the worst of it."

"The best of it, you mean," Shawna teased him, sounding further away now and weaker than ever.

My brother's reply was typically wry. "We'll agree to disagree on that. But listen, Laura, don't go getting in one of your righteous huffs about being left behind tonight. First of all, it's his ranch. He's your boss and he can make whatever personnel decisions he deems right. It don't mean he doesn't trust you. In fact, he just left you in charge of the whole ranch in the middle of a storm. I'd argue that means he *does* trust you, quite a lot. Not everything is a personal insult, alright?"

He might have a point, and with the rain continuing to pelt down, being warm and dry inside seemed pretty good. I felt bad that Jesse was out in it, and he would have felt bad if I was. I could understand that.

"I'll go easy on him," I promised, finding that my annoyance had mostly melted away. Jesse could still learn to consult me rather than assuming he knew everything, but it didn't seem worth arguing about as much as it had earlier. "Anyway, that's what's going on here. I just wanted to let you know and say thanks, Shawna. It wouldn't have happened without you."

"Oh, I think it would have," she disagreed. Her words had started to come slower, like the conversation had tired her out. "It might have just taken a bit longer. I hope it goes really well, Laura. He sounds like he's a good one."

"Yeah, I think he is. I'll be up in a few more days and I'll update you again then."

"Perfect. Bring him along if you can. I'd love to meet him."

I didn't know if Jesse would be ready for that. I hadn't mentioned a thing about Shawna's prognosis to him yet, and it wasn't really a happy time to be introducing him to the rest of my family. On the other hand, it might be the only chance he got to meet her, and she was definitely worth meeting.

"I'll see what I can do," I promised. "Take care, Shawna." I left it at that, trying not to get too emotional. She knew what I meant.

After we hung up, I turned the TV on, waiting for Jesse to come back. The hour grew later with no sign of him and my eyelids began to get heavy. My blinks started to get longer and slower, and at some point, I must have fallen asleep because the next thing I knew, a pair of strong arms was setting me down into my bed, a bare chest floating above me in the darkness.

"Jesse?" I mumbled his name sleepily, trying to force my eyes open.

"Yeah. Go back to sleep, Laura. It's late. Everything's fine. I'll see you in the morning, alright?"

I hummed in agreement, rolling over in the warmth of my bed, and drifting back into sleep immediately.

Rain still dripped down my window when my alarm went off the next morning. We'd have to make our rounds and check that nothing had been damaged in the night's storm, but otherwise, it would be a pretty slow day, the rain inhibiting a lot of our usual work. That should give me a chance to work on the holiday side of things instead. It might even give me and Jesse a chance to finish our conversation from the night before.

All in all, I felt pretty good as I got out of bed, ready to make a start on things, but that all changed when I picked up my phone and saw the message waiting there for me, sent to our family group chat.

Shawna passed away just after 2:30 this morning.

# Chapter Ten

~**Jesse**~

The morning came far too soon. It had been well after midnight when I got back the night before, soaked and exhausted. The Fishers' cattle hadn't wanted to go out into the storm, understandably enough, and one of the horses bolted once we finally got them moving. A deep creek bordered the property on one side so we had to make sure the horse didn't get stuck and it took nearly an hour to track him down once the cattle were safe.

The TV in the living room was still on when I arrived back home and I took a quick peek in to find Laura fast asleep on the couch. She must have tried waiting up for me but hadn't quite made it. Our early starts made late nights that much harder, and I just hoped she hadn't been waiting because she was still upset with me about not letting her go in the first place. I wouldn't apologize for it, not when I knew just how miserable the whole night had been.

Too wet to be of much use, I went to my room first to take off my drenched clothes and give my hair a quick rub with the towel before throwing on some sweatpants and going back out to move her to her own bed for the night. She somehow managed to look both adorable and sexy when I laid her down. When she murmured my name, I was tempted to just climb in beside her, but we both needed the rest. That would be more likely to happen in separate beds.

Despite that precaution, I still could have used more sleep. Since I didn't drink coffee, obviously, I would have to break out one of the energy drinks I kept for these very rare occasions when I needed a boost. As soon as I had dressed, I headed to the kitchen, but on the way, I passed Laura's closed door and could hear her talking to someone, sounding upset.

"Laura?" I knocked quietly and pushed the door open just a crack, not wanting to disturb her but also wanting to make sure she was alright. She stood at the window, still in her clothes from the night before, her back to the door. It didn't look like she'd heard me.

"You know what he's like, Tonia. He'll say there was no need to wake everyone up when there was nothing they could do. I'll be leaving as soon as I can, but I thought you'd want to get over there..."

She trailed off as the person on the other end spoke, loud enough that I could hear their voice but not enough that I could hear what was being said.

"Yeah, you go get ready, I'll call Billie. Will you pick her up? Okay, I'll let her know. We'll let Mom and Dad sleep a little longer. I'll see you soon."

She hung up and immediately started to dial another number, still not aware of my presence.

"Laura?" I repeated her name and this time she heard me but she held up her index finger, asking me to wait. For the brief second that she turned towards me, I thought I got a glimpse of tears in her eyes, sending a shot of adrenaline through me that negated the need for caffeine. I was wide awake now.

"Hey, Billie." She paused for a second before cutting her sister off. I'd gathered enough from what I'd heard and from my previous conversations with Jim Callahan to guess that she'd been speaking to one sister before and now had the other. Laura spoke briskly, just as she did when dealing with ranch business. "Yes, I know what time it is. I just got up for work and saw that Dex had messaged all of us. I thought you'd want to hear it from me rather than reading the message."

She didn't say what the message said but it seemed like she didn't have to. A string of sounds I couldn't even be sure were words came through the phone and Laura covered her eyes with her hand. When she spoke again, her voice was strained, her earlier businesslike tone completely gone.

"I know. Tonia's heading over now to pick you up, Cam will take Charlie to a friend's and then he'll be there too. I'll be leaving here as soon as I'm dressed but it'll be a few hours before I can get there." Whatever Billie said next made Laura laugh, in a choked, desperate kind of way. "I know but he's got to be out of his mind right now. We can cut him some slack for the text."

They exchanged a few more words before Laura hung up and turned to me fully, her eyes red and watery.

"I'm sorry, Jesse, I've got to go up to Houston for a few days. I don't know how long I'll be gone."

I walked into the room now that she'd acknowledged me, wanting to help her out even though I didn't know for sure what she needed just yet. "Back up a second. What's going on?"

"It's my sister-in-law, Shawna. Dex's wife. She died a couple of hours ago."

The words hit me like a bucket of ice water, the blood freezing in my veins. Light flashed before my eyes and I could see the kitchen floor again with my mom on it, and the policeman at our door who came to tell us about the car accident. The loss hit me all over again, plunging me back into the grief that never fully went away, sharp and cold and stealing my breath away as I struggled to find the surface of it.

"I'm... I'm sorry," I managed to stutter, pushing the pain down with all my might. No matter how it affected me, this wasn't about me right now. I had to focus on Laura. "How did she... what happened?"

"Cancer," Laura explained, wiping at her eyes ferociously. "We knew it was coming, just not today. I've got to get dressed. I've got to go."

"Of course." I backed out of the room while she started to get ready.

In the kitchen, I picked up the phone to call Tyson. I'd told him he could sleep in that morning after our late night, but I was going to have to take it back. Rain was still coming down and there was no way I would let Laura drive herself into the city in her current frame of mind.

By the time I'd finished explaining the situation to him and making sure he had all the instructions for the day, Laura had appeared in the doorway. "I'll let you know when I'll be back as soon as I know. I don't know when the funeral is yet."

She had a small overnight bag with her, crammed full. I could guess she hadn't folded anything, just shoved it all in to try to get away faster.

"I'm coming with you," I told her in a tone that should make it clear I wouldn't take no for an answer. "I'll drive you wherever you need to go."

"You don't need to do that..."

"Yeah, I do. You're upset and the weather's terrible and I don't want you on the road by yourself. Someone from your family can drive you back after, and if they can't, call me and I'll come get you."

The fact that she didn't argue any further offered me the best proof so far of just how affected she was. We dashed from the front door to the truck in the rain and were out on the highway in no time, the wipers working hard to keep the windshield clear. All we could see was grey sky, tail lights ahead of us and the occasional headlights coming the other way. It felt a bit like being in a bubble, and I could guess Laura felt it even more. Grief had a funny way of disconnecting you from the world.

We drove in silence for a while, my eyes fixed on the road while Laura stared blankly ahead, occasionally reaching up to wipe her face dry. The heavy lump in my stomach got heavier and heavier as the shock began to fade and more practical thoughts began to return.

This pain she felt right now, the pain her whole family must be in, especially her brother, I'd sworn to myself I wouldn't feel again. I wouldn't be that lost little boy ever again. I wouldn't let anyone else close enough that their death would destroy my whole world. People died, all the time, sometimes out of the blue and sometimes slowly, but the one constant was that they died, leaving devastation and heartache behind them.

Knowing that, knowing it to be truer than anything else in this world, I'd worked hard to build my walls and keep my emotional distance. I could hear that someone had died and think it was sad, but it wouldn't shatter me, nor would anyone else be heartbroken when something happened to me. I'd lived my whole life since I left home based on that principle, up until the day Laura Callahan walked through my door.

Now, in her sad, lost eyes, I could see all the reasons why we shouldn't get any closer. I could be friendly with her and I could be her boss, but it couldn't be more than that and I had let myself forget it. We'd been playing with fire, but this sad event brought it all rushing back, bringing me back to my senses.

Somehow, I was going to have to let her go.

~Laura~

As much as I hated to admit it, I was glad that Jesse insisted on driving me. My vision kept blurring with my tears which made it even harder to see through the rain that streaked down the windshield in front of us, brushed to the side by the rhythmic motion of the wipers.

The pain in my heart physically hurt, the grief in my chest making my body want to cave in on itself, and I could barely begin to imagine how my brother must be feeling. Even though we knew this moment would be coming, far sooner than anyone wanted, it still felt unexpectedly cruel. Just the night before, she had been talking to me, laughing and listening and giving me her strong support and wisdom just like she always had, and now she was just gone. I'd never hear her voice again, never be able to share another joke or talk through another problem, and the injustice of it hit me all over again, just like it had when she first got her diagnosis, just like it had only a few days ago when she told me the end would be coming soon.

Jesse remained silent in the driver's seat, giving me space to think and grieve, supportive but not intrusive. I wanted to tell him about Shawna, I wanted him to know what kind of person she'd been and why the world would be less without her in it, but it felt too raw, too fresh. I needed to process it more first but I didn't want to shut him out either.

We still hadn't finished our conversation from the day before about his past and we still had over an hour on the highway before we reached the city. Maybe by seeing me so emotionally vulnerable, he might be willing to open up a bit more too. It seemed possible.

"Shawna is the first person really close to me who has died," I admitted to him, clearing my throat as the last word got stuck there. "I guess I've been pretty lucky so far."

He nodded slowly, his eyes still on the road and the muscles in his cheek tightening. "It's something we've all got to deal with sooner or later."

His experience was 'sooner', apparently, and I brought that up as delicately as I could. "You were ten when your dad died?"

He'd mentioned being ten years old and not understanding what an inheritance was, so I made an educated guess.

He nodded again, taking a deep breath. "Yeah, but my mom died before that, when I was seven."

"Shit." I said the word out loud before I could stop myself, wincing at how crude it sounded. "I mean, I'm sorry. What happened?"

That answered one of the questions I'd had the night before, about where his mother had been when his father died. I couldn't imagine losing both parents at such a young age. When my daddy had his heart attack a couple of years ago, the thought of losing him terrified me, and I was an adult by then.

With short sentences, devoid of any kind of real emotion, Jesse explained how he'd come across his mother after her aneurysm. He told me how there'd been no warning, no time to prepare, and fresh tears came to my eyes, those ones for him rather than me. At least with Shawna, we'd had a chance to prepare and say our goodbyes. It didn't help a lot right now, but I could see how in the future, we'd be happy we had that time, Dex especially.

"My dad took it hard," Jesse went on to explain. "He had no idea what to do with me and my sister. My mom always looked after everything: the banking, the grocery shopping, cleaning the house, dressing us, feeding us, you name it. He went to work, came home and sat on the couch for a few hours and read us a story before bed. To go from that to being solely responsible for two young kids was like an overload to his system."

I could understand that since my own family had been similar. My daddy ran the ranch but my mom ran the house. He would have been lost without her, but if something had happened, my aunts and uncles and grandparents would have stepped in to help, not to mention family friends.

Hopefully, Jesse's dad had been the same. "Did y'all have other family nearby?"

Unfortunately, he shook his head. "My parents were both only children of older parents. I had one grandfather still alive at the time, my mom's dad, but he was in assisted living of his own, in rough shape thanks to diabetes he didn't take care of properly. He couldn't help."

"So, your dad remarried?" It must have been pretty quick if Jesse'd had a stepmother three years later, and he confirmed that.

"I don't know if they actually even liked each other that much, but her husband had left her with two kids of her own, and she wanted stability while he wanted a maid. They got married not quite a year after my mom died."

"And how did she treat you while your dad was still alive?" I already knew what happened afterwards, but surely his dad wouldn't have allowed him to be mistreated?

"Like second-class citizens, both me and my sister. Her boys got new clothes while we had to wear ours until they wore out and she was afraid people might notice. I remember my sister's toes being red from her shoes because they were too small, and I had to ask my dad for money to buy her new ones because our 'mother' wouldn't do it."

I couldn't imagine treating innocent children that way, and I wanted to know more about Jesse's sister too. He'd never mentioned her before at any time over the past month while he knew all about my family. I wondered why they weren't close, but I tried to stick to the story in order and not jump ahead.

"Your dad didn't know what was going on after that?"

Jesse took a deep breath, his eyes still looking ahead at the road. "I think he knew but he didn't want to admit it. He was deeply unhappy in his own way and he didn't know how to deal with it. He started drinking more, coming home later, keeping his blinders up so he wouldn't have to acknowledge how bad things were. One day, he came home and my sister wasn't there. My stepmother had arranged for her to spend a week with a friend on her farm without telling him. Personally, I was happy about it because I figured she'd have more fun with her friend than she would at home, but for some reason, my dad chose that moment to get really offended that his wife was passing off her responsibility for his kids on someone else. He said he was going to get her and bring her home. The whole house shook when he slammed the door on his way out."

He paused there for a moment but I had a feeling he hadn't finished yet so I stayed silent, waiting to hear what happened next. Nothing prepared me for what he had to say though.

"The police said he must have just lost control. They didn't find any alcohol in his system, surprisingly. The car went off the road on the way back into town and hit a tree. My sister was sitting in the front seat and they both died instantly."

My stomach bottomed out so strongly that I had to grip onto the door for support. "Oh, Jesse. That's awful."

That word didn't begin to encompass it, but I couldn't think of any better ones. How brutally unfair that he should have to go through two traumatic losses like that when he was still just a boy. His whole family wiped out, just like that. I couldn't begin to imagine.

"It wasn't good," he acknowledged grimly, in a massive understatement. "You know the rest of what happened after that."

I knew some of it, certainly, but I had a feeling we'd only scratched the surface of how all of that must have affected him.

Jesse glanced over at me for the first time since he started talking. "I don't usually tell people about this stuff, Laura. I don't need any pity. I've dealt with it. But I wanted you to know that I do get what it's like to lose someone and I'm sorry for you and your family that you're going through it. Don't worry about getting back to the ranch until you're ready. We'll make do without you."

His tone made it clear that he didn't want to discuss it any further and I had to respect that, at least for the time being. He'd just shared something deeply personal with me and I appreciated him confiding in me more than I could express.

Soon, the outskirts of the city appeared, and I directed him to the hospital, a route I unfortunately knew from memory. He pulled up into the drop-off zone, making it clear he had no intention of coming in, which I completely understood. He'd already gone so far out of his way.

"Thank you for the ride," I told him as I unbuckled my seatbelt and grabbed my bag. "I'll be in touch as soon as I know anything more about when I'll be back."

His expression looked almost wistful as he nodded, and I got the odd feeling that he didn't really expect me to come back at all. It almost looked like he was saying goodbye for good. "Take all the time you need. The ranch will still be there when you get back."

Only after he'd driven away did anything strike me as odd in the way he'd phrased that. He said the *ranch* would still be there, but he didn't say he would. Hopefully, that was just another example of me overthinking things, and in any case, I couldn't worry about it now. With a deep breath to steel myself, I headed inside to find my family.

The hospital room looked the same as when I visited just a few days earlier, bright and colourful despite the rain on the window, full of flowers and cards and Dex's art. The daisies I had brought were right where I left them, still fully in bloom, but the bed in the middle of it all lay empty.

My brother, brother-in-law, and my sisters sat in the corner of the room, away from the bed, their chairs arranged in a circle, speaking quietly but calmly until they saw me come in. Billie was on her feet first, throwing herself into my arms while fresh tears flowed freely, everyone feeling the pain of the loss again with my arrival. Tonia and Cam were next, each of us trying to give and draw strength from each other in equal measure, and finally, I collapsed into my brother's strong embrace, sobbing even harder as I felt him shuddering against me.

"I'm... sorry..." I tried to say but it mostly came out as a wail, unintelligible and painful.

"I am too," he said, his arms still tight around me. "She wasn't just mine. She was part of the family."

He had that right. We all loved her, and the fact that Dex acknowledged our pain even through his own only made me hurt for him all the more.

"What's happening now?" I asked after a few more minutes, when I finally managed to pull myself away. Cam had dragged over another chair for me and Tonia stood ready with a box of Kleenex that I gratefully took. We all sat down, the air between us feeling thin and fragile.

Tonia answered for Dex, her hand on his arm protectively. She had always been the organized one, so he'd asked her a long time ago if she would help with the arrangements if things got to this point. "Mom and Dad are on their way and so are Shawna's parents and her brother. Mom and Dad will take Dex home so he can get some rest and we can pack this all up."

She indicated the room around us as Dex chewed on his lip, obviously uncomfortable with the idea of leaving. His pale face had bags beneath his eyes, his usually bright blue eyes looking faded and sad. He probably hadn't slept all night.

"And Shawna?" I grabbed another tissue to catch the tears brought on by simply saying her name out loud. I wanted to know if I could see her again but I had no real idea what happened when someone died. As I told Jesse, I'd never been through this before.

Tonia was on top of that too. "She wanted to donate anything that might be useful, although, with the cancer, that won't be much. The doctors will see if there's anything they can use and then the funeral home will come and collect her. We'll have a viewing in two days and the funeral in four."

We talked quietly for the next twenty minutes about the funeral and all the arrangements, trying to focus on the practical matters to keep the more emotional ones at bay, until more people began to arrive and the floodgates opened again. I watched in awe and admiration as my brother comforted Shawna's family even through his own pain. My mom held Dex for a long time, her heart obviously broken for her little boy.

As I sat there watching it all, even through all the heartache, I felt grateful as well. Grateful to have others to understand how I felt and grateful for Dex that he had so many people who loved him who would help him through this, no matter how steep a hill that might seem to climb. Yet again, my thoughts drifted back to Jesse, going through his own losses so young with no one there to support him. How he could have managed to pull himself through it floored me.

Eventually, as they had to, things began to move along. Our parents took Dex home with them where they would make him eat and sleep. We let Shawna's family go through all the cards in the room to see if there were any they wanted to take, and when they had gone, Tonia, Cam, Billie and I began to pack up the rest in boxes that Tonia had brought, always thinking ahead.

"How is the gallery doing?" I asked as I gathered up Dex's drawings. He and Shawna had opened their own gallery a couple of years earlier to sell Dex's artwork. It had been a slow start but he'd gained some loyal fans and Shawna had big plans for it. However, with all the time they'd spent in the hospital lately, I couldn't imagine he'd had much time for working.

"I went in the other day to check on it," Tonia admitted. "The manager told me it's been a little slow since Dex hasn't been producing anything new, but they've still got enough stock to keep going for a while. Shawna had a good business plan in place. It should be all right."

I hoped so. Besides Shawna, art was the one thing Dex had always loved. Hopefully, he could continue to find some kind of joy in it. He would need something to wake up for each day.

Moving on to the flowers, I picked up a cute, bear-shaped mug with a cactus in it. Shaking my head, I held it out to my sister. "Billie, this has to be from you."

"What makes you think so?" she tried to ask innocently, but we all knew the truth. For a brief moment, smiles appeared on everyone's faces.

Dex, Tonia and I were all very close in age, Dex and Tonia being less than a year apart, but Billie was four years younger than me. Growing up, she'd always complained about being left out of things because she was too young, and Shawna had commented once about how Billie looked like a cactus when she got in one of her huffs. "Be careful, her prickles are out," became a common way to diffuse the tension in the house, since it always made Billie laugh even when she tried to stay mad. Shawna had always done her best to make sure Billie would always be included.

"I just gave it to her two days ago," Billie admitted as I carefully packed it away in one of the boxes. "That was the last time I was here. I thought we'd have more time."

We all had. The end had come shockingly fast.

"I spoke to her yesterday, but I was planning on coming in person today," Tonia told us. "She asked me to bring in a few things for her. She thought she still had more time too."

My call with her the night before quickly replayed in my head. "Yeah, she even asked me to bring Jesse with me the next time I came up."

Three curious faces all turned to me, and I quickly realized my mistake. "Why would you bring Jesse to meet Shawna?" Cam asked.

"Have you been holding out on us, Laura?" Tonia put things together way too quickly, as usual. "Do we all need to be meeting this Jesse too?"

As much as I loved my sisters, that definitely wouldn't help matters before Jesse and I had a chance to define our relationship further. "You'll meet him when there's a good reason to. Right now, there isn't."

"Then why would Shawna want to meet him?" Billie pointed out before turning to Tonia. "She's definitely lying."

"Good luck, Laura," Cam told me sympathetically, shaking his head as Billie and Tonia whispered together. "Or maybe I should say good luck to Jesse."

"You're stuck with us for the next four days," Tonia reminded me. "Eventually, you'll crack and tell us the truth."

I would, I knew that for a fact, but I would draw it out for as long as I could first. As long as they were speculating about me, we could keep the hopelessness we all felt over Shawna's absence at bay, and as we bickered and teased each other, I could almost hear her laughter in the back of my mind. Even though she'd gone, she'd always be a part of us, and no matter how much it hurt, I would always be grateful that I'd been lucky enough to have her in my life.

Chapter Eleven

~Jesse~

My muscles ached as I returned to the house at the end of the day. I'd worked myself hard that day, just as I had the two days before that. The rain from the storm that went through had loosened up some of the ground in the farthest field, bringing down part of the fence with it. We'd spent the last two days fixing it and I worked even longer hours than usual. I didn't mind since I had nothing to get back to the house for, and if my body screamed at me in protest, it helped to drown out the other voices in my head, the ones that missed Laura and disagreed with the decision I'd made to take a step back from the path I'd been about to go down with her.

Even while I worked, though, I couldn't stop my mind from wandering. I had never met the woman who passed away, never even knew she was sick, so logically, I knew it had nothing to do with me, but the timing of her passing felt like more than coincidence. It felt like the universe holding up a great big stop sign to me, reminding me of what would ultimately await if I chose to give in to the temptation that Laura had brought into my house and my life since the day she arrived.

Eventually, however, I had to go home, to the house which had felt quieter and colder the last few days. I threw my frozen dinner in the oven before heading to my room, same as always, but everywhere I went, I could feel Laura's absence, showing me yet again how much I had come to rely on her presence in such a short time. I certainly hadn't missed Jim Callahan like this when he moved out for good.

After changing my clothes and throwing a load of laundry in, I finally let myself check my phone, bracing myself before I did. Laura had messaged me late on the same day I dropped her off in Houston to say that she expected to be back on the weekend and she'd let me know for sure when she knew more. I sent her a quick thanks in reply for keeping me updated but left it at that. Since then, I hadn't heard a word.

The screen remained empty, filling me with both relief and disappointment at the same time. Placing the phone back on my dresser face-down, I made my way back to the kitchen.

I'd only just sat down with my dinner when a loud knock sounded at the door, and my back muscles protested as I jumped in surprise. I hadn't expected any visitors, and I definitely didn't expect the person who stood at the door.

"Hey, Jesse." Mary-Beth gave me a warm, sympathetic smile. "I was out this way and thought I'd drop in and see if you wanted to car-pool up to the city tomorrow. We'll be leaving the kids at home so you don't have to worry about being overrun."

It felt like she was speaking a different language, her words made so little sense to me. "Tomorrow? The city?"

My confusion seemed to be contagious as Mary-Beth's forehead creased. "Shawna's funeral. You're going, aren't you?"

That helped to clear things up some, but not entirely. Laura hadn't mentioned a thing about it to me, which I pointed out. "I wasn't invited."

Mary-Beth huffed in either disapproval or disbelief, I couldn't tell which. "Since when do you need an invitation to support someone important in your life? It would mean a lot to Laura if you were there. Half of Sandy Creek is going, I'm not even sure why they're having it in Houston in the first place, except that she's going to be buried there, I suppose."

My heart had begun to thud heavily in my chest, my fingertips turning cold at the mere idea of it. I had never been to a funeral. My mom had a small one but my dad didn't let my sister and I go, thinking we were too young, and when my dad and sister died, my stepmother hadn't bothered with one. I heard her talking to one of her friends, calling it an unnecessary expense. She'd complained bitterly about even having to pay for the cremation.

Since then, I'd avoided funerals whenever anyone I was acquainted with passed away. Since I was never that close to anyone, it had been easy enough to do. Put on the spot like this, I didn't know what to do.

Would Laura really want me there? Her family was her priority, rightfully so. Maybe that explained why she hadn't mentioned it to me in the first place. Or maybe she suspected how uncomfortable the whole thing would make me, based on the conversation we had in my truck. On the other hand, Mary-Beth didn't know about any of that and there was no easy way to explain it to her without going into my background, which I really didn't want to do. Telling Laura had been one thing, and not a very easy thing at that, but no one else needed to know.

As I tried to figure out what to say, Mary-Beth took the decision out of my hands. "We'll pick you up at eight. No jeans. See you then."

She walked away before I could get a word in, leaving me completely flummoxed. In a daze, I returned to the kitchen and sat down in front of my food, but I couldn't bring myself to take another bite.

Fuck, maybe I should go. It would be difficult, but just because I'd decided there couldn't be any kind of romantic relationship between us didn't mean I didn't care about her at all. It would be a friendly, supportive gesture before I told her about my decision. Abandoning my meal for good, I called Tyson to tell him I'd be gone again the next day. Most ranch owners did take the occasional day off but that had never been my style before and I felt guilty about it even as he assured me it would be fine.

"You got something to wear?" he asked me curiously when I explained where I would be going. "I ain't ever seen you in anything but jeans."

That *was* a bit of an issue. "Actually, that's part of the reason I'm calling. I don't suppose you've got anything I can borrow?"

"Not that'll look right on you," he replied with a laugh. "Let me get on the horn to Kayla and see what I can do. I got your back, Jesse."

"Thanks."

Not much more than an hour later, Kayla and Tyson were both at my door with three different suits they'd procured from God knows where, along with shoes in a few different sizes. Kayla insisted I try all the suits on and chose the one she thought looked best.

"You men are hopeless," she laughed as she took the other two suits with her on the way out the door. "I'd hate to see you trying to pick out a suit for your wedding."

Luckily, I wouldn't ever have to worry about that. I didn't expect Tyson would either, but I was surprised to see him blush at her comment anyway. After thanking them both for their help, I called it a night, leaving the suit hanging over my bathroom door.

At quarter to eight the next morning, Mary-Beth and Wayne pulled up in their minivan, and she gave me a nod of approval as her eyes scanned me from head to toe. "You'd almost pass for a city boy, Jesse. I'll let you sit up front with Wayne, I didn't get a chance to vacuum all the Cheerios out of the back seat yet."

Mary-Beth kept up a constant stream of chatter from the back for the whole drive to the city, which I appreciated. She didn't seem to need any kind of reply most of the time, and when she did, Wayne would throw out a few words to keep her going. The sun shone brightly, unlike the last time I made the drive. Was that better for a funeral, or not? I really couldn't say.

Men in suits directed us into the church parking lot, already full to overflowing by the time we arrived. I recognized a lot of the trucks in the lot, backing up Mary-Beth's assertion that we wouldn't be the only folks from Sandy Creek in attendance. A steady stream of people headed to the entrance, the women in black dresses and heels, the men in suits that looked like mine. Even so, I felt out of place, barely knowing a thing about the woman whose memory we were there to honour. If

Mary-Beth hadn't been there to nudge me along, I would have been tempted to stay in the van and wait.

Inside, the mood was suitably sombre as people milled about, greeting each other sympathetically. In the entrance, a framed pencil drawing of a young woman rested on an easel, a warm smile on her face, and Mary-Beth smiled wistfully as she laid eyes on it. "That must have been one of the first sketches Dex ever made of Shawna," she whispered to me. "He's a talented artist."

I knew that much from Laura's stories about her family, and the sketch confirmed it. It wasn't polished, more like a first draft than a finished product, but he'd captured a feel of her anyway. It felt like she was smiling right at me.

We took a seat near the back, most of the pews already filled, and just before the service started, the Callahan family walked in to take their place in the front. Dex was hard to miss; he could have easily been a male version of Laura with the same blue eyes and dark hair, not to mention the stooped posture of someone who'd been kicked down by life. His parents flanked him as he walked in, followed by another couple with a young boy, which must be one of Laura's sisters, then Laura herself along with her other sister.

Laura's eyes scanned the room as she entered, smiling gratefully at the gathered crowd, and that smile deepened as she caught sight of Mary-Beth. A second later, her eyes moved to me and they widened in such surprise that I had to wonder if she really hadn't wanted me there. But in the next second, her expression softened, and she gave me a nod and a smile that sent a rush of warmth through me, replacing the coldness that I'd felt ever since she left.

Apparently, I hadn't done a very good job of convincing myself that nothing further would be happening between us. That would only make the conversation we needed to have later more difficult, but I put it out of my mind as the service got underway. The day was most definitely not about me.

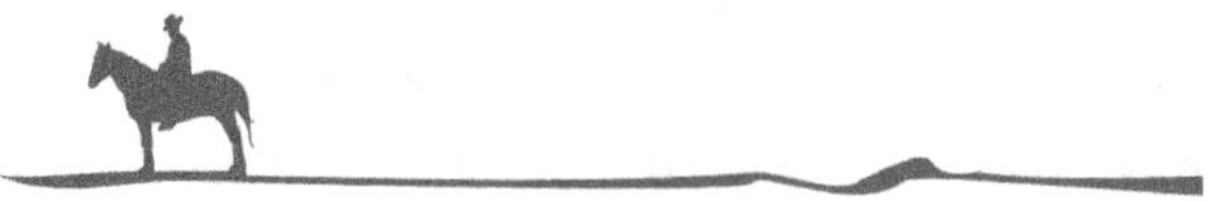

~Laura~

The last few days had been surreal; I couldn't think of any better word to describe it. It seemed like time had stopped, like it shouldn't be possible for the world to just carry on the same as it always had, and yet, things kept moving forward anyway. One minute we'd be in hysterical laughter over something and the next, we'd be sobbing. Everything felt heightened yet nothing seemed entirely real.

If I felt that way, I couldn't begin to imagine what must be going on inside Dex's head. He let us take over and endured our efforts to feed and entertain him, but the spark had gone from his eyes and I had to wonder what it would take to bring it back again.

In the meantime, my nephew, Charlie, proved a great distraction. Too young to understand anything that was happening, he carried on as he always had, making us all laugh and giving us something to focus on. Cam took him home every night while Tonia, Billie and I stayed at my parents', the whole Callahan family under one roof again as we tried our best to wrap Dex in love and support.

We had to talk about other things too, and of course, it didn't take long for my sisters to bring up Jesse. After putting them off as long as I could, teasing them with hints and innuendos, I finally ended up confessing the whole story as the three of us sat around on one of the guest room beds the night before the funeral. The only things I left out were the details he'd shared with me about his childhood. Those were his stories to tell, not mine. I simply said that he'd lost people close to him at a young age and had to grow up fast, and I told them about the advice Shawna had given me and how she'd suggested his initial standoffishness stemmed from fear of being hurt.

"We haven't had a chance to talk about what we want out of the relationship yet, but I really like him. More than I've ever liked anyone before," I admitted, saying the words out loud for the first time. I hadn't even entirely admitted it to myself yet.

"I can tell. You've never had that dopey look on your face before," Tonia pointed out with a laugh.

"What look?" I tried to rearrange my expression into a more neutral one, which only made them laugh.

"The same one Tonia wore when she and Cam got back together," Billie interjected, throwing our older sister a teasing smile.

I quickly shook my head in horror. "No. It can't be that bad. *Nothing* could be that bad."

"I was never dopey!" Tonia threw a pillow at Billie first, then me, which quickly devolved into a full-out battle, the three of us shrieking as pillows went flying until our mom appeared at the door and reminded us that Dex was trying to sleep. That quickly quieted us down.

My sisters weren't ready to let the conversation go yet though. Tonia leaned back against the headboard, holding a pillow against her stomach. "In the past, you always said you never got serious with anyone because you couldn't see a future with them. You didn't want the same things. I'm guessing that ain't the case with Jesse."

That was an understatement if I'd ever heard one. We wanted *exactly* the same thing: the ranch. That had been our friction point to begin with, but it could end up working in our favour. He'd promised to split the ranch with me if my plans worked, but if we were together, really together, we wouldn't have to split anything. We could just share it, both of us living in the house and raising the family there that I'd always imagined.

"Oh my God, you've got it so bad!" Billie exclaimed, pulling me out of my daydreams. "I'm sorry, Laura, but that might be the dopiest look I've seen yet."

I took the teasing in good humour since I couldn't really argue with it. I *did* have it bad. I missed Jesse and I hoped he was missing me too.

"He'll be at the funeral tomorrow, right?" Tonia asked. "I really need a face to go with all this swooning."

I quickly shook my head. "No. I haven't told him about it."

"Why not?!" my sisters exclaimed in unison.

"We're not even technically dating or whatever you want to call it. He's got the ranch to run and I don't want him to feel obligated to come if it's going to be difficult for him emotionally. He's still got his own stuff to deal with."

"If he cares about you, he'll be willing to do what's difficult," Tonia countered. "He'll want to support you."

I knew she had a point, but maybe that was exactly why I didn't tell him: I didn't want to know where I fell on his priority list just yet, because while I could see a future for us, Jesse hadn't actually told me anything about what he wanted.

So, when I walked into the funeral the next day, overwhelmed in the best way by the turnout of people who had come to support Dex and pay their respects to his wonderful wife, those chocolate-brown eyes of Jesse's were the last ones I expected to see looking back at me. I only had time to vaguely register the suit he wore and how handsome he looked in it before I had to move on, heading to the front of the church where we all took our seats next to Shawna's family.

My heart thumped heavily as I tried to focus back on what the day was about rather than obsessing about why he had come and what it might mean. Still, as I looked up at the casket and the beautiful sculpture next to it that Dex had created during Shawna's treatment, showing her weighed down by her illness but not defeated by it, I could almost hear my sister-in-law's voice in the back of my head: *Talk to me about something else. I'm so tired of everyone crying.*

She wouldn't mind me pining after my hot boss at her funeral. In fact, if she were there with us, which I hoped she was in some way, she was probably checking him out for herself.

There wasn't a dry eye in the place as person after person got up to share their stories about Shawna. Dex didn't speak in person but he and Shawna had pre-recorded a message to be played where he talked about how special she was to him, holding her hand as she sat next to him. At the end, she thanked everyone for coming and made an appeal to all the single women in the crowd or anyone with single friends. "I can personally recommend Dexter Callahan as a husband. If you don't mind a little paint here and there, I promise he's a keeper."

I stayed close to Dex afterwards as people came to speak to him, my sisters and I forming a protective line of defense in case he got overwhelmed, but we didn't need to worry. He did his best to comfort everyone else, not giving in to his own sadness. Shawna would have been very proud of him.

"Whoa, check out the guy in the suit by the back door," Billie whispered to me and Tonia under her breath. "He's gorgeous. I've never seen him before, I wonder who he's here with."

"They're *all* wearing suits," Tonia pointed out, but as I glanced over, I had a pretty good idea who had caught her eye.

"The one in the black and blue tie who keeps pulling on his collar?" When Billie nodded eagerly, I had to try not to gloat. "That's Jesse."

"What?!" Immediately, both their heads whipped around as I groaned.

"Can we try to have a *little* decorum? This is a funeral, after all."

"I thought you didn't tell him about today," Billie reminded me, still glancing back towards the door.

"I didn't. He must have heard about it in town." Since he'd been sitting next to Mary-Beth, I had a pretty good idea where he would have heard it from, but I still couldn't quite believe he came. A few minutes later, Mary-Beth and Wayne came over to give Dex their love, followed by a rather uncomfortable-looking Jesse. He looked wonderful in his suit, but it also didn't look entirely like him.

"Jim." He held his hand out to my father, since he was the person in the family he'd met first. "I'm real sorry about what your family is going through."

"Thanks for coming, Jesse." My daddy looked just as surprised as I was to see him there. "Let me introduce you to the rest of the family."

Jesse politely shook hands with my mom, Dex, and my two sisters before getting to me. Billie didn't seem to want to let his hand go.

"And of course, you already know Laura," my daddy said, looking between the two of us.

"Yes, I sure do." His brown eyes looked down at me with an almost cautious expression, as if he didn't know how I'd react to his being there. "I hope you're doing alright, Laura."

"I'm okay, thank you. Thanks for coming." It felt strange to be so formal with him, aware of everyone's eyes on us. It was a far cry from our nights riding on the ranch or being together in the house, where the world consisted of only the two of us.

"We'll be having dinner back at the house after the burial," Tonia interjected, not even trying to pretend she wasn't eavesdropping. "You're welcome to join us."

Jesse looked over at her as he replied. "I appreciate that, but I came up with the Parkers and they'll need to get back to their kids." His eyes drifted back over to me. "I can come back and pick you up tomorrow if you're still planning to head back then."

"I am, but you don't need to make another trip. You've got work to do. Billie offered to take me."

"Oh, was that tomorrow? I think I'm actually busy." Billie gave me an apologetic smile before turning to Jesse. "She'll be ready in the morning. Let me write down the address for you."

I watched helplessly as Billie gave Jesse directions and he promised to arrive around nine to get me.

"What?" she asked me innocently after he'd gone. "You said you guys still need to talk, right? No better place to do that than when you're stuck together in a car for hours. I'm just helping move this along, because I swear, if you let that man get away, I'm disowning you."

"Agreed," Tonia added. "If I weren't already married..."

"What's that, Sugar?" Cam asked, walking over at that precise moment and raising his eyebrows at his wife questioningly.

"Nothing," Tonia quickly replied as we all giggled. "Nothing at all. Come on, it's time to go."

It seemed it really was time for things to move on, in more ways than one.

~Jesse~

My mouth felt dry as I hopped out of the truck to open the door for Laura the next morning and I swallowed uncomfortably, trying to put on a normal-looking smile. I'd been dreading this conversation ever since I dropped her off at the hospital five days earlier, but now that the time had come, I knew I couldn't put it off any longer.

Laura came out of the house before I'd even finished parking, her overnight bag in her hand, dressed in her jeans and a pretty blouse, less formal than the day before but still equally gorgeous. I'd also switched back to my usual jeans and boots, feeling much more like myself, and I gave my belt a little tug, trying to adjust my jeans without being too obvious as my body reacted to the sight of her.

"Good morning." I managed to get the door open just before she got to it. "You've already said your goodbyes?"

She certainly seemed eager to get going, and she laughed as she pulled herself up into the passenger seat, placing her bag on the floor at her feet. "If you came to the door, they'd have you staying for breakfast, my mom feeding you till you're ready to burst and my sisters interrogating you about every detail of your life from birth until this morning. If you'd like that to happen, we can go back."

Without a word, I pushed the door closed, leaving her laughing again on the other side of it. Jogging back around to the driver's side, I put the truck back into gear. "I don't know if you're joking, but I'm not sure it's a risk I want to take. I do have to get back to work today."

"You didn't have to come and get me," she reminded me, and I winced as I heard how that sounded.

"I know. I'm happy to, but I'll be happy to get back too. The other guys have been asking about you too. They miss you." That was the honest truth. Everyone had commented on how quiet it seemed without Laura around. I hadn't been the only one to notice.

She fell silent as I maneuvered us back out of the city and onto the highway. With that being my third trip this week, Houston was almost starting to feel familiar, but all the traffic made me eager to get back to the open space of the ranch. I wasn't cut out for city life, just like I wasn't cut out for other things either.

"I didn't expect you to come yesterday," Laura finally spoke up once the traffic had eased.

That had been clear by her reaction to seeing me there. "I hope I didn't cross any lines by being there. Mary-Beth didn't give me much choice."

I glanced over in time to see her smile, that warm, beautiful smile I'd been missing over the past few days. "I can imagine. It's not that I didn't want you there, I just didn't want to put any pressure on you to come. I know death can make people uncomfortable, and you have more reason to have a problem with it than most. Besides, you didn't know Shawna."

"It sounds like she was something special." Listening to all the people at the funeral talking about Laura's sister-in-law, I had almost started to feel like I knew her. I certainly knew the look of hopelessness I could see in her husband's eyes when I shook his hand afterwards.

"She really was," Laura agreed. "But we're all special to the people who love us. We all touch *somebody*. Shawna just had a lot of some-bodies."

On that point, I felt less certain. It had crossed my mind the day before that if I were to die, only a handful of people would be affected. There'd be Tyson and the other ranch hands who might notice, and I couldn't imagine any of them crying over me, which was just how I wanted it. I'd be sorry if they died too, but not devastated. It seemed far safer that way, but that was before Laura. In such a short amount of time, she'd snuck into my heart and my thoughts, and if I didn't want to cause her grief or be the broken man sitting in the front row, I'd have to stop things before they went any farther.

That was what I needed to talk to her about and the reason why my mouth had been dry ever since I caught sight of her. I hated the idea of hurting her and I hated the idea of cutting off what had been a completely unexpected connection and the best part of my life for the last month, but it would hurt far less to do it at that point than if we let ourselves get in any deeper. Grabbing my water bottle, I let the cool liquid fill my mouth as I braced myself for the words I had to say, the ones my body was resisting with all its might.

"Is your brother going to be alright?" That seemed like a good way to ease into things, starting with things she could relate to.

Laura sighed, wrapping her arms across her stomach. "Honestly, I'm not sure. Shawna has been his whole life for so long. He's held it together this week but he's not the same. He just seems... empty."

That was a good word for it. Again, I knew that feeling very well.

"I know it'll take some time," she quickly added. "He's got other things in his life he cares about. His work and family and his friends, they'll all help, but I just don't know. I want to imagine him being happy and carefree again, but it's hard to picture. Do you ever really get over something like that?"

I didn't know if she was asking me personally, but I offered my own perspective anyway. "I don't think you do. You go on because you have to, but the part of you that dies along with them, it never comes back."

Laura nodded sadly, her arms tightening around herself. "Tonia said it must be like losing a limb or something, but then, in a way, that's a reason to still have hope, isn't it? Because people still live full, happy lives missing a limb. Maybe they can't do everything they used to and it'll never be the same as it was, but they learn different ways of doing things instead. It doesn't have to mean they can never do anything ever again."

The comparison had some merit, and I could build on it to try to explain where I was coming from. I had to put it out there before I lost my nerve. "Laura, I've been thinking a lot about what's been going on between us. All of this - the funeral and the memories that come with it - well, it's helped me to put some things in perspective."

"Okay." In my peripheral vision, I could see her turning towards me, her arms uncrossing as she gave me her undivided attention. "What are you thinking?"

"Well, to borrow your metaphor, when I lost my mom, it was like losing both my arms. It hurt so much that it felt like it would never heal. When my dad was taken, there went my leg. My sister took the other one. It took me a long, long time to figure out how to do anything for myself again or to feel like I could ever be whole again."

She leaned a little bit closer. "The fact that you did says so much about how strong you are. They'd be so proud of you now."

I hadn't expected those words from her and I found myself blinking back my emotion as I tried to push through to what I really needed to say. "The thing is, Laura, I've got nothing left. I've got no more limbs to lose. The wounds have healed as much as they're going to, the scar tissue has covered over the worst of it, but I can't put myself in that position again. I can't take the risk. One more cut would cut me apart."

"That's why you don't let people close," she guessed, her eyes still fixed on me even though I stared straight ahead at the road. "That's why you don't let them in."

"Call it self-defense. Call it cowardly, and you're probably right, but I owe it to you to be honest with you, Laura. You're incredible, so this has nothing to do with whether or not I want you, because I think I've made it pretty damn clear that I do. But the things you deserve, the kind of love I saw at that funeral yesterday, I can't give it to you. I don't have it left in me to give."

I paused there to see if she would say something, to see if she would guess what I was trying to say, but she remained silent, waiting for me to finish.

"So, I think that it'd be best for us both if we took a step back here, before we do something we'll regret."

With the words finally out of my mouth, I exhaled in relief while simultaneously bracing for whatever her response might be. Laura had fought me over plenty of things in the past month, big and small. I knew how worked up she could get and I knew how stubborn she could be, and that was before we were even dealing with anything as personal as this was. I really couldn't anticipate how she might react.

The silence probably lasted less than a minute but each second felt like an eternity. Finally, she took a deep breath of her own, leaning back from me. "I appreciate the honesty, so I'm going to be equally candid with you. I think you're incredible too. When I came back to town, my focus was entirely on the ranch. I wasn't looking for anything romantic and, well, let's face it, I thought you were gay."

The reminder makes us both smile, if only for a brief moment.

"What's been going on between us, as you called it, came out of the blue for me. I've never felt anything like this before and I think it could be a lot more. I think we could be really good together. As we've just seen, life can be too damn short sometimes, and if we don't take our shot while we get it, we might miss out entirely."

"Laura..."

She didn't let me speak. "Hold on. You had your say, now let me have mine. I hear what you're saying and I respect the way you feel. You've got to do what you need to do to protect yourself, but I'm not going to deny the way I feel either just to make this more comfortable for you. This is what I want, I'm stating that plainly. I want you. But if you don't feel the same, I'll accept that. I'm a big girl, so give it to me straight, Jesse: when you say you want to take a step back, what does that mean, exactly?"

She yielded the floor to me at last while also putting me on the spot. I'd be lying if I said it didn't affect me to hear that she wanted me and that she'd never felt this way about anyone before. Of course that meant something to me, and I felt the same way about her too. It just didn't change the basic facts and the rules I'd made myself to live by.

It didn't change how terrified I was about losing someone again.

So even though it made my chest ache, I forced the words out anyway. "It means we should go back to staying out of each other's way. We're colleagues and housemates, but nothing more."

Her jaw clenched, perhaps in anger or perhaps simply in disappointment, but she didn't put up a fight. She said she'd respect my decision and she did. "Fine. I guess that's the end of that, then. Were there any repairs needed at the ranch after the storm?"

She switched immediately into business mode and we spent the rest of the drive talking over work. After her time away, we had only two weeks left until her first clients arrived, so she had a lot to do. It should help us to keep out of each other's way, as I said.

But somehow, as we pulled back into the ranch and got ready to go back to normal life, even though I'd gotten exactly what I asked for, I couldn't help feeling like I'd come out of our conversation as the loser anyway.

Chapter Twelve

Jesse went straight out to work as soon as we got home, telling me to take the rest of the day off if I needed to, but I didn't want that at all. I needed to get back onto the land, beneath the big sky and breathing the fresh air, even with the smell of manure mixed in. It had always been in my blood but even more so after the last month of being back there again. I missed it more than ever while I'd been away, and I knew in my heart that I'd never be able to be away from it for a long time ever again.

Not to mention that if I sat around the house with nothing to do but brood for the rest of the day, I might drive myself crazy.

It would be a huge understatement to say that the conversation in the truck hadn't gone the way I'd been hoping. I'd been thinking about it the night before after Tonia and Billie weighed in on how I needed to lock Jesse down. We were sitting around my parents' living room after most of the guests had gone home, and the topic of conversation came back around to Jesse's unexpected appearance at the funeral. I appreciated their enthusiasm, but I had my doubts about coming on too strong. Jesse still hadn't said anything out loud about wanting more, I pointed out, which prompted Dex to speak up. We hadn't even realized he'd been paying attention.

"Sometimes, actions speak louder than words. Shawna always said if

I'd just told her I thought she was beautiful, she wouldn't have believed me, but when I drew her, she couldn't deny what she saw. The weird thing was: I didn't even realize how I saw her until I drew her either. I think Jesse showing up today says a lot, even if he ain't ready to admit it out loud yet."

I trusted my brother's opinion on the male psyche more than my sisters', even if I knew not all men were as sweet as Dex, and I'd carried that hope with me as I joined Jesse in the truck that morning, ready to confess my feelings. However, when the time came for us to have 'the talk', it didn't go that way.

He wanted to pull back right when I was ready to dive in, and that hurt no matter how 'incredible' he said he found me.

He said it had nothing to do with not wanting me, which I had to believe based on our chemistry in the bedroom, but he wasn't willing to put his heart on the line anyway, and no matter how much I might want to, I knew I couldn't force him to do it. If he didn't feel ready, I couldn't change that, but I made my position clear anyway. Life could change on a dime, he knew that better than anyone, so beating around the bush seemed counterproductive. He could stew on that information just as I would have to come to terms with the fact that he was willing to walk away from what we had, or at least what we'd been on the verge of having.

So, after changing my shirt to one I wouldn't mind getting dirty, I headed out to the field to join the men. The other hands all greeted me with a hint of uncertainty, not sure if they should be respecting any mourning period, but I didn't want anyone tiptoeing around me. I'd already grieved in private and I would continue to do so, but what would help me most would be getting back to normal as soon as possible. As soon as I made that clear, teasing Tyson about his inability to drive a fence post straight, the others quickly relaxed and we were back to joking around and working hard in no time.

As things began to wrap up that afternoon, I told Jesse I would head back to the house. "I need to get caught up on the holiday side of things.

We'll have paying customers here before we know it."

"Sounds good." He avoided looking directly at me, as he had most of the day. "I've got some things to finish up out here and then I'm going into town tonight, so I'll be out of your way."

That was new. He hadn't gone into town in the evening since I'd been there, other than the night he came to the bar to find me. However, as his employee and nothing more, I had no reason to ask for more details, so I didn't. "Alright. I'll see you tomorrow, then."

He gave me a nod before turning back to his work, and I headed back to the house. With my laptop in my room, I went through the emails that had come in for my new business venture over the last few days while multitasking around the house, responding to messages between unpacking and getting supper started. Expecting Jesse to be out in the field for a while still, I threw a load of laundry in, including the clothes I had on, stripping down to my underwear in the laundry room before heading back to my room to grab something comfy to put on for the evening.

I came out of the room just as Jesse entered the hall at the opposite end, skittering to a stop as he got a look at me. For a second, I thought he might actually trip over his feet and land flat on his face as we both stared at each other in surprise.

I recovered first. "Sorry. I didn't think you'd be back yet. I was just..."

"Yeah, no, I... I get it. Go... go ahead."

He gestured to my bedroom door which stood between the two of us and, straightening my shoulders, I walked over to it as confidently as possible. He'd seen me wearing less before, after all. There was no reason this had to be awkward, and if he felt uncomfortable, then maybe that wouldn't be entirely a bad thing.

At my door, I paused, looking back at him over my shoulder. "I'm making some chilli for supper. There'll be extra if you'd like some. I make it pretty hot, though."

"I... uh, no, thanks. I've got plans, like I said."

I gave a shrug, shifting my hips just a little and noticing the way his eyes were immediately drawn downwards. "Suit yourself." With that, I closed the door behind me, giving in to a moment of satisfaction at just how flummoxed he looked.

As I went to grab my yoga pants and sweater, the feeling quickly faded, though. No matter how much fun it might be to tease him with a glimpse of what he was missing, the fact remained that I was missing out on it too. It frustrated me more than I could say that we both liked each other, we both wanted each other, and nothing would come of it.

However, I wouldn't sit around feeling sorry for myself either. That had never been my style. If Jesse meant what he said, then hoping he'd change his mind wouldn't do me any good. I'd found one man who could excite me while also sharing the same goals and lifestyle, so why shouldn't I be able to find another one if I wanted to?

I didn't have to go chasing it, but I wouldn't hide from it either. Starting in just a couple of weeks, a steady stream of customers, a lot of them men, would be coming to the ranch, looking for a way to connect with the way of life I had always loved. There would be riding lessons and roping lessons and campfires at sunset, all the kinds of things I found romantic. Who could say what might happen then?

~Jesse~

If I didn't know Laura so well, I would have thought she did it on purpose. Coming in from the field, I planned to get changed as quickly as possible and head out for the evening, avoiding any potentially awkward conversation. Although Laura had handled me breaking things off calmly and maturely, it still seemed wiser to give her a bit of space until the initial sting of it had passed.

I certainly did not expect to find her in the hallway in her bra and panties, looking like all my best dreams from the past few nights coming true right in front of me.

If it were another woman, I might have thought she did it to mess with me, but Laura didn't play games like that. She'd always told me exactly what she thought and exactly what she wanted, so even if she *could* have faked the surprised look on her face when she saw me, I didn't think she had. That left me dealing with the fact that quite possibly the most beautiful woman I had ever seen was in her underwear on the other side of the door, just a few feet away from me, and she'd be willing to take it off for me again if only I could be the man she needed me to be.

If only I could forget all the pain that loving anyone had ever brought me.

With a pained sigh, I headed to my room instead. A quick change of clothes later, I headed back out of the house and to my truck, ignoring the mouthwatering aroma of Laura's chilli bubbling away on the stove.

The Sandy Creek bar was pretty quiet at that time of night, even more so than usual, so I saw Wayne and his friends as soon as I walked in. He waved me over and shoved a basket of wings in front of me as soon as I'd taken a seat, calling over to the bar to get me a drink without leaving his seat.

On the drive back from Houston, Mary-Beth had fallen asleep in the back seat, leaving me and Wayne on our own to talk, and he'd asked me why he never saw me out in town.

"The ranch keeps me busy," I explained, which was mostly true. "It's a 24-hour-a-day job."

"You've got to take a break sometime," he argued. "I love my wife and kids, and I work hard, but I still need a bit of time to just relax and be more than a husband and an employee too. If you don't, life has a funny way of passing you by."

In light of the funeral we'd just attended, those words seemed more relevant than ever.

"You should come sometime," he continued, just as persistent as his wife when he wanted to be. "You gotta eat, don't you? Me and some of the guys always do wings on a Thursday. We'll save you a spot."

"Maybe sometime." I tried to keep my response vague, but he wouldn't accept that.

"Tomorrow's Thursday. Why don't you come then?"

An excuse pushed its way to the tip of my tongue, but before I spoke it out loud, I gave it another moment's thought. Knowing that I intended to talk to Laura on the drive the next day, it might actually be good to have a reason to get out of the house in case things were strained between us. I supposed that, just this once, I could make an exception.

"Glad you could make it." Wayne slapped me on the back with a warm smile once I'd got settled in the booth against the far wall, opposite the bar. "This is Joey, Tom and Steve. Guys, this is Jesse."

I nodded politely at all of them before digging into the food in front of me. My stomach had been growling ever since I smelled Laura's chilli, and it gave me a good excuse to not have to make small talk either. The TV over the bar was showing a football game so no one talked much about anything other than the game for the next fifteen minutes or so, which was perfect for me. Unfortunately, when half-time came, the focus turned to the one topic of conversation I would rather avoid.

"I hear you got Laura Callahan working for you," the guy across from me said. I felt pretty sure Wayne had introduced him as Tom. "That's got to be interesting."

Something in the way he said the last word rubbed me the wrong way. "How do you mean?"

"We all went to school with Laura," he explained. "We've all seen her stubborn side."

"She never liked anyone telling her what she could or couldn't do," Joey added from the far side of the table. "I can't imagine her taking orders too well."

"People change," Wayne pointed out. "Maybe she's different now."

They all looked over at me for confirmation and I couldn't help smiling as I thought about the various arguments we'd had about the ranch.

"Oh, she's stubborn as hell, but she knows what she's talking about. When she makes suggestions, I listen. She'll take feedback and admit when she's wrong, too. Honestly, I couldn't ask for a better employee. I don't know if you've heard about this whole working holiday program she's starting up?"

The men all nodded. "I know a few folks keeping a close eye on it," Steve told us. "If you do well, others will jump on the bandwagon. You could find yourself with some competition."

That didn't worry me. I only wanted Laura to be happy.

Fuck. As soon as that thought crossed my mind, I had to stop myself from groaning. That didn't sound like something a boss should be thinking.

I wasn't the only one drifting towards more personal matters either. "Is she seeing anyone?" Steve asked. "I heard she's looking good these days." Wayne shot me a nervous glance, no doubt having heard the whole story from Mary-Beth about me coming and finding Laura in the bar last week. It surprised me that Steve wouldn't know about it, but I never paid attention to gossip either. Maybe he was out of the loop.

In any case, I had no claim on her, not after what we'd discussed that day, so no matter how much it pained me to say the words out loud, I had no choice. "No, she's not in a relationship. The ranch takes up a lot of her time, though."

"Even better," Joey laughed. "Someone hot that you don't have to spend a lot of time with? That's the dream, isn't it?"

They all laughed before Wayne changed the subject, to my relief. First, I had to deal with Laura looking all kinds of tempting back at the house, and then I had to deal with other men speculating about getting together with her. Someone somewhere seemed determined to make this as difficult for me as it could possibly be, no matter how much I tried to convince myself that I'd made the right call. I stayed for another hour or so to watch the end of the game before heading home. That time, I entered the hallway more cautiously, but Laura seemed to be in her room. I could see the light beneath her door, and though there almost seemed to be a magnet pulling me towards it as I walked by, I forced myself to keep going.

I'd spent the last few nights alone in the house, but now that she was back yet equally as far out of reach, my bed felt even emptier than before. Hopefully, missing her would get easier. If not, I really didn't know what I was going to do.

~Laura~

One of the constants of life was the way time continued to march on, no matter what. Shawna's passing couldn't slow it and neither could the man of my dreams telling me he didn't see a future for us.

The sun still came up the same way each morning as Jesse and I made polite small talk in the kitchen over breakfast. Mornings bled into one another as we worked out in the fields, herding the cattle, vaccinating the calves and looking after the horses. After lunch, I devoted my attention to the working holiday business, making sure everything was in place for our first guests. The bunkhouse came to life as I decorated it in a retro Western style, comfortable but not luxurious. The guests should feel like they were roughing it a little bit compared to their high-class lives in the city but they shouldn't want for anything. My extra staff got hired, food ordered, more bookings were made, and almost before I knew it, we were just one day away from the first arrival.

The evenings passed a little slower than the busy days, even though my work often carried over past dinner. Jesse and I no longer went out riding together. He told me he'd taught me everything he knew, but of course, that had never been the whole reason we did it. It had been about having an excuse to spend time together too, and now that he no longer wanted to, the foundation for it crumbled. No matter how many times I offered, he refused to eat my cooking. We ate together sometimes, talking about ranch business rather than anything personal, but he always insisted on making his own meals. At least it wasn't *all* frozen dinners; he actually started doing some basic cooking on his own, inspired by some of the things I'd shown him. I tried to encourage it without pushing too hard.

One night, I went out on a date. Mary-Beth set me up with one of Wayne's friends, a guy I remembered from high school, and though I tried to give him the benefit of the doubt that he'd improved since then, by the end of the night, I knew it wouldn't be going anywhere. I told him so just as honestly as I always did, and Mary-Beth told me a couple of days later that he'd mentioned to a few people that I thought too much of myself. *Charming.*

It didn't particularly bother me, though, not when I had so much else to focus on, and the look on Jesse's face when I casually mentioned I had a date had given me more satisfaction than the date itself did. He obviously didn't like it, but he didn't do anything about it either. He seemed completely determined to stick to his resolution and again, I didn't push it. I had no interest in trying to manipulate him into wanting to be with me. Either he did or he didn't, and the only one who could make that call was him.

The morning of the day that our first guests would be arriving, we had breakfast together, as usual. All my plans were in place, so sitting around waiting for the guests to show up and getting nervous wouldn't do me any good. I planned to work out in the field with Jesse as usual until lunch time and then head over to the bunkhouse to double check everything one last time. The first group booked in was a half-dozen executives from a company Tonia had worked with a few months earlier. I planned on starting with a short horse ride that afternoon to get them comfortable, followed by a cookout to really break the ice.

"You're welcome to stop by and grab some food and say hi if you'd like," I told Jesse as I reviewed the itinerary with him. "Our customers will probably be thrilled to meet a real live cowboy."

"I doubt that, Laura," he scoffed good-naturedly. "These are success-ful businessmen, not little boys."

"Men who *were* little boys once," I argued back. "They might try to cover him up, but that little boy is still there inside them, shaping their life whether they know it or not."

Jesse's brown eyes met mine across the table and I realized too late what else that could sound like I was talking about: the little boy inside him who'd been through so much, he couldn't let himself love again.

"I'm sorry, I didn't mean..."

"I know." He cut me off as he got to his feet. "Time for work."

The shuttle bus pulled up just after three o'clock that afternoon. We offered transportation from the city as an add-on and this group had taken advantage of it. They'd also taken our instructions about what to wear to heart as there wasn't a suit in sight. Most of the men wore jeans that looked brand-new as they stepped out of the vehicle and took a look around at the wide-open space and the bunkhouse behind me.

"Welcome to Sandy Creek." I put on my widest smile, eager to make a good impression. I'd dressed the part too, wearing my cowboy boots and hat, my hair hanging down over my shoulders, the top buttons of my shirt left undone. These men were buying into the experience of country life, and if part of that meant flirting with a cowgirl, I'd happily play that part, especially since a couple of the six men who gathered around me were rather handsome. "I think that my sister told you that you're our first group, but don't think that means I'm going to go easy on you. If anything, I'll be testing out just how far I can push y'all."

They all smiled back at me, only a little nervously.

"We're going to get started right away so take your bags into the bunkhouse and pick a bed. There are no single rooms; hands on the ranch have to share. Use the restroom if you need to and then we're going to go for a ride."

Jesse had let me take the ranch's six best-trained horses for our newcomers to use and I'd brokered an arrangement with another nearby ranch to let us borrow some of theirs when we got larger groups in. We wouldn't be riding every day, but I knew they'd expect it as part of the experience, so I planned to lead with it.

It took a while to get the men ready to go. Two of them had ridden before, once or twice, but the others hadn't, so even just getting mounted took some time. Once they were all secure on top of their horses, I gave them a quick lesson on stopping and starting and how to avoid getting thrown off. With that, we were ready to go.

The weather had decided to cooperate, to my delight. Although summer had almost arrived, the heat hadn't fully hit yet and the gentle, warm breeze felt inviting rather than stifling. An easy trail went between the fenced fields, a trail Jesse and I had travelled down many times together, but I put that out of my mind as I focused on setting a good pace and making sure no one got into any trouble.

At the top of the small hill in the east corner of our land, I brought us to a stop and let them look out over the land as I gave a brief history of ranching in this area and our ranch in particular.

"How much is the land worth?" one of the older men wanted to know.

That was exactly the mentality we were trying to counteract with this experience, and I did my best to explain that to him. "I could put a dollar figure on it, but the true worth of it isn't something you can buy. It's something you feel. The value is in working the land the same way people have done for generations, connecting with it and pushing your personal limits. I'll ask you that same question again on your last day here and you can tell me how much you think it's worth."

We circled back around down another trail where we could see Jesse and a couple of the other hands working with the cattle. One of the men asked if we could stop to watch and I used the opportunity to answer the questions they had about the cows and the cowboys' work.

"What are those things in the cows' ears?" another man asked.

"Those are their ID tags. All calves are tagged before they're three weeks old and they also need to be vaccinated. We've just finished a first round of that for the ones born first and we'll do another round in a few weeks for the later arrivals. Calving season is a busy time on the ranch. Most of those you can see with their mamas now are about six to eight weeks old. They'll be drinking from mom for a while still."

They all seemed impressed as I answered every question thoroughly, and I could almost pretend not to notice how good Jesse looked on his horse whenever I happened to glance over his way.

By the time we returned to the bunkhouse, the cook had fired up the grill, and the men all made appreciative noises as they got a look at the spread already laid out.

"Everyone go in and wash up before we eat," I ordered, trying not to giggle as I watched them all stagger away from the horses, their legs a little sore from the unfamiliar activity.

Over beers and burgers, I learned more about each of them and about their business. They all seemed like nice guys and by the time I said goodnight to them all, I felt optimistic about the week ahead. One of the ones I'd pegged as handsome right off the bat, Luke, seemed particularly attentive, wanting to know all about me.

Jesse never showed up, but that was okay. He'd have another chance at the farewell barbecue in a week's time, and for the amount of money these guys were paying, I felt certain I could convince him to at least drop by and thank them for coming.

Until then, I wasn't going to let anything Jesse did or didn't do get me down, not when things were off to such a good start to earning my half of the ranch, fair and square.

Chapter Thirteen

~Jesse~

Laura seemed to be in a good mood over breakfast the next morning, which I took to mean that her first day had gone well.

She didn't comment on me not turning up for her cookout. I had debated about it, nearly heading over a half-dozen times but ultimately changing my mind and staying put. This had always been her project, not mine, and I didn't want to take any of the credit for it that rightfully belonged to her. The guests should see her as being in charge rather than answering to me, but I didn't know how to tell her that without it sounding condescending, so in the end, I made no explanation at all. She could simply think it came down to me being antisocial if she wanted to.

"You know, you don't have to get up this early," I pointed out. "Your guests aren't going to be up for hours yet."

Laura shrugged as she ate the melon she'd cut up for herself, popping the pieces deftly into her mouth before licking her fingers clean. I shifted uncomfortably in my seat as my body reacted to the sight. "I don't mind getting a bit of work done with y'all first. It's kind of crazy how quickly something becomes a habit. It hasn't even been two months that I've been getting up this early and already, my body thinks it's normal."

I knew what she meant. It also felt kind of crazy how quickly having her there had become normal to me and how much I craved being around her. And yet, when we were in the same room, like we were right then, I had to hold myself back too, denying just how much I wanted her.

It killed me when she announced she had a date the week before, even though I simply nodded and stood by while she went on her way. It would be bound to happen eventually. I wasn't the only man with eyes to see just how incredible she was, and she owed me nothing. Even so, it stung a little bit, if only because I had absolutely no interest in being with anyone else. I could go to the bar in Austin if I really wanted some companionship, but the idea of being with anyone who wasn't Laura held no appeal. I didn't just want sex; I wanted sex with *her*, but I couldn't let myself have that either, not when it would mean promising her something I didn't have in me to give.

Somehow, I had to move past this, like Laura already seemed to be. I simply hadn't figured out how yet.

Over the next few days, Laura really put the men to work. She had them cleaning out the horse stalls and replacing a section of fence on one of the far fields. We needed new ditches dug to replace the irrigation pipes to another one of the fields and she put them to work on that too. I let her borrow Tyson to give them an introduction to herding cattle and he absolutely loved being the centre of attention. He came back walking a few inches taller, looking awfully proud of himself.

They certainly didn't get as much work done as six experienced hands would have in the same amount of time, but they did achieve some concrete results and, as Laura had pointed out to me in her initial proposal, we didn't have to pay them a dime. *They* paid *us* instead. It almost felt dishonest, but they must be getting something out of it too, and I had to admit that if things carried on this way, her plan looked very likely to succeed. Since I was a man of my word, I could very well be signing over half the ranch to her in ten months' time.

There really didn't seem to be anything she couldn't do.

She'd planned another barbecue for the group's last night, and now that the working part of the holiday was over, I had no excuse to stay away. I couldn't undermine her authority when the work had finished, so after getting cleaned up from my own work for the day, I put on my boots and hat and headed down the road to the bunkhouse.

The smell of grilled meat hit me first, followed by a burst of laughter, and when I rounded the corner, the sight that greeted me filled me with both pride and a deep, intense possessiveness.

The group all sat around one of the large, round, wooden picnic tables that Laura had bought, plates full of steak and corn on the cob and baked potatoes, open bottles of beer in front of them, and all eyes were on Laura. She'd taken off her hat, leaving her brown hair sparkling in the sunshine, her cheeks slightly flushed and her eyes animated as she told them a story I'd never heard before about a junior rodeo she'd taken part in here in town.

She had them eating out of her hand, everyone hanging on each word, and in the expressions of the men I could see, it looked like far more than a professional interest. One of them even reached out and put his hand on her arm as she made them all laugh again.

"Jesse!"

I hadn't realized that I'd stopped moving until Laura looked up to spot me hovering in the background and called my name. She quickly beckoned me over with a smile and a wave of her hands.

"Guys, this is Jesse Greenbank, the owner of the ranch. You've seen him out in the fields this week, working hard, as always."

Some of the men stood up and others remained seated as I went over to shake their hands. The one closest to Laura, the one who had touched her, stayed where he was.

"Thanks for all the great work you did this week," I said as Laura directed me to a seat and went to fill a plate for me. "I hope y'all ain't gonna be too sore."

They laughed as a few of them stretched out some of their muscles, wincing at the reminder.

"It felt great to be working with my hands," one of the older men told me, displaying his hands that didn't have a single callous on them, making mine look like worn leather in comparison. "Even though I hurt, I can't remember the last time I slept so well."

They peppered me with questions about the cattle and what would happen next in the ranch's work cycle as we all dug into our food. I seemed to have everyone's attention other than the man next to Laura who kept up a private side conversation with her the whole time, and every time he made her laugh, it felt like a knife twisting into my gut.

"What about Laura, though?" I asked the group, trying to put the attention back on her so the guy next to her couldn't monopolize her attention any longer. "How amazing is she?"

Her cheeks turned delightfully pink as the men began to sing her praises, all of them saying how the experience wouldn't have been the same without her. "You've got yourself a winner here," the older man told me. I had a feeling he must be the one in charge of the group. "I hope you're paying her what she's worth."

"I'm not sure that amount exists." The words came out of my mouth before I had a chance to think them through, but no one disagreed with me.

"Alright, all this praise is going to go to my head. Anyone need any more food or another beer?" Laura stood up and headed back over to the food table, and my jaw clenched as the guy next to her immediately got up to 'help'. The other men continued to chat about their experience and ask me questions, but I couldn't take my eyes off Laura and her admirer.

Hearing that she had a date had been bad enough. Watching someone else come onto her was even worse, and just like it had in the bar a few weeks ago, the night that I gave into my feelings for her in the first place, the urge to do something about it became nearly overwhelming.

And when he leaned closer to her, resting his hand on her hip as he whispered something into her ear, I couldn't hold back any longer.

"Excuse me." I got to my feet in the middle of someone asking me a question, leaving them mid-sentence as I headed over to the pair who had their backs to me. His hand was still on Laura's hip and I had to clench my fists to keep from pulling it off. "Is everything okay here?"

They both turned to me, Laura with surprise on her face and the guy with suspicion. He must have heard something in my tone that gave him a clue as to why I was asking. Sometimes, men just understood each other that way, and his response confirmed my own concerns.

"I don't think we need any more help, thanks." His grip tightened rather than pulling away, staking his claim with the certainty of someone who thought he really had a chance.

Laura simply picked up the plates of food she'd been putting together, stepping out of his reach and around me. "Luke's right, we're all finished."

She began to head back to the table and I let her go, but when Luke tried to follow her, I grabbed him by the shoulder, holding him back. "How about you give her a bit of space?"

"I don't see how this is any business of yours." His eyebrows raised in challenge, showing me he had no intention of backing down.

"It's my business because that's my employee that you're hitting on while she's trying to do her job."

"She's on her own time now," he pointed out, accurately. "And I don't think she'd have any trouble telling me to back off herself if that's what she wanted."

The implication that she was actually encouraging his flirting had me seeing red more than ever.

"Jesse, can I talk to you for a second?" Laura had come back over after putting the food down on the table, sneaking up on us just as I had on them a moment ago.

"Of course." If she was with me, she wouldn't be with him, so even if she planned to tell me off, it seemed like the better option.

"You guys go ahead and finish that all off," Laura told the group, gesturing to the remaining food and drink as we walked away. "You've earned it!"

As soon as we were around the corner, I tried to start speaking, but she shook her head, heading back towards the house, making it clear she didn't want to be overheard. Her silence only lasted until we got through the door; as soon as it closed behind us, she dove in, crossing her arms in accusation.

"What the hell was that?"

I had the same question. "That jerk was all over you."

"His name is Luke, he's a paying customer, and he's a nice guy. You have no right to come in there and try to act all macho and intimidating." Her pursed lips made it clear just how unimpressed she was.

I didn't see it that way. "He was flirting with you."

"Yes, he was! And I was flirting back. So what? It's just a bit of fun, and even if it wasn't, it's got nothing to do with you, Jesse. You made that very clear. If I want to spend the night with him, I can. We're roommates and nothing more, remember? You can't have it both ways, so what is it you want?"

She was one hundred percent right, but I couldn't help the way I felt anyway and I took a step closer to her as I tried to open up to her about exactly how I felt. "I hate this, Laura. I hate being at odds with you. I hate being close to you and not being able to touch you. I hate the idea of that guy being with you. If you want someone to satisfy you, it should be me."

Her eyes widened in surprise, neither of us expecting those words to come out of my mouth. "What does that mean? You've changed your mind about being in a relationship?"

"No." I couldn't go that far. No matter how frustrated I felt, I simply couldn't cross that line. "I can't."

"So... what, then? You want sex?" She didn't say it angrily. It simply sounded like she wanted to understand.

Of course I wanted to sleep with her again, but not in the seedy way it might sound. "If you were serious about that Luke guy, that'd be one thing, but you said yourself it's just a bit of fun. If that's what you want, if you just want someone to make you feel good in the way you know I can, then I don't see why that can't be me. I could do a better fucking job than he could, I know that."

Laura put her head in her hands, her own frustration clear, but I couldn't tell if it was sexual frustration like I felt or if she found my proposal entirely inappropriate.

"So, we use each other for sex?" she clarified, rubbing her hands down her face in a way that only made me want to run my hands over her instead. "No strings, no other feelings involved?"

"It'd be on your terms, but basically, yeah." Since I couldn't explain it any better, I left it at that.

"You're crazy," Laura declared, shaking her head in disbelief.

"I know." I couldn't blame her for thinking so. I had never felt less balanced than I did at that moment, but putting it all out there made me feel a little more in control too. If she told me off in no uncertain terms, I could try to convince my body that it really had no more chance. At least I'd know for sure.

That wasn't what she did, though. Still shaking her head, Laura let out a deep sigh. "I guess I must be crazy too."

Before I could ask what she meant by that, she stepped towards me and pulled my lips down onto hers.

~Laura~

People said that insanity was doing the same thing over and over again and expecting a different result. Jesse and I had been there before: his jealousy driving him to make a move his heart wasn't ready for. I knew he wanted me and I knew equally well that he hadn't changed his position. If there had been any doubt, he just told me so himself. He wouldn't or couldn't offer me any kind of commitment beyond that night, so if I kissed him with the expectation that it would lead to a change of heart, I really would have to consider myself delusional.

That wasn't why I did it, though. I kissed him simply because I wanted him. I kissed him because while Luke had been charming and flirty and made his interest very clear, as soon as Jesse appeared at the bunkhouse in his boots and hat and broken-in jeans, everyone else faded into the background. I kissed him because I had spent almost two weeks lying in bed each night remembering the way it felt to have those rough hands of his on me and to see the look in his eyes when he lost control, the same look he gave me when he offered to make me feel good.

It wouldn't mean anything and I understood that, but I wanted it anyway. I'd worked hard all week and deserved a reward. No strings, no feelings other than the ones he made my body feel. Free from expectations, we could simply let go and enjoy each other in the way we already knew that we would.

Eventually, I would have to move on and find someone who could offer me the whole package, something more fulfilling in the long run, but until that man came along, why not let myself indulge in something I knew wasn't good for me, as long as I remembered not to expect anything more than he offered.

Once the dam had broken with the kiss, we couldn't keep our hands off each other. We didn't even bother to take our boots off, stumbling down the hall with our lips still connected, my hands undoing his belt as he fumbled with the buttons of my shirt. My back hit the hallway wall, and then his did, spinning around each other almost like a dance as we got nearer to our destination. My room was closer than his, so I pushed him in there, not wanting to waste any more time.

Finally breaking apart, I went over to the window to close the curtains, just in case, while Jesse tugged his boots off. Both of us undressed as quickly as possible, our eyes on each other, almost racing to see who could get naked first. He beat me by just a few seconds, coming over to remove my bra himself, his cock already erect, looking just as eager for what was to come as I felt.

"You look incredible." His normally deep voice sounded even throatier than usual, the need in it so strong I couldn't miss it. Those perfect, calloused hands skimmed over my curves, sending pleasure through me as he traced every line. "God, I've wanted to touch you. Every time I see you, I have to hold myself back."

He did a good job of hiding it, but then again, maybe I did too. The idea of being naked with him again had crossed my mind far too often, far more than I would ever admit.

"You can choose the position," I told him, reaching down to wrap my hand around his warm, stiff cock, revelling in the way his eyes closed in pleasure as I did. "I think it's your turn."

He let me take control the other times we'd done this, and I had to admit to being curious about what he would do if it were his choice. No matter what, it would be good, and with the way my body throbbed with need, it honestly didn't matter to me. I just wanted him inside me, the sooner, the better.

When he didn't immediately answer, I thought he might refuse and ask me to choose again, but it turned out he must have simply been considering his options, because when he answered, he sounded firm in his decision. "On your hands and knees."

I wouldn't be able to see him that way, but maybe that was the point. We were there to make each other feel good, not stare deeply into each other's eyes. With my body pulsing in anticipation, I climbed up onto the bed without a word, spreading my legs for him and smiling in satisfaction when I heard him inhale shakily.

"Fuck, Laura." My hips straining towards him, I expected to feel his cock at any second, but when he made contact, his tongue touched me instead. "You taste so damn good."

I couldn't answer that, couldn't do anything other than moan and whimper as he licked at me in a way that both teased and satisfied me. His hands rubbed my ass as he buried his face between my legs and I forgot all about the reasons we hadn't been doing this. All I knew was how good it felt to have that perfect specimen of a man focused on me, his touch and his own sounds of pleasure, muffled against my skin, sending ripples of desire and satisfaction through me, pulling me higher and higher until I could barely keep my balance.

"Please, Jesse," I panted as my arms began to tremble. "I need…"

I didn't have to say the words. He already knew, and his mouth vanished, leaving me right on the edge, aching and cold, until his cock drove into me, filling me up in one fell swoop. With his fingers on my clit, I came hard, convulsing around him as he groaned.

"Fuck," he managed to mutter, the word drifting through my subconscious as my body floated on the waves of my orgasm. "How do you feel so good?"

I wanted an answer to that too. What made this so much better than any other man I had been with before, even when I knew it was only sex and nothing more?

There wasn't time to figure it out, not when he began to move, his cock sliding in and out of me as he gripped my hips, filling every inch of me at the most incredible angle. My hands clawed at the bedspread as I tried to keep my balance, my body already building towards another release as he handled me just right, just the way I wanted it.

"I know you can give me more than one." Jesse's right hand moved back to my clit as his pace increased. As his cock drove into me harder and faster, his fingers pressed down on me, making me moan again. "Come with me, Laura. Let me feel you one more time."

For him, I could certainly let myself go again. For him, I didn't really have a choice. His breath grew shorter as his own orgasm drew near and knowing he felt it just as much as I did helped to bring me back to my peak. When he gave a low, primal groan, his fingers still on me and his cock buried inside me, I did just as he said, coming one more time right along with him, our bodies in perfect sync.

We stayed there like that for a few moments, him standing behind me, still connected, his hands resting gently on my body, until the last shockwave through my body had faded and I could see straight once again. Gently, I leaned forward, pulling myself off him, trying to ignore how empty it felt without him there.

"Well, thanks. I enjoyed that." I gave him a smile as I sat down on the bed, turning to face Jesse and trying to ignore how incredibly sexy he looked standing there naked, his cock slick with my pleasure. "I guess I'll see you in the morning."

Jesse's eyebrows drew together, his expression uncertain. "I don't gotta go right now. I could stay for a while."

"That's not necessary. We both got what we wanted and I should head back to the barbecue. They'll be wondering where I went."

"Let them wonder, then." He moved towards me, leaning down to reach for my hand, but I shook my head.

"I'm finished here, Jesse. You can do what you like now, but I'm heading back. Just sex, right?"

Climbing off the bed, I grabbed my clothes off the floor and headed to my bathroom to clean myself up.

Insanity would be letting myself think his desire to stay meant that he'd change his mind, that it meant anything more than what he'd said it did, and I wouldn't make that mistake again. The sex had been just as incredible as before, but I expected nothing else. So long as I kept my physical desires separate from my emotional ones, I could stay in control, and for now, that itch had been scratched.

With a clearer head, I could get back to work.

~Jesse~

The change from complete satisfaction to all-consuming frustration happened so fast, I nearly got whiplash. The way Laura casually walked away after what had to be acknowledged as pretty amazing sex, thanking me for playing my part and then dismissing me, left me feeling disposable and disappointed, even though I knew she had only followed my own stipulations. I told her I wanted sex without the emotion, the kind I usually had with my hotel bar pick-ups, and so she gave it to me, effectively showing me that, when it came to her, I didn't want that at all.

What *did* I want, then? The answer to that was frustratingly opaque. I wanted to be able to give her what she truly wanted from me. I wanted sex like we just had but I wanted her in my arms afterwards too. I wanted her to be mine, for people to know she was mine and to not have to worry about the guests flirting with her. I wanted to be able to take all the things she offered me - the friendship, the warm home and amazing meals, the sex, and more - without feeling like I could never adequately repay them.

I wanted to not be the broken little boy anymore, but he'd been running the show for so long, I didn't know how to take back control. No matter how hard I tried, I couldn't see a way to push past that fear of losing her to simply be in the moment. Other people did it all the time but they didn't know how it felt to lose everything. From the bottom of my empty heart, I envied their ignorance, and perhaps that was what I wanted most of all: I wanted the bliss of not knowing how quickly it could all be taken from me if I let my guard down.

Since that would never be possible, I couldn't see a way forward, and I went to bed that night more frustrated than ever. What I'd hoped would break some of the tension between us had only made it worse, at least for me.

Laura had a few days before the next group arrived, so after working with the housekeeper to get the bunkhouse ready and gleefully showing me the enthusiastic reviews her first group left, she headed up to Houston overnight to visit with her family. The usually welcome solitude of the empty house felt almost oppressive as I got cleaned up from the day's work, and I found myself calling Wayne Parker.

"If you and any of the guys feel like watching the game tonight, I've got plenty of room out here on the ranch."

He eagerly took me up on it, especially when I offered to provide the beer. Armed with snacks, three of them were soon seated around my living room, and I had to admit it kind of made a nice change. It helped to keep my mind off Laura, anyway, and that had been its primary purpose.

When she returned the next evening, she found me reading alone in the living room, refusing to admit to myself that I'd been waiting for her, and she came to sit next to me on the couch.

"Would it be alright if I had someone come and stay with us for a few days? Here in the house, I mean?"

My chest immediately tightened at the idea of her bringing another man there, even though she had every right to do so. Had she met someone in Houston? Rekindled an old flame, maybe? She wouldn't be doing it just to make me jealous, she wasn't that type of person, so it must actually be something serious. My mind whirled with the possibilities, each one making me a little more nauseated.

"It's your house too," I reminded her through the bitter taste in my mouth, trying to be mature about things. "When?"

"Once the next group has gone. I want to be able to give him my full attention."

I really didn't need any further details. Every jealous bone in my body screamed at me to tell her no, to tell her that anything this man could give her, I could do better, but my mind knew that wasn't true. When it came to a little satisfaction of the kind Luke had wanted from her, sure, but not if there was more to it than that. "That's fine," I heard myself saying. "I can move upstairs if you want more privacy."

Laura gave me a funny look. "I ain't kicking you out of your room, Jesse. He can stay upstairs."

Upstairs? He wouldn't be staying with her? Confusion and hope both rose in me as Laura began to smile.

"Who exactly do you think I'm bringing here?"

"I don't have a clue," I admitted as I began to see I must have jumped to conclusions. "Who is it?"

"My brother, Dex."

That made a lot of sense, and relief flooded through me as Laura shook her head with an indulgent smile on her face.

"You really thought I'd be bringing a man I'd just met here?"

I didn't want to answer that. I didn't want to think about it a second longer now that I knew it wasn't true. "How is your brother doing?" I asked instead.

As I hoped, that managed to distract her. "He's been better," she told me with a sigh, leaning back on the couch. "He's having trouble working. He's having trouble sleeping. This place has always inspired him, same as it has for me in a different way, so I thought that if he spent some time here, it might get his creative juices flowing again."

"It won't have too many memories?" I knew from the things both Laura and Mary-Beth had told me that Dex had started dating his wife in high school, so I imagined she would have spent some time there in the house with him.

"It does but I don't think that bothers him. He wants to feel close to her but he also needs a change of scene. We can even put him to work if he feels like it. It might not help, but it's worth a shot."

I certainly knew about how work could help to maintain a sense of normality, so I quickly agreed and we talked over the logistics for a while along with her plans for her next holiday group before she stood back up.

"I'm going to get ready for bed. Tomorrow's another busy day." Heading towards the hall, she paused in the doorway for just a second. "I wouldn't ever try to hurt you on purpose, Jesse. I hope you know that."

She was referring back to my assumption that she'd be bringing a man there to sleep with her, and I acknowledged her assurance with a sheepish smile. "I know. You have every right to be happy, though. I don't expect you to stop living your life on my behalf either."

The words we didn't say lingered in the air between us, how we both wished things could be different, but the gap between what she deserved and what I had to give still seemed too wide. We said good night and both went to our own rooms, only feet away from each other but feeling like we were miles apart.

Chapter Fourteen

~Laura~

My second group of guests left the ranch in the late afternoon after a final trail ride. The group had been bigger and a mix of men and women, which meant less individual time with each guest and far less flirting than the first group. It had rained in the morning, and when two of the group took their horses off trail and started to get scared about slipping in the mud, I had to dismount to go help them out. Of course, I ended up taking a spill in front of the entire group, caking the entire backside of my jeans in mud.

I laughed it off, telling them that working on a ranch wasn't all glamour and prestige, and they all seemed to have had a good time in the end, but by the time their bus drove off, I was more than ready to get in the shower and clean off before Dex arrived.

Jesse got back to the house at almost exactly the same time I did, approaching from the other direction at the end of his work day, and he stopped to let me go in first.

"No, go ahead," I tried to say, not really wanting him to get a look at the back of me.

He gave me a confused smile, tipping his hat. "Ladies first."

"That's not necessary. You've had a longer day."

"You've been dealing with people," he countered. "That's worse than wrangling animals any day."

I planted my feet more firmly. "Just go in, Jesse."

"After you, Laura."

We stood there, facing off at the bottom of the steps, until, with a sigh, I gave in. "Alright, fine."

As I walked up the steps to the porch, Jesse burst out laughing behind me, exactly as I'd been trying to avoid. "What in the world happened to you?"

I turned back to glare at him. "You know, a gentleman wouldn't laugh at me. Chivalry doesn't end with letting a lady go in the door first."

"I'm sorry, but it looks like you took a mud bath." He didn't sound very sorry at all as I pulled off my boots at the door, trying not to shake too much of the caked dirt off my pants. It didn't work; little pieces flaked off anyway. "Come on, take your jeans off, Laura. You don't want to leave a trail through the house."

"You want me to strip right here at the front door?"

I meant the question as a joke, trying to match his tone, but the words seemed to shift the mood between us anyway. When he answered again, the humour had gone from his voice, leaving it sounding tighter. "Makes more sense. I'll get a bag to take your clothes to the laundry room and you can go get cleaned up. You ain't usually shy about it."

That could refer to the time he'd caught me in my underwear in the hallway before, or the times I'd been naked in front of him. Either way, the reminder sent a rush of heat through my body. It had been more than a week since the last time we'd had sex, and with Dex coming, we wouldn't have another opportunity for a while. Maybe it wouldn't hurt to indulge just one more time.

"You know, my shower's big enough..."

I didn't even get the sentence out before I caught sight of Dex's truck at the end of the drive.

"Shoot, he's here!"

Startled by my mid-sentence change of topic, Jesse blinked in surprise before looking over his shoulder to see the same thing I'd just seen.

"Alright, move, Laura. Clothes off and go get ready. I can play host until you get back."

Giving him a grateful smile, I pulled my clothes off as quickly as possible and raced down the hall to my room. Fifteen minutes later, showered and changed and much fresher, I came out to the kitchen to find Dex and Jesse at the kitchen table, Dex with a cup of coffee in his hands. I thought I had noticed the smell in my room, but I figured it came from my machine.

"Oh, Dex, you shouldn't... I forgot to mention..."

Jesse quickly got to his feet, offering his seat to me instead. "It's fine, Laura. I'm going to get changed myself."

He left the room before I could say anything else and I sat down in his abandoned chair, leaning over to give my brother a hug. "How was your drive?"

"Fine." With his lips, he gave me a smile, but his eyes didn't change. "It's strange to be back here."

Glancing around the kitchen, I tried to see it from his perspective. It had taken me a while to get used to it too when I first came back, but now, it just felt like home. "It's different," I agreed. "The only thing constant is change, right?"

As soon as the words were out of my mouth, I winced at my tactlessness. Dex was the last person in the world who needed to be reminded of that.

Noticing my reaction, he reached over and patted my hand. "Don't feel like you gotta second guess everything you say, Laura. That ain't you, and I know what you mean. Most of the time, anyway."

His smile felt a little more genuine that time and once again, I found myself in awe of how, despite the one hurting worst of all, he still managed to take the time to make everyone around him feel better.

"Where did you get the coffee from?" I asked, doing my best to change the subject to something safer.

"Jesse went into your room and got it for me while you were in the shower. I know you like your coffee, but keeping the machine in your room feels a little obsessive." He meant it as a joke, but I would need to tell him why I had it in there. I didn't want him to feel bad, but I didn't want Jesse to be uncomfortable either.

"Jesse doesn't like the smell. I keep it in there so he doesn't have to smell it. I can be considerate now and then, believe it or not."

"I know you can." Dex looked down at the cup in his hands in consideration, but when he spoke again, it was on a different topic. "I gotta admit, I'm a bit surprised you guys are still in separate rooms. After what I heard between you and Shawna..."

"I thought you didn't hear anything incriminating!" I reminded him, and he chuckled, sounding a little livelier than before.

"Let's just say I heard enough. So, what happened? Things didn't work out?"

I sighed, leaning forward to rest my chin on my hands. "Do you want the short answer or the long answer?"

"How about we go for a ride tonight and you can tell me as much as you want to? I can't promise I can help like Shawna could, but I can listen."

That sounded amazing to me, but I hadn't invited him there to lay all my problems on him. "I'm supposed to be taking care of you, not the other way around."

Dex shook his head, looking back down at his coffee again. "I don't think either of us need taking care of. We can just hang out, annoying each other like we used to."

I could get behind that. "In that case, I'll make us a quick dinner and we can go."

Jesse joined us for dinner, eating his own food, as usual. The conversation stayed casual, centering around the ranch and how my business venture was going. Unlike my sisters, Dex could actually stay on topic without throwing innuendos in. Jesse seemed relaxed around him, which made me happy, and he told us to enjoy ourselves as we left the house afterwards to go for our ride.

Dex was as rusty on his horse as I had been a couple of months earlier, so we kept the pace slow as we toured the ranch, pointing out places we both remembered from our childhood, until Dex asked to hear all the details about Jesse. "What's going on, Laura?"

It didn't take any more than that. I told my big brother the whole story, leaving out only the more intimate parts and glossing over the details of Jesse's losses. I would never share those without his permission.

When I'd finished, I waited for him to say something. Where Tonia and Billie would have said the first thing that popped into their heads, Dex had always been more considered, and he took his time to think it over now.

"I get where he's coming from," he finally said, which weren't at all the words I'd hoped to hear, but coming from my brother, I had to respect them. "And I appreciate that he didn't try to lead you on once he'd made his decision. He sounds like a decent guy."

"He's more than that." Decent didn't begin to cover it. "He's smart and hard-working and so good at his job. He takes me seriously but he also laughs at me. He isn't capable of caring just a little bit; that's why it's got to be all or nothing. He tries so damn hard to do the right thing, even when he's wrong."

I left out the other part, about what a giving and satisfying lover he was, figuring my brother didn't need to hear that. I'd already got my point across.

"So, that's where we are. I don't know what else I can do. I've told him how I feel and he's told me how he feels. We're at an impasse."

"I can see that." Dex gave me a nod of understanding. "For the record, I think you've done the right thing, Laura. You've been honest but you can't force him to be ready if he's not."

I appreciated that validation, but I'd hoped for a little more. I wanted a plan of action like Shawna gave me, but that wasn't Dex's style, and I wasn't quite so tactless as to complain about it. I knew he had way more reason to be missing her than I did. "So, you think it's hopeless? I should just let it go?"

"Let me think about it over the next few days," Dex suggested. "I can get to know Jesse a bit better for myself. I ain't making any promises, but I'll give you my honest opinion before I go."

I really couldn't ask for more than that. "Thanks for listening, Dex. I'm glad you're here."

"Me too." We both looked out over the ranch, taking in the view that had always meant so much to both of us. It always brought me a sense of peace no matter how wrong things might seem otherwise, and I hoped that, if nothing else, he would find a little bit of that peace there too.

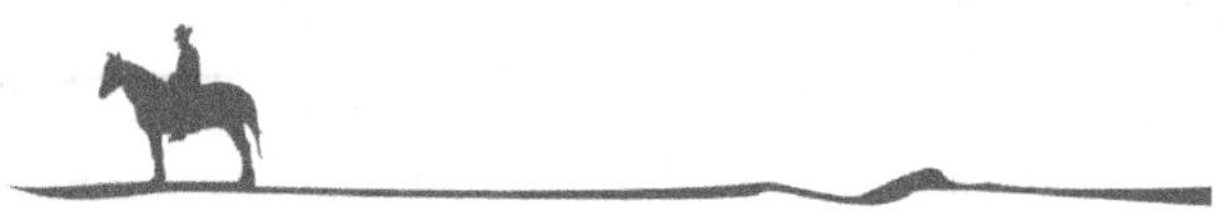

~Jesse~

As a houseguest, it would be hard to find fault with Dex Callahan. Though he'd grown up there, same as Laura, he never acted like the place belonged to him, unlike his sister. He offered his help where appropriate, both around the house and on the ranch, but never overstepped. Despite what he must be going through, he did his best to set me at ease without expecting me to do all the talking, and the fact that he both understood and felt comfortable teasing his sister only added to my enjoyment at having him around.

With another person there, things didn't have a chance to get awkward or tense between me and Laura. We could be ourselves without worrying about crossing any lines, and it evened us out so much that when Dex announced he'd be going back up to Houston the next day, after only five days with us, it genuinely disappointed me.

"We'll have to go for one more ride tonight before you go," Laura suggested.

Dex nodded in agreement. "I was hoping you'd say that. I'd actually like to take some photos to help with some painting I'd like to do when

I get home."

I could see Laura's pride over the fact that he'd found some inspiration, and I was glad for him too. He seemed to be handling things pretty well so far, but I knew how quickly that could fall apart. Grief had a funny way of lulling you into a false sense of security, thinking you'd moved past it, and then knocking you down all over again.

As we cleaned up the remains of our dinners, Laura's phone rang and she excused herself to answer it in the living room while Dex and I finished washing the dishes.

"You're doing a great job here with the ranch," he told me as we both looked out the kitchen window at the beautiful early summer's evening. "I know it hit Laura hard when our daddy went and sold it on her, but she would have been stretched pretty thin trying to hit the ground running, fixing the things that needed to be fixed *and* putting all her big plans in place at the same time. You've given her a solid foundation to work off of, and I think you complement each other pretty well."

Coming from a member of the family who'd owned this place for generations, that meant a lot, and on the last point especially, I had to agree. "She would have managed it somehow, but from a selfish point of view, I'm glad it's worked out this way. We make a good team."

The woman in question came back into the kitchen a moment later, full of apologies. "Dex, I'm so sorry, that was Mary-Beth on the phone. She and Wayne and the kids have all come down with some kind of bug and she needs a bit of help. I know it's your last night here, but…"

"Go on," Dex encouraged, not letting her finish. "Go and help your friend. I'll be fine."

"But you wanted to get the pictures," she reminded him, clearly looking torn.

There seemed to be an easy enough solution to that, even though a few months ago, I probably wouldn't have got involved. "I can take Dex out for a ride. I ain't got no plans tonight."

Laura's grateful smile warmed me from head to toe. "That would be great, Jesse. You don't mind?"

Surprisingly, I really didn't. "Not at all."

"Alright, in that case, wish me luck! I'll try not to bring any germs back with me." She headed for the door while Dex and I put the rest of the dishes away. In companionable silence, we grabbed our boots and hats and headed out to the barn to get the horses saddled.

He didn't need any help, having grown up around horses just like Laura had, and we set an easy pace over to the hill at the far end of the fields where the best views were found. When we got there, I watched him taking photos on his phone's camera, trying to see the view through his eyes.

"I imagine you're seeing something a bit different than I am," I finally admitted. "All I see when I look out there is the fence that needs to be replaced and the irrigation ditch that needs to be finished."

Dex smiled as he stuck his phone back in his pocket, relaxing astride his horse as he took in the view with his own eyes rather than through the camera's lens. "I can see it just like I'd paint it, the background shapes and colours first, the details added later. For a long time, I didn't realize that not everybody sees the world that way."

That was really interesting. I tried again, attempting to look past the practical. "You mean like the way the house makes a line against the sky there?"

"Exactly." Dex nodded in approval. "You've got the sharp angles and the softer, rolling feel of the hills and the clouds. Greens and yellows and blues."

I could see it, sort of. Still not the same way he did, I imagined, but a little more than I had before. "So, you'll paint this when you go back to the city?"

His lips tightened as he continued to look out over the land. "I'm going to try to do something with it. Not a painting, probably, but something that incorporates the feel of it. I've got to get some more pieces ready for the gallery, but I ain't felt much like it lately. Working here, I can keep my hands and mind busy, but in my workshop, when I create a piece, it's all about the emotion, and that's where I'm having trouble."

I understood that, far better than I would have liked to. "Sometimes, it's easier to block it all out."

His hat dipped as he nodded in agreement. "Unfortunately, art doesn't come from what's easy. The most successful pieces nearly destroy me at the best of times. And this... well, this ain't the best of times."

That was an understatement if I ever heard one. Though I had no experience in talking to people about stuff like this, I heard myself asking the question anyway: "How are you coping?"

I recognized the way he exhaled, the way the words got choked up as he tried to get them out. "It's pretty rough. I thought I was prepared, or as prepared as I could be, but it's worse than I imagined. She was everything to me. It ain't even the big things I miss the most. I miss 'em, don't get me wrong, but it's the little ones that catch me off guard. Hearing something I know would make her laugh and not being able to share it with her, or just walking into a room and expecting to see her, but she's not there. It's like a papercut on my heart each time; not enough to kill me, but enough that the sting never lets up."

Once again, I knew exactly how that felt, not only from losing my family, but the way it felt when Laura went away. Not that it hurt as bad as the kind of hurt he was talking about, but I missed those little things too, far more than I expected to. What he said made complete sense to me.

His next words, however, took me completely by surprise. "But no matter how bad it gets, no matter how much it hurts, even if it lasts the rest of my life, I wouldn't give up a minute of the time we had together."

"Really?" I winced as I heard the way the word sounded as it came out of my mouth. My tone was heavy with disbelief, but the truth was, I didn't see how that could be true. "I mean, not even if you could go back to when it all started, before you fell for her? Before you got attached?"

Dex shook his head, still looking out into the distance. "If I could go back in time and talk to that teenage version of myself, you know what I'd tell him?"

I honestly didn't have a clue. "What would you say?"

"I'd tell him that Shawna Armstrong is going to break his heart. I'd tell him about the day she first got her diagnosis, the day we found out the cancer came back, and the day she found out she'd never get to have a baby. I'd tell him about the tears and the anger and the gut-wrenching feeling of not being able to do a goddamned thing to make it better. I'd tell him about the day they took her away for the last time and how he's going to have to say goodbye. I wouldn't sugarcoat a single bit of it."

There were tears in his eyes, and in mine too as I heard the pain underlying each and every word. Though I didn't have the memories he described, I could smell that coffee on the kitchen floor again and see the sympathy in the police officer's eyes when he knelt down to tell me my family was gone. I could feel the aching emptiness of it, the vulnerability and the despair.

Dex hadn't finished yet, though. "And then I'd tell him to ask her to the dance anyway."

Those words made so little sense to me, they might as well have been in another language, and I stared at him in utter confusion. "Why would you do that?"

"Because that's not the whole story. Not even close. I wouldn't tell him about the first time she kisses him or how it feels to walk with her hand-in-hand. I wouldn't say a word about the excitement of buying their house or how she'll be the most beautiful bride there's ever been. I'd keep it from him about how waking up next to her makes the whole world feel right or how she'll help him open the gallery he always dreamed about, believing in him more than anyone in their right mind ever would. I wouldn't tell him any of that, because those parts are the real story. Those are the parts nothing could ever spoil, the memories that will make all the hard times worthwhile. I'd tell him he's the luckiest man in the whole world, no matter how it ends, and to just enjoy it while it lasts, because that woman right there, she's the one who's going to make him live. And if we ain't living, what the hell are we doing here?"

As he spoke, as he painted a picture of his relationship, I couldn't help superimposing my own memories of Laura over it. Running into her in my kitchen the first time we met. Delivering the calf with her on her first day and how well we worked together right off the bat. The evenings we spent riding, and kissing her for the first time after bringing her home from the bar. The way it felt to be inside her and how nothing else in the world seemed to exist in those moments. The way I'd felt more alive ever since the day she burst into my life, completely unexpectedly.

She frustrated me, she challenged me, and she satisfied me, but she never left me indifferent, no matter how hard I tried to keep her out of my heart.

Was Dex actually right? Would the good times be worth it, no matter what might happen in the end?

I had to accept that, for the first time, it felt possible. And if anyone knew what he was talking about, it would be a man who had just been through the very worst of it.

Almost as if he could read my mind, he looked over at me, offering me a wry smile despite his watery eyes. "No one can promise to never leave us. But Shawna gave me everything she had, as long as she was able to give it, and if hurting now is the price I have to pay for everything I got, I'd still call it the bargain of a lifetime."

I couldn't think of a single thing to say to that, so I simply nodded to let him know I'd heard what he was trying to tell me. He'd certainly given me a lot to think about, and as we headed back to the house, my mind continued to race. Could I really take the chance, after all this time, and put my heart on the line again? After all my indecision, would she even still want it?

I supposed, in the end, there was only one way to find out.

~Laura~

Mary-Beth looked dead on her feet when I arrived, which I figured she must have been in order to call me in the first place. Her makeup wasn't even done, which shocked me most of all. I thought it might have taken the world ending for that to happen. She was the kind of person to help anyone out at the drop of a hat but would almost never ask for help herself.

"My parents are down and out too," she explained as I marched her straight to her room to go lie down. "We must have all spread it to each other."

Wayne was already in bed and he mumbled a barely-comprehensible greeting to me, saying something about armadillos in cowboy hats as I got Mary-Beth settled next to him. I made him drink some water and made sure they had some Tylenol on hand before leaving them to rest in peace.

The kids were a bit more restless, also feverish and unhappy. I got them something to drink too and gathered them all together in one bed, holding the youngest one while I told them stories about a cowgirl and her best friend who happened to be a horse, and how they rescued animals. It took a little while, but eventually, they all gave in to their body's desire to sleep and I moved them back to their own beds, breathing a sigh of relief when none of them woke up. After cleaning up the living room and the kitchen, I left Mary-Beth a note to tell her to call me in the morning if she wasn't feeling better, and left the house

By the time I got back out to the ranch, the sun had set and Jesse and Dex had both gone to their rooms. My curiosity about how their evening went would just have to wait, and after getting ready for bed, I soon fell into a deep sleep of my own.

In the morning, Jesse seemed a little more talkative than usual over breakfast as he asked about the Parkers and we talked over the day's schedule. Another group would be arriving for their stay the next day, so I had some last-minute prep to do, but otherwise, it would be as 'regular' a day as there ever was on the ranch. I planned to take a lunch break with Dex before he headed back to the city.

"Thanks again for letting Dex come and stay."

"I enjoyed getting to know him," Jesse replied, and I believed he meant it too. "He's a good guy."

He would get no argument from me there. When it came to my family, I had definitely been blessed.

Jesse was too busy to stop for lunch with us, or he just claimed to be so that Dex and I could have a bit of time alone, and my brother surprised me by telling me that he and Jesse had a good talk during their ride.

"He actually talked to you? About personal stuff?" I honestly didn't know if Jesse did that with anyone other than me.

"I think I did most of the talking," Dex admitted. "But it felt good to get some of that stuff out, and it felt like we understood each other. I like him, Laura."

I liked him too. That had never been the issue.

"You said you'd let me know before you left if you thought Jesse and I had any chance of working out," I reminded my big brother. "So?"

Dex laughed at my blunt question, but he gave me an honest, thoughtful answer, as usual. "It's pretty clear by watching the two of you that he cares about you. It's also pretty clear he's holding himself back. I tried to tell him, in not so many words, that when you find something special, you shouldn't let fear hold you back."

"You talked to him about me?" As much as my brother loved me, I hadn't expected him to actually say anything on my behalf. He didn't usually get involved.

"Not exactly," he replied, whatever that meant. "I just tried to find the parallels between our situations. I couldn't even tell you exactly what I said. It almost felt like Shawna was whispering in my ear, giving me the words she thought he might need to hear. I know that she's rooting for you guys too."

I didn't doubt that for a second. "Thanks, Dex."

I waved from the porch until I couldn't see his truck anymore down the drive, and then I went back to work. By the time the end of the day rolled around, I had started to feel a little achy, and after I'd changed my clothes back in my room, I gave Mary-Beth a call.

"We're doing so much better," she told me. "Thank you for last night, you're a lifesaver."

I assured her it had been no problem before asking the most pressing question on my mind. "How did it start for you guys?"

When she described my overall feeling almost exactly, saying she felt that way the day before she got sick, before it really hit, I groaned and she immediately caught on. "Oh, shoot, really? I'm so sorry, Laura! If it helps, it only really lasted for a full day."

That was good news, but one day would still be tricky, especially with my next group arriving in the morning.

"Call me if you need anything," she insisted. "I'm sorry!"

Remembering the hug I'd given Dex before he left, I texted him just to warn him to be on the lookout for symptoms. At least I hadn't interacted too closely with anyone else, so hopefully, the spread would be limited.

"Laura?" Jesse knocked quietly on my door. "You coming out for dinner?"

The question surprised me, since it went against his whole 'do our own thing' ethos, but I answered him readily enough. "I think I better stay away from you tonight. I might be coming down with whatever the Parkers had and I don't want to make anyone else sick."

"What do you need?" He immediately focused on the practical, as I would have expected. "Can I bring you something to eat?"

"That would be great. Just a sandwich or a salad would be perfect. The bigger problem, Jesse, is what to do about the group that's coming tomorrow."

"Let's worry about that tomorrow when we see how you're feeling. I'll be right back."

He returned in about twenty minutes, having made me not only a sandwich, but a bowl of soup too, carrying it all on a tray that I recognized. My mom had used it to bring us food when we were sick in bed, and she must have left it behind.

"You didn't have to go to so much trouble," I admonished him, even as my stomach rumbled at the smell of the thick tomato soup. "And none of it was previously frozen!"

He chuckled at my teasing. "I'm not sure out of a can is much better, but I'm glad if it helps. Let me know if you need anything else."

I promised I would and kicked him out before he breathed in too many germs. After a quiet evening, I had a restless sleep, my body feeling alternately too hot and too cold, and by the morning, I had to face facts: I was definitely sick.

"We'll have to cancel the group for today," I moaned when Jesse knocked on the door to see how I was. He stayed at the door while I sat up in bed, my covers wrapped around me. "It's on my list to train someone to be on standby for me, but I haven't got to it yet. It's going to look so unprofessional."

I hardly ever got sick. It hadn't seemed too likely when I had made my schedule, so I hadn't made hiring my backup a priority.

"There ain't no need to cancel," Jesse assured me. "You were just doing a welcome ride today, right, and the cookout?"

He had been paying attention to my schedule, I noticed. "That's right, but they can't do that on their own."

"They don't have to. I can do it."

He wouldn't have surprised me more if he'd suggested that the President of the United States come and lead the group instead. "You?" I squeaked in surprise.

Jesse's eyebrows raised in mock offense. "Why is that so unbelievable? I know how to ride, don't I? I can tell them about the ranch."

He did and he could, but after all his comments about how this was entirely my project and how he didn't want to deal with people, I still couldn't quite believe he was offering. "What about your own work?"

"They can manage without me for the day." Jesse's expression had turned to one of amusement. "Why are you trying to talk me out of it?"

"I'm not, I'm just surprised is all."

"Don't be. We're a team, aren't we? You've got my back and I've got yours."

He must have meant that in a professional sense. Personally, it went against everything he'd ever told me he wanted. "Well, if you're sure, that would be amazing, Jesse. Thank you."

"It's no problem. I'll go out and do some work with the hands now before the group gets here. If you need anything, you can text me."

Once again, I was flummoxed. "You never have your phone on you."

"Well, I can carry it today, can't I?" He shook his head, as if *I* were the one behaving strangely. "Get some rest, Laura. I'll check in on you later."

He left me on my own after that, wondering if the whole thing had been some kind of fever dream. I couldn't be completely certain, but assuming it had really happened, I gratefully sank back down into bed and fell back to sleep as my body tried its best to make me better.

Chapter Fifteen

~Jesse~

Leading Laura's group for the day went a lot better than I would have expected. She had everything planned out meticulously, so all I had to do was turn up, say a few words, and get everyone on their horses. The group consisted of the executive team of a small oil company and their spouses, so I wouldn't have to worry about any of them flirting with Laura once she got back on her feet. That made me feel even better.

She had been asleep when I went to check on her at lunch time, so I'd left some food and water on a tray by her bed. The group were all happy to call it an early night after the cookout when I reminded them they'd be expected to be up and ready by eight o'clock, and I made up a quick plate of leftovers to bring back to Laura when I returned to the house.

"Laura?" I knocked quietly on the door, not wanting to wake her if she was still sleeping.

A muffled "come in" came through the door, so I pushed it open to find her still in bed but awake, barely.

"How are you feeling?" The fact that she was still in bed told me most of what I needed to know, but I still wanted to hear it from her. At least the food that I'd left earlier had disappeared.

"Like a porcupine."

I hadn't expected that answer, and I gave a startled laugh. "Come again?"

"All prickly," she added, as if that explained everything.

"Right. Okay." Clearly, she was still feverish. "I've got some more food for you. Have you had something to drink?"

I handed her the glass of water I'd brought in with me, and she took it willingly, taking a good, long drink before placing it on her bedside table.

"Jesse?"

"Yeah?" I made room on the table for her food, aware of her blue eyes following my every move. After closing her curtains, I sat down on the edge of her bed, keeping a good distance between us.

She waited until I was settled to ask me her question. "Where does water come from?"

Another laugh made its way out of my mouth. "The tap, Laura."

She thought about that for a second before shaking her head. "I mean before that."

"The tank?"

That didn't please her either. "No, before that too. Where does it start?"

I had a feeling no answer I could give was going to satisfy her. "I thought you were the one with the Master's degree. Shouldn't you be able to tell me?"

She sighed far more dramatically than necessary as she snuggled down further into the bed, pulling her covers up to her chin. "I used to be smart."

I had to smile. This was almost as good as seeing her drunk, which I hadn't had the pleasure of experiencing yet. Her filter appeared to be completely turned off, and Laura didn't have much of a filter to begin with. "I think you're still pretty smart. You just need some more sleep."

"Smart women don't fall in love with men who don't love them back."

That stopped me in my tracks, a cold wave of trepidation rushing through my body. What did she mean by that? Her eyes had closed, as if she might go back to sleep right there and then, without offering me any explanation.

It felt wrong to ask any follow-up questions in her present condition, where she might not even know what she was saying, but on the other hand, if she did remember this conversation and I simply left it there, would she take that as agreement on my part?

I decided to keep things general rather than talk about us specifically. We did need to talk, but not like this. "Some people might say that falling in love is never very smart. There are a lot of ways it can go wrong."

"So, why do we do it, then?"

She was really asking the hard questions that evening. "I guess because when it goes right, it's worth it. That's what I've heard, anyway."

"But you don't think so." She didn't phrase that as a question. It sounded like something she knew for certain.

I had been thinking about that very topic for most of the last two days, ever since my talk with Dex. When I imagined talking about it with Laura, I didn't picture it like this, with her sick in bed, her eyes closed, and me not even sure she would remember a word of it, but life wasn't all picture-perfect moments. Sometimes, you just had to take what you were given.

"I used to think that. Now, I'm not quite so sure."

She gave an adorable little snort of derision. "Since when do you change your mind?"

I had to laugh at that. "Are you kidding? All you've done since you got here is change my mind. You got me to consider selling half the ranch to you. You talked me into this whole working holiday plan, which is working out brilliantly. You've got a way of making me see things from a different point of view."

"I see your point of view too." Her words were even more mumbled that time, but she still seemed to be following along with the conversation perfectly well, so I kept talking too.

"What do you see?"

She sighed, nestling her face against the pillow. "I would be sad if you died."

That blunt response made me laugh again as she cut straight to the heart of the matter. "Well, thanks, I think."

"But you don't care if I do."

Again, her words were blunt, but that time, they made me wince. Hopefully, she didn't actually think that, but I'd have to set her straight anyway. "That ain't true. I wanted not to care, but the truth is, it's too late for that. I already care a whole lot. I feel happier when I get to see you and I miss you when you aren't here. Just about every part of my day is better with you in it, and if something happened to you, it would hurt me a hell of a lot. So, it seems like I already got all the things I didn't want, without getting to really enjoy the good side of it."

That had been the thing I realized most of all after my talk with Dex. He talked about what he would go back and say to himself at the start of his relationship, and I tried to put myself in that same position. If I could intercept the version of me two months ago, before I walked into that kitchen and ran straight into Laura Callahan, would I tell him to turn around? Would I give up everything we'd shared together because she might eventually leave me? Would I have been better off never getting to know her laugh, her intelligence, her body, and the way she made me feel?

Or would I tell him that if he walked through that door, he might find a whole new life, one better than anything he'd ever imagined before?

"That's really not very smart," Laura murmured.

"No, it sure ain't. I'm hoping it ain't too late for me to get a bit smarter though."

I waited for her to reply to that, but no answer seemed to be coming. Her breathing evened out, letting me know she'd gone back to sleep, and I got up to refill her water glass, leaving it on the table next to her untouched dinner. Before leaving the room, I leaned down to kiss her warm forehead.

"We'll talk about this more tomorrow, Laura."

Hopefully, she'd be feeling better by then, and I could tell her the words I'd really wanted to say, when I could be sure that she'd remember them.

~**Laura**~

I wouldn't have said I felt one hundred percent in the morning, but I felt much, much better. The whole previous day had passed in a blur, drifting in and out of consciousness, feeling hot and sweaty one minute and cold and shivery the next. Jesse had been in and out of the room even though I couldn't be sure if I'd actually spoken to him; I just knew that food and water kept appearing, telling me he must have been there.

I had vague snippets of memories of having a conversation with him where we talked about how he was feeling, but that seemed so unlikely, I must have dreamed it.

Already in the kitchen when I got there at twenty after four, Jesse looked up from his toast in surprise. He hadn't shaved that morning and the stubble lining his jaw looked even more sexy than usual, but his eyes were full of concern. "Are you sure you should be out of bed?"

"Is that a nice way of saying that I look awful?" I went to the fridge to grab some yogurt and fruit, trying to get back into my usual routine. One day out of commission had been plenty for me and I wanted to get back to work.

Jesse huffed in amusement. "Don't go putting words in my mouth. I ain't ever thought that."

I peered up at him over the fridge door, ready to make a sarcastic reply, but his expression was so serious that the words died in my throat and a rush of heat, completely unrelated to the fever, ran through my body. Did he actually mean that the way it sounded, or was I reading too much into it?

"I don't need you this morning," he continued, as if he hadn't said anything out of the ordinary. "Stay in and do work on your computer if you want to be productive. If you feel up to meeting your group at eight, go ahead, but if you don't, let me know and I can take over again. There's no need to push yourself, Laura. The world won't end if you take another day to recover."

He sounded so firm and determined that I couldn't even summon the will to argue. I sat down at the table next to him instead. "How did it go yesterday?"

He gave me a summary of the trail ride and the cookout, along with a quick rundown of the personalities of the group, leaving me rather impressed. He'd really been paying attention.

"I saw that you brought me some dinner from the cookout," I told him. "Thanks for that. Sorry I missed you."

His chocolate-brown eyes looked over at me curiously. "You don't remember me bringing it in? You talked to me for a while."

Did I? The day was so jumbled up in my head, mixed between dreams and memory, that I couldn't be certain. Eventually, I had to shake my head. "I don't think so. I was pretty out of it."

He nodded, looking down at his plate with what almost seemed like disappointment. "I thought that might be the case. Anyway, I gotta get to work. You know where to find me if you need me."

As he got to his feet, I quickly added some further thanks. "I really appreciate you taking over yesterday, Jesse, and looking after me too. You went above and beyond."

"You would have done the same for me," he said simply. "I'll see you later."

I would have done the same, certainly, but that had never really factored into anything before. It almost felt like something had changed between us, like the distance he'd always insisted on keeping had lessened just a little, but I couldn't explain why or how. Maybe I was simply still a little delusional and seeing things that weren't actually there.

As he'd suggested, I went back to my room and got caught up on my emails, still having a few hours until the guests were expecting me. As I went through my correspondence, more memories started to come back to me, completely out of context. An image flashed across my mind of Jesse sitting on the edge of the bed, his body lit only by the light from the hallway, his face in shadow and the scent of barbecue and horses drifting over to me. *You've got a way of making me see things from a different point of view*, I thought he said.

Did that really happen? It felt detailed enough to have been real, but I couldn't place it within a wider conversation.

The group staying with us that week were all friendly and fun, though I could have sworn some of the women looked disappointed when they realized I'd be working with them that day rather than Jesse. It gave me a strange feeling; not quite jealousy, since I knew none of them would have any more chance with him than I did, but I felt a sense of loss all the same at the knowledge that he would never be mine either.

With that particular group, I'd decided to put them to work reestablishing the ranch's vegetable garden. My mom had always kept a huge garden, growing pretty much all the vegetables we needed right there, but in the two years since my parents had left, it had been neglected, the weeds and wild grass taking over. It would be a big job to clean it all out, but I had the free labour to do it, and once we got it up and running again, it would cut down on the food I'd need to buy to feed our holidaymakers too.

As a reward for the day's hard work, I took them over to the barn in the afternoon to meet some of the calves. Jesse was still there, working hard even after the other hands had clocked out for the day. Mucking out the horse stalls, his strong body twisting and bending, several of the women found the sight far more interesting than the calves, and I could hardly blame them.

I feel happier when I get to see you and I miss you when you aren't here. Those words popped into my head, in Jesse's voice, though I had no visual memory to accompany them. They just floated there in the darkness, warm and soothing. Had I dreamed that, or had he actually said them? What could we have been talking about that he would have said something like that?

After returning the guests to the bunkhouse where the cook had their supper waiting, I wished them all a good night and headed back to the house. Jesse's boots were still missing, meaning he mustn't have come back from the barn yet, and I hovered at the door, considering whether I should go and help him finish up or if he would simply tell me to go back and rest, when another phrase suddenly rang in my ears, as clear as if he were right behind me.

Just about every part of my day is better with you in it, and if something happened to you, it would hurt me a hell of a lot.

I couldn't be making all of it up. My imagination had never been particularly strong, my mind geared more to the practical than the creative. The words were in my head so clearly, in his voice, hearing every inflection and the way he paused, uncertain whether to continue, that it had to be true. He must have said those things, but why? What did they mean?

Rather than trying to figure it out for myself, I might as well go straight to the source. Turning back around, I headed back down the porch steps and towards the barn.

I found him where I'd left him earlier, just a few stalls further down, a pitchfork in his strong hands, and when he looked up and saw me coming on my own, his pleased expression sent another flush through my body, no matter how much I tried to fight it.

"What did you mean by what you said?" I blurted out as I got within a few steps of him, getting straight to the point.

Not having the benefit of being aboard my train of thought, Jesse had no idea what I was talking about, and his eyebrows knit together in confusion as he stopped what he was doing, letting the pitchfork rest on the ground as he leaned forward on the handle. "What I said about what?"

"You said you care about me. That you'd miss me if I went away."

His expression didn't clear, exactly, but he began to understand me anyway. "I thought you didn't remember any of that."

"I don't remember all of it," I admitted. "Bits and pieces are coming back. What were we talking about, Jesse? Why did you say that?"

"You told me I wouldn't care if you died," he explained wryly. "I was setting you straight."

Did I really say that? I didn't remember that part at all, but I could see where it would have come from, and if we were being that blunt with each other, I might as well let it all out. "I thought that was the whole point, though. You don't want to get hurt again, so you won't let yourself care. That's why you don't want to be with me."

"That's what I told you," he had to agree. "And that's what I thought I wanted, but like I told you last night, it ain't working. I already care for you, whether I wanted to or not."

That didn't sound like much of a compliment. "So, I forced you into it somehow?"

"No, that's not..." He shook his head, taking a breath. "Look, Laura, I don't have any practice with this. I don't know the right things to say, but there were some things your brother told me that really made me take a long, hard look at what's been going on between us and how I feel."

So, I had Dex to thank for this confusing conversation? I wasn't sure yet if I owed him a kiss or a punch in the arm.

"I ain't got it all figured out," Jesse admitted. "But there are a few things I know. First off, I don't just wanna have sex with you. Without anything else, it feels incomplete and unsatisfying."

Did he really just say that having sex with me was *unsatisfying*? I crossed my arms as Jesse winced.

"I told you, I ain't got the right words. It's not unsatisfying when it happens; far from it. But afterwards, when you went and kicked me out, it felt wrong. I've never wanted more from any woman before, but from you, I do."

That sounded a little bit better. I let my arms loosen, waiting to see where he would go next. His eyes darted between me and the floor and the ceiling as he did his best to explain himself to me.

"The only reason I can think of why I would feel that way is that I'm already falling for you, even though I didn't mean to. I thought nothing would be worth exposing myself to that kind of hurt again, but that was before I knew you existed. When I think about what it's been like over the past few months with you and what it could be like if I just get out of my own way, then I think it might be worth it after all. Because if you walked away from me right now, you'd break my heart anyway. Every night I go to bed without you feels like a waste."

My heart had begun to race but I forced myself to stay silent, waiting for him to finish, biting my tongue to keep from interrupting as long as I could.

"And yet, I wouldn't take it back. I wouldn't give up knowing what it feels like to have you in my arms just to go back to the life I had before. There might be lows but the highs are so much higher than I ever thought they could be, and for me to stand here and say I don't want the most incredible woman I ever met to love me because someday, she might not be there to love me anymore, sounds like the stupidest damn thing I ever heard. I know I'm probably not making a lick of sense, but..."

"Jesse." I stepped forward with tears shining in my eyes, unable to hold back any longer. He'd had me right from the second he said he was falling for me; the rest of it was just icing on the cake, each word warming me not only by what he said but by the care and thought he'd obviously put into it. "I know what you mean. And I meant what I said too: I'll never hurt you on purpose. I can't see the future and I can't promise it'll never hurt, but I *can* tell you that I've never felt anything like this before. Not being with you feels like a waste to me too."

He leaned closer to me, the pitchfork still between us. "You're not mad at me for taking so long to figure it out?"

"That depends. What exactly have you figured out?"

He'd said a lot of amazing things, but he still hadn't spelled out exactly what he wanted, and my heart pounded in hope and anticipation as I waited for his conclusion.

Jesse's eyes looked down on me, filled with affection, a hint of amusement, and a great deal of heat. "I'm pretty sure I love you, Laura Callahan. And if it's okay with you, I'd like to show you exactly how much."

~Jesse~

I'd never said those words to a woman before. I never thought I would.

I hadn't said them to *anyone* since I was ten years old. After everything I'd lost, I truly thought I didn't ever want to have a reason to say them again, that love was best avoided since it had only ever brought me pain. But after three days of looking at it from every possible angle, trying to see what I was missing, I had come to the conclusion that there was nothing else this could be.

I loved her.

Laura filled up all the parts of my life I hadn't even known were empty and made everything feel better and deeper and more significant. And if she loved me too, if we could make each other happy, then it seemed ridiculous to make us both suffer by not being together just because we might suffer one day. The thought of losing her still scared me, as did the idea that she would ever have cause to grieve me, but not being with her terrified me even more. The thought of her being with someone else cut me too deep, as I'd made pretty clear with the way I kept getting between her and anyone who showed any interest in her. All the signs had been there, I'd just been too stubborn to recognize what it meant.

But now that I knew it, I told her as plainly as I could, forcing out those words that took more courage than anything I'd ever done before. My hands were trembling as I held onto the pitchfork to keep myself steady.

I put my heart on the line, a heart that was already scarred but not quite as useless as I'd thought, and I just had to hope she would say that she wanted it.

Those gorgeous blue eyes looked up at me with surprise, as if she couldn't quite believe what she'd heard, and then, without warning, she launched herself into my arms, pressing her lips against mine and trapping the pitchfork between us.

It couldn't exactly be called an answer, but I wasn't about to complain. I'd missed her so much: the feel of her, the smell of her, the taste of her, all of my senses combining to drink her in as I pulled the pitchfork out from between our bodies, tossing it to the side so that nothing stood between us, pressing myself firmly against her as we devoured each other. My hands went to the sides of her head, my fingers threading through her hair as our kiss deepened, my tongue entering her mouth the way I hoped to soon be inside her in other ways. Her hands grabbed at my shirt, her fingers digging into my back as her hips moved against me, driving me crazy with the thought that she wanted me too.

She'd been missing this too.

"Is that a yes, Laura? You're going to let me show you?"

Her whispered reply, breathy and full of desire, had all my blood rushing to my cock. "Show me. Please."

We should go into the house. It really wasn't that far, and anyone could walk into the barn at any time, like Laura herself had just done, but in the heat of the moment, the distance seemed insurmountable. I pulled her further into the stall with me instead, closing the door to give us a bit of privacy, though it only came up to my chest.

"Jesse." She moaned out my name as I spun her around, pressing her against the side of the stall, my hands on her breasts and my erection grinding against her ass. From our previous encounters, I knew she liked it a little rough, and my need for her was so strong, tenderness wasn't really on the cards. There would be time for that later: lingering moments in bed, kissing and caressing every inch of her, but at that moment, I just wanted to claim her. I needed to.

Sweeping her hair to one side, I kissed down the side of her neck, my fingers moving down to her jeans to undo them. As soon as I could, I slid one hand inside her pants, between her legs to where her heat and dampness had already started, as ready for me as I was for her. Her ass rubbed against me, her hips undulating as she sought some relief from the aching need that gripped her just as strongly as it did me. Firmly, I yanked down her jeans and her panties, rubbing my hand over her ass and giving it a light, encouraging smack that had Laura whimpering in pleasure.

The tightness in my own jeans was almost unbearable as I undid my belt, trying to move as quickly as possible to get us both where we truly wanted to be. Laura's hips angled towards me in anticipation, her hands reaching up to grab onto the rails that divided this stall from the one next door, as if she expected that she would need to hold on. That was certainly my plan too.

Finally, I got my cock loose, and my fingers returned to the perfect heaven between her legs, sliding across her wet opening, up to her clit as she moaned and sighed, and when I replaced my hand with my cock, pressing into her from behind, my hard length disappearing into her perfect body, it felt even more right than it ever had before.

It felt like home.

With one hand sliding up beneath her shirt to cup her breast and the other holding her hips in place, my fingers close enough to reach her clit, I thrust into her, hard and fast, over and over. Each time I entered her was perfect, yet never enough. I could never get enough of her. As the friction increased, our bodies merging together again and again, her cries of pleasure echoed up into the high ceilings above us.

"I want you so fucking badly, all the time," I whispered in her ear, removing my hand from beneath her shirt to place it on top of hers, holding onto the rail along with her to steady myself as my pace increased. "When I see you working out in the field, it's like torture."

"You.. hardly... even look at me," she gasped between my thrusts, her body writhing against me.

"Exactly. Because when I do, I think about this and I get hard, which makes it difficult to move around."

She gave a shaky, breathless laugh. "Well, now I'm going to think about this every time I'm in the barn."

I grunted in agreement, but I couldn't bring myself to regret it as my fingers found her clit again. "Worth it."

"Fuck, Jesse!" She called out my name one more time as she came, her body trembling around me.

I slowed down just enough so I wouldn't overstimulate her, pulling her face towards me gently so I could kiss her lips, and when I thought she was ready, I picked up the momentum again. With her body even more slick than before, it didn't take long for me to feel my own orgasm building, but when she spoke again, her words were what drove me over the edge.

"I love you too," she whispered, and my control broke, my cock pumping deep inside her as we both held onto the rail, trying not to lose our balance.

Even though I'd already fallen for her, fully and completely.

Panting and sweaty, we lingered there for a few moments as we caught our breath, and finally, I pulled out of her, turning her around gently so I could see her face. The pleasure and happiness in her eyes took my breath away all over again as I pressed my lips to hers, not in need that time, but with adoration.

"Do you really mean that?" I felt pretty sure she wouldn't have said it if she didn't, but even so, hearing those words in the heat of sex wasn't quite the same as when she fully had her wits about her.

Laura didn't hesitate. "Of course I do. I don't know exactly when it happened, but I'm so in love with you, Jesse."

"And you ain't just saying that to get your half of the ranch?"

She burst out laughing, her infectious giggle making me grin like an idiot. Fuck, I loved to see that light shining in her eyes when I teased her. I loved every single thing about her, but her smile had to be my favourite.

"If that was all I wanted, none of this would be necessary," she teased me right back. "My plan is going to work, so you owe me half the ranch no matter what."

It certainly looked that way. She had blown me away, in every way.

Her expression turned more serious as she looked up at me, her fingers gently stroking my face. "I came back to the ranch because I always thought it was meant to be mine. I thought you took it from me, but now, I think it was meant to be yours too. We're right where we're supposed to be, both of us."

I couldn't disagree. Nothing had ever felt so right.

"I came here for a piece of land, but I found so much more. Thank you for trusting me, Jesse."

In my eyes, all the praise belonged to her. "Thank you for being patient with me. I might not be the quickest to put things together, but I ain't afraid of a little hard work either. I'll do my very best to make you happy, Laura."

"You really don't have to try very hard at all to do that." She smiled at me again, her eyes shining, until, with a laugh, she looked down at our bodies, our jeans still both down around our knees. "I guess we should head back to the house and get cleaned up. How about you do the laundry and I'll make us some dinner?"

I could hear the hope in her voice as she offered to cook for me, and I had no intention of disappointing her. Not ever again, if I could help it. "That sounds perfect. Let's go and make a start of it."

~Laura~

By the time I got changed and had supper ready, Jesse had taken care of the laundry and showered, returning to the kitchen with his hair still damp, looking sexy as sin. Excitement bubbled up inside me at the sight of him, worse than any crush I'd ever had before, and the idea that we were actually, finally, on the same page had my stomach fluttering and my chest swelling with happiness. It still seemed far too good to be true.

"That smells fantastic," he murmured, coming up behind me at the stove, his warm body pressing up against my back as he wrapped his arms around my waist, his chin resting on my shoulder. "Though I'm tempted to skip it and head straight to bed instead."

The shot of pure desire that ran through my body with those words, settling right between my legs, made it clear I wouldn't mind either, but I simply laughed. "If that's your plan, we better keep our strength up and eat something first."

"It is definitely my plan, Laura." He squeezed me tighter against him, letting me feel that he was already half-hard again, before reluctantly letting me go. "What else do we need?"

I directed him to set the table while I finished up my quick mushroom stroganoff, one of my mom's favourite comfort food recipes. I could picture her standing there in that very kitchen making it, almost as clearly as I could picture myself standing there making it for my own kids. The past and the future both seemed very close, tied together by the amazing man who said all the right things as I placed his plate down in front of him.

"I'm almost more impressed that you let me cook than I am about you saying you love me," I teased him. "I wasn't sure if it was ever going to happen."

"You don't know how many nights I sat here salivating over the smell of your cooking," he told me, shoving a large forkful into his mouth and groaning in pleasure as the flavours hit his tongue. "Almost as many times as I fantasized over the sight of you cooking it."

"So, what exactly did Dex say to you?" Although my brother had mentioned their conversation, I couldn't imagine the exact words that had managed to break down Jesse's walls at last. I certainly hadn't managed it. "I have to send him the world's biggest fruit basket, apparently."

Jesse chuckled, still half-focused on his food and half on me. "Honestly, it wasn't any one thing in particular. Most of what he said, I've heard from other people, but I think I just wasn't ready to hear it before. I never trusted the people who said it. But knowing what Dex has just been through, how much he's hurting but hearing him say that he'd do it all over again if he could, combined with my feelings for you and how much you tempted me all on your own, it just kind of made everything make sense. The stars aligned, I guess: he said right what I needed to hear, right when I needed to hear it."

The stars did seem to have aligned, in more ways than one: Jesse coming to work there in the first place, the whole situation with my dad selling the ranch and the deal Jesse and I struck, me moving in with him. If just one different choice had been made, things might not have ended the same way. Life could knock us down, yes, like it did to Jesse as a child and like it had just done to Dex, but it could also surprise us in wonderful, unexpected ways. We couldn't count on the good times always being there, so all we could do was make the most of them and enjoy them while they lasted.

Hopefully, my brother still had good surprises in his future too.

"So, I don't want to scare you off or anything, but you ought to know, Jesse, I've got plans for the future. It's best if we get on the same page right off the bat. How do you feel about kids?"

He'd just another bite of his supper in his mouth, and he nearly choked on it in surprise. Taking a drink of water, he looked over at me in amusement. "You really don't waste any time, do you?"

I shrugged unapologetically. "I'm not saying it has to be right this second. I'm just saying we should talk about it so we know in advance if there are things that ain't gonna work. I'd rather know now if we have any sticking points."

He shook his head, the smile slowly fading from his face. "To be honest, I never saw that in my future."

My stomach immediately dropped, the picture I'd just had in my head of raising my family here growing a little bit weaker.

"It comes back to the same reason I held myself back from a relationship. The idea of losing a child, or of leaving a kid without their dad, same as I was, is pretty hard to fathom. It ain't something I'm going to be ready to jump into, Laura. You're going to have to be patient with me, again, but I understand it's something that's important to you, so if we were to get to that point, I'm not ruling it out."

Not exactly a firm commitment, but I understood that for him to even agree to that much was a big step for him. I could be patient, if that was what he needed.

"What are your other conditions?" he asked, the humour beginning to creep back into his eyes. "I know you have a whole list, Laura. Lay it on me."

"I wouldn't call it a *whole* list," I protested, making him laugh. "There's really just one other condition, one that always sent the men I met in Houston running."

Jesse's eyebrows raised curiously. "And what's that?"

"That they gotta be okay with living on a ranch with me out in the middle of nowhere, getting up at four in the morning and working hard all day long, birthing calves and digging ditches, riding and roping, satisfying me at night, and then get up ready to do it all again the next day."

He laughed again, longer and deeper that time. "And that didn't have them lining up around the block?"

"I guess it's not everyone's idea of fun," I admitted with a shrug, trying to hold back my own grin.

"No, it ain't. But luckily for us, I think our ideas about what's fun are pretty damn similar."

His gaze dropped to my body, making it clear that we were no longer talking about the ranch, and with supper almost finished, I had no intention of putting him off any longer. "Why don't we see if you're right?"

Jesse needed no further encouragement. Abandoning the remains of our meal, he pulled me down the hall to his bedroom.

What happened between us out in the barn had been amazing, easily one of the hottest experiences of my life. I would never look at a horse stall in quite the same way again. In his room, though, it felt completely different. Though we still wanted each other just as much, we took it slow, knowing that we were in no rush. Jesse insisted I lay back and let him please me, whispering dirty words of encouragement from between my legs, and when he'd satisfied me with his tongue, he got to his knees and slowly slid into me, his whole body covering me as his hard cock filled me up.

"I could have been missing this," he whispered, his tone somewhere between awe and disbelief as he thrust into me slowly and deeply, his face just inches from mine, his brown eyes drinking me in. "I could have been alone tonight, just like all those other nights we wasted. Why did I ever think that made sense?"

"I'm not sure, because nothing has ever made this much sense," I whispered back. His firm body above me and inside me, and the look of love in his eyes as we moved together, it all added up to one thought in my head, more certain than anything I'd ever known before.

This had always been my home.

Chapter Sixteen

~**Jesse**~

"When's the last time you skipped out of work early?" Laura teased me as we pulled away from the house, waving goodbye to Tyson who would look after things in our absence.

"Technically, as the owner, I can do whatever I want," I pointed out. "I set my own hours, so there's no such thing as leaving early."

"And your hours are usually 14 hours a day," she retorted, accurately. "Today, you only worked ten, so I'm counting this as early."

It had been almost two weeks since I stopped pretending like I didn't want a relationship, since we both stopped trying to resist what had always been between us, and it had been ever better than I could have imagined. Waking up next to Laura each morning, sharing my meals with her, working with her, and going to bed together each night felt completely natural. It felt like nothing had changed and like everything had, all at the same time.

That evening, we were heading up to Houston to have dinner with her family, which was a slightly daunting prospect. She promised me it would be entirely informal, just a casual barbecue in her parent's backyard.

"We used to do this all the time," she explained when she first asked me to go. "It was a regular thing until Shawna got sicker and she and

Dex started missing them. It didn't feel quite right doing it without them there, and obviously, since the funeral, we've all had other things on our minds. But we've all agreed it's time to get back into it, and just because I don't live in Houston anymore doesn't mean I'm going to miss it."

She had warned me when she took the job that she might need to take these regular trips, and she even planned her working holiday schedule around it. The previous group had left two days earlier and the next group would arrive the next day. Everything was already set, so she could enjoy the night off without needing to worry.

Her family obviously meant a great deal to her, and since *she* meant a great deal to *me*, it meant I would make it a priority too, even if I had no idea what I might be getting into. Never having had a family of my own as an adult, it would be an entirely new experience.

"My sisters are completely inappropriate," she warned me with a laugh. "They have no filter and will say whatever's on their minds. In other words, they're a lot like me."

In that case, I should like them just fine. I already knew Dex a little bit and Jim from his time on the ranch, so I wouldn't be going in completely blind, but Laura had told me that she'd never brought anyone to these family get-togethers before. Bringing someone new along meant things were pretty serious, so I knew I'd be under a lot of scrutiny to see if I deserved a place at the Callahan family table.

"Daddy already thought you were worthy of the ranch," Laura reminded me. "So, you're halfway there."

The Callahans' ranch-style house was in a nice residential area, feeling closer to a small town than to the city's downtown core. By the time we arrived and stepped out of the truck, we could already smell the meat on the grill.

"Are we late?" I asked. That wouldn't be the best impression to make.

"There's no set time," Laura assured me. "It's always a fight between Cam and Dex to see who's going to man the barbecue anyway. Dex has first dibs as a natural-born Callahan, but if he's ever late, Cam always jumps in."

That sounded like an argument to stay out of as I followed Laura into the house. After stopping to wash up, we headed out to the backyard.

A chorus of greetings rang out as we arrived, the scene about as wholesome and heartwarming as I could have imagined. Mr Callahan was playing catch with his two-year-old grandson while Mrs Callahan and her other two daughters arranged a picnic table full of food. The other two men stood over at the grill, chatting, but everyone turned to face us as we walked in.

Laura made a general introduction, not wasting any time. "Everyone, you've already met Jesse. Go easy on him, alright?"

With that, she left me on my own, going over to say hello to her parents, and Tonia and Billie quickly took her place beside me.

"You must be so pleased with the way the holiday business is working out," Tonia started as soon as she'd said hello. "The feedback I'm hearing on my end is amazing. You guys will have a waiting list in no time."

"Well, that's Laura's project, not mine, but it certainly seems to be..."

"Did people really think you were gay?" Billie interrupted, unable to hold back her curiosity.

I blinked in surprise as I tried to absorb the change of subject. "Yeah, I guess so. I had no idea until Laura..."

Tonia cut in, pulling my attention back to her. "If you hired a few more cowboys who look like you to help lead the groups, you could definitely expand into the bachelorette market. It's got a lot of potential, you ought to consider it."

"Well, right now the holidays include a lot of hard work. I'm not sure if that's something we're..."

"You really are very handsome," Billie blurted out. "Have you ever done any kind of modelling?"

"Uh, no. Thank you? That's not something I..."

"You really should take a look at it. Destination bachelorette parties are a thing, and for the right kind of woman, it would have a lot of appeal."

"It's never too late to start. Have you ever tried acting?"

"Hey, Jesse." Dex's voice cutting through the chatter came as a welcome relief, since I really didn't know which conversation I was meant to be following. "Can we have your help for a minute?"

I gave my apologies to Tonia and Billie, gratefully escaping to join Dex and Cam at the barbecue.

"You'll get used to that," Cam told me with a laugh, holding out a beer in greeting. We'd met at the funeral but hadn't had a chance to say much more than hello. "I won't say it's ever easy to keep up with them, but it'll become more normal."

"I thought Laura was the bluntest person I'd ever met," I admitted. "Now, I ain't so sure."

"They're worse as a group," Dex told me, with Cam nodding in agreement. "One-on-one, they're easier to handle."

The affection in both their tones made it clear that no matter how overwhelming it got, they didn't actually see it as a bad thing.

"How long have you and Tonia been together?" I asked Cam. As another outsider, I figured he would be the best guide for me as I tried to navigate my way around the Callahan clan.

He grimaced as Dex chuckled. "That's kind of a long story. We were together in high school but we broke up and it took a while before we got back together."

"He thought he was out, but he ended up getting sucked back in," Dex summarized sarcastically.

"Best decision of my life," Cam added, his eyes full of affection as he glanced over at his wife and son.

I could relate to that. As the night went on, there was a lot of food and even more laughs. Laura sat next to me, protecting me from the worst of Tonia and Billie's questions, though they really weren't that bad. As Laura said, they were a lot like her, just saying what they thought, and I preferred that over having to try to look for hidden meanings.

As the evening began to wrap up, I managed to get a couple of minutes alone with Dex to thank him for the conversation we'd had back on the ranch and let him know that I'd taken his advice to heart.

"I just told the truth," he said, playing it off. "I'm glad if it helped."

Laura came over to join us, her arm slipping around my waist. "I told Jesse we owe you a fruit basket or something."

"Keep your fruit," Dex laughed, shaking his head. "But actually, I've got something for you guys. I almost forgot."

He went out to his truck to get it, leaving Laura and I mystified. "You have any idea what this is about?" I asked her.

She shook her head. "Honestly, it could be anything."

Dex returned a couple of minutes later with a canvas under his arm, making me more confused than ever. "I noticed Laura had done some decorating at the house," he explained. "It's looking good, but I thought it could still use something more."

As he turned the canvas around to show it to us, Laura gasped in surprise while several different emotions swelled up inside me: pride, gratitude, and most of all, happiness, pure and simple.

He'd painted the view of the ranch from the hill, the one he'd taken pictures of that night when we had our talk, but in the foreground, he'd added two figures. On horseback, our backs to the viewer but our bodies angled towards each other, Laura and I looked to be caught in a private joke, her leaning back with her beautiful smile while I leaned forward, my gaze fixed on her.

The painting was technically stunning, but more than that, he'd captured the push and pull between us, the give and take, and it felt like a moment I recognized even though it had never happened, or at least not that he'd witnessed.

The rest of the family all exclaimed over it while Laura and I stood there, stunned into speechlessness. Laura recovered herself first, looking up at her brother in confusion. "When did you do this? I only told you guys that Jesse was coming here like two days ago."

"I started it as soon as I got home from staying with you," Dex admitted. "I had a feeling it might work out."

"This is amazing," I told him honestly, my voice coming out a little choked up. "Thank you."

Everything I'd ever wanted in life was encapsulated in that image: the ownership of the land, everything that could be seen belonging to me, but there was so much more I had never expected. In Laura's smile, I could see our whole future, a future I'd never even dreamed of.

I didn't plan to waste another day of it.

~Ten months later~

~Laura~

I kept the smile pasted on my face, waving as the bus pulled down the drive until I was sure they could no longer see me. As soon as they were out of sight, I let the smile drop, my shoulders slumping with an exhausted sigh. Some groups were easy: friendly, hard-working, ready for a good time and to put in some real labour. My most recent guests had not been one of those groups. Someone's daddy thought it would be a good idea to send his spoiled son and his rich friends to see what 'real work' was like, and they couldn't have been less interested. Aside from hitting on me, they spent most of their energy complaining about the smell and having to step around the cow patties in the field. We had two calves born during their stay and they didn't even want to watch. I could already imagine the reviews about how uptight I was for expecting them to do actual work.

I couldn't win them all, though; I'd certainly learned that in the time I'd been running the program, so I chalked it up to experience and got started with helping the housekeeper to strip the beds in preparation for the next group.

Besides, nothing seemed so bad when I got to go home at the end of it to the amazing man who worked harder than anyone I knew.

While I'd been busy with the working holidays, he'd put all my other suggestions in place, and everything had been going even better than I could have anticipated. With that day being the official one-year mark since we made our agreement, Jesse had asked his accountant to put together the final figures to satisfy my curiosity, but we both knew without seeing them that I had won our agreement. Half the ranch would officially be mine, just like it always should have been. Sometimes, fate just couldn't be denied.

By the time I'd finished helping in the bunkhouse, my stomach had started to growl and I headed to the house to put something together for lunch, knowing Jesse would be there to join me soon. However, when I walked in, I could already smell bacon sizzling and my stomach rumbled even louder. After removing my boots, I headed to the kitchen to see what was going on.

The sight of Jesse in his jeans, belt, and deep blue work shirt took my breath away just as much as it did the very first time I saw him. Maybe even more, now that I knew just how good he looked underneath it all. He whistled a country song as he put together some BLT sandwiches for us, and when he caught sight of me from the corner of his eye, he looked over with a grin that still made my stomach flip.

"Hey. The last calf came this morning. Mom and baby are doing great, but I had to come in and get changed, so I thought I'd make lunch too."

I'd been teaching him how to cook, for fun, and he was actually really good at it. He tried hard, like he did at everything, and when he cooked for the Parkers a couple of weeks ago, Mary-Beth teased me that the student had surpassed the teacher.

"It'd be nice if I was better at something," Jesse replied, giving me a wink. "She's so damn good at everything else."

Mary-Beth had been thrilled when Jesse and I got together. She insisted that we come out to the Sandy Creek bar with her and Wayne to put the rumours about Jesse's sexuality to rest. He said he didn't care what anyone else thought, but we both knew how people liked to talk. The news of our first appearance there spread like wildfire, so showing up together would be an easy way to quash the speculation once and for all.

Or at least, I thought it would be easy. We hadn't counted on Dale.

Although Jesse and I drove in together, he got called over by Wayne and some of his other friends who were checking out some modifications that one of them had made to their trucks. "I'll meet you in there," I told him, having no interest in cars myself. "Have fun."

Mary-Beth already had a table for us and after saying hello, I went up to the bar to order a drink for me and Jesse. It took less than a minute for Dale to sidle up next to me. He must have had some kind of radar.

"Back on your own, I see?" he greeted me, though I hadn't given him any encouragement. The beer on his breath was so strong, I could nearly get drunk off the fumes. "I could have told you that things wouldn't work out with Greenbank."

This should be good. "And why would that be?"

"Everyone knows he'd prefer one of the ranch hands to someone like you. Even though you act like a man sometimes, you still ain't one."

That was really his idea of hitting on me? I felt sorry for him more than anything else. "Are you jealous, Dale? Were you hoping he'd take a shine to you instead?"

As I expected, he took offense to that, as insecure men often did, blustering in denial. "I'm as straight as they come, Laura. You give me one night and you'd never doubt it again."

His hand went to my ass and before I had a chance to do anything about it, someone pointedly cleared their throat behind us, giving me déjà vu. We'd been there before, only this time, I had no intention of diffusing the situation. Jesse could handle himself.

"You've got one second to get your hand off her," Jesse growled, and a quick glance over my shoulder showed me that the other guys were all still with him. Dale was vastly outnumbered, not to mention outclassed, and the smart thing would have been to walk away. Unfortunately, being smart had never been his forte.

"She don't belong to you," Dale argued, incorrectly. His hand moved to my hip instead, pulling me closer to him. "She can make up her own mind."

I certainly could, and I gave it to him plain. "Dale, I'm here with Jesse. If you like being pain-free, I'd take a step back if I were you."

He didn't take my advice. "Just give me one night and I can show you what you've been missing."

"That's one." Almost faster than I could blink, Jesse grabbed Dale by the shirt and pulled him away from me, so hard that he fell over, hitting the ground as everyone in the bar turned to see what was going on.

Embarrassed and far too drunk to know when to walk away, Dale scrambled back to his feet. "I ain't afraid of you, Greenbank."

"No? Well, you should be, because if you *ever* talk to my woman that way again, you'll get a lot worse than this."

Jesse's punch came so fast that it took everyone in the bar by surprise, but especially Dale. He reeled back, howling in pain as he clutched his jaw, and a crowd quickly gathered, eager to see what would happen next.

Jesse, however, had made his point, turning his back on Dale dismissively as he joined me at the bar, his arm sliding around my waist possessively. "You okay?"

I didn't usually condone any kind of violence, but I had to admit I was pretty turned on right at that moment. "Of course. I think you just put the rumours to rest all on your own."

"Well, just in case I didn't…"

He leaned in to kiss me in front of the entire bar, and though Mary-Beth told me later there was plenty of hooting and hollering, I didn't hear a thing. The only thing I was aware of was him.

He brought our sandwiches over to the table as I washed my hands. Only when I sat down did I notice the thick envelope in the middle of the table. "What's this?"

Jesse's chocolate-brown eyes were warm with anticipation. "The year-end figures from the accountant. I thought we could look at it together."

"Why didn't you lead with that?!" I pushed my untouched sandwich away to grab the envelope, sliding my finger beneath the flap to open it as Jesse chuckled.

"Well, I'm still gonna eat. You can tell me what it says."

There were a lot of rows of figures and charts, but it didn't take long to find the one I was looking for: Jesse's year-one projections from his loan application compared to our actual results. Even though I'd expected it, seeing it in black and white still made the whole thing feel more real, and satisfaction flowed through me as my eyes devoured the statistics.

I placed the papers down on the table facing him with that one on top and jabbed a triumphant finger at it. "There! One hundred and twenty two percent of the target!"

"Is that all?" Jesse asked, licking a bit of mayonnaise from his lips. "I thought it would be more."

I stared at him in disbelief. "What do you mean 'is that all'? It's fantastic!"

He gave me an indulgent chuckle. "Of course it is. You've just done such a good job, I thought it would be more."

"Well, there were a lot of initial costs," I reminded him. "Building the bunkhouse and kitting it out, the cookers, buying the extra trail horses, the staffing. But now that most of that is done, the profits will only go up. It's just going to get better from here."

"Yeah, I think it is." His soft smile made him even more handsome, if that were even possible.

"So, I guess that means you've got some more paperwork to complete," I reminded him. "Fifty percent of the ranch is officially mine."

He looked down almost nervously. "About that, Laura: I don't know if the paperwork will be necessary."

"What do you mean?" He couldn't be backing out, could he? That wasn't the Jesse I knew, but I didn't know what else he could be talking about. "That was our deal."

"It was," he agreed, still not looking at me. "But I've been thinking about a different one instead."

"A different deal?" He had totally lost me now. "What deal? Why?"

He focused on the last question first. "Well, you've done so much more than I thought possible here. I mean, all of this, but more than this." He reached out to gesture at the papers but ended up sweeping them off the table and onto the floor instead. "Shit, sorry."

I tried to reach down to get them, but he gently pushed me back as he got down onto the floor to pick them up instead, reaching to grab the ones that had dropped under the table. His head disappeared for a second, and when he came back out, he looked up at me with a sheepish, shy, hopeful smile.

It took me a second to put it together: the look on his face, the fact that he was down on one knee, and the fact that he had no papers in his hands. Instead, a small box had appeared, out of nowhere.

"Signing all those papers seems like a waste of time when we could just sign one and achieve the same thing. Fifty/fifty partners for the ranch, and for everything. Forever."

He flipped the box open to reveal a beautiful diamond ring, one large stone in the centre, almost completely encircled by a group of smaller diamonds in the shape of a horseshoe.

"Will you marry me, Laura?"

I had been as patient as I could. I knew I wanted to marry him almost from the very start, but I knew that with his past and the fears he still had, it would take him a while to get there too. For a year, I'd been patiently waiting, knowing that he loved me but not knowing when, if ever, we'd get to that point, and now that it had finally come, I could barely believe my eyes.

"You're sure?" I asked, the words popping into my head and out of my mouth before I could stop them.

Jesse let out an amused laugh. "Don't I look sure? I didn't just find this ring under the table by accident, you know."

That was a good point. He must have planned this, for a while now in order to get that ring made, but I still couldn't quite believe it.

"And you want kids and everything? The whole deal?"

Jesse shifted his weight, trying to stay comfortable while kneeling on the floor. "That's the only reason it took me so long to ask. I wanted to be sure I could give you everything you want, everything you deserve, and yeah. I'm ready now. I love you, and I know I'll love our whole family just as much. Love might not stop pain from coming, but it's worth it anyway. You're worth it, Laura."

Those words finally convinced me that he really meant it, and I threw myself into his arms, knocking him off balance as we both tumbled to the kitchen floor, laughing even as my eyes filled with happy tears. "Of course I'll marry you. You won't regret giving this a chance, Jesse."

Those were the words I said to him a year earlier when we made our deal in the first place. Then, he told me he wasn't sure about that, but as he slid the ring onto my finger before looking up at me with all the affection I could possibly dream of, he sounded a lot more certain. "There aren't many things for sure in life, but this one is. I'll never regret this, Laura."

As he kissed me, both of us still laying on the floor of the house where I was born, I knew he meant it, and I knew I felt just the same. No matter what came next, he and I were always meant to be.

Epilogue

~Four months later~

~Laura~

Once Jesse proposed, we both agreed there was no need to wait much longer, so with Tonia's help, we got the wedding pulled together in a matter of four short months. It would take longer to schedule some time for the honeymoon since our working holiday calendar was so full, but that didn't matter to me; I had never cared about fancy trips or spending time away from the ranch. Being there with Jesse would be all the honeymoon I needed.

My mom practically squealed with excitement when I told her we wanted to get married on the ranch. She had always imagined marrying her children off from there, but Dex's wedding had been on Shawna's ranch instead and Tonia and Cam got married in the city. With my dad selling the ranch, she thought she'd missed her chance.

The first time she and my dad came down to stay with us, it had been a little strange for all of us to have them as guests in their former home, but when my dad spent the day with me, helping out with one of my groups, he finally admitted to me that he'd been wrong.

"I never would have thought about doing something like this, Laura. I should have given you a chance to pull the place out of the hole I'd gotten it into. I just didn't want to burden you with it, and I truly thought you'd be happier without all the worry, but I underestimated you. I'm sorry."

For a Callahan, saying he'd screwed up was a huge deal.

Despite my own stubbornness, I could be gracious in victory. "I believe that you thought you were doing right by me, Daddy, even if you should have talked to me about it first. And besides, I really can't complain with the way things have turned out."

That couldn't be more of an understatement. I'd rather have Jesse in my life than be outright owner of the ranch any day.

On our wedding day, my daddy stood by to walk me down the aisle while my sisters, Mary-Beth, and Tyson's fiancée, Kayla, fussed over my dress, getting everything ready. After years of swearing he'd never get married, seeing how happy Jesse and I were together had softened Tyson's stance, and he'd finally admitted that he and Kayla were already a couple anyway. They didn't have a date set yet, but I imagined it wouldn't be long, and I hoped that when Jesse and I had kids, they'd have some neighbour kids to play with, just down the drive.

My dress was based on the one my great-grandmother had worn when she got married right there on the ranch ninety years earlier. I kept the vintage lace designs, updating the frame to something simple and elegant with spaghetti straps and a scoop back. Beneath my dress, I wore my cowboy boots, and Jesse would be wearing his too. Dex had been touched when Jesse asked him to be his best man, and Tyson, Wayne and Cam would also be standing up for him. For a guy who had no real friends when I met him, Jesse sure had his pick of them on his wedding day.

When they declared me ready, we all headed out to the back lawn where all our friends and family had gathered. Rather than a plain arched canopy, we had a horseshoe-shaped one, matching my ring. Mary-Beth was my maid of honour, mostly because if I chose between Tonia and Billie, the other one would never let me live it down. One of Mary-Beth's daughters was our flower girl while Tonia's son, Charlie, got to be the ringbearer. I couldn't feel any more surrounded by love, and just before we headed down the aisle, I raised my eyes to the sky to thank Shawna for all her help in getting us to that day. She would be watching, I knew it.

When I finally laid eyes on Jesse, my heart nearly burst with happiness. He truly looked like a dream come true in his tan suit, his firm frame filling it out perfectly, and the toes of his boots poking out underneath. I had told him he could wear jeans if he wanted; after all, I found him extremely sexy that way, but he insisted on dressing up too, and seeing him standing there, I was glad he had. We'd have some amazing pictures later on, and I couldn't wait to get him out of that suit later on.

His eyes stayed fixed on me as I walked up the aisle, and after my daddy shook his hand, Jesse took my hand with an awed expression. "I thought the day he trusted me with his ranch would be the happiest day of my life, but this is so much better."

"I could say the same," I teased him, and we both smiled as we turned to face the minister.

There, on the piece of land we both loved, Jesse and I promised to love and honour each other for as long as we lived. Whether that would be long or short didn't matter as much as how well we would do it, and when Jesse kissed me to seal our vows, I had no doubt that he would never give it less than his best.

~Jesse~

In all my life, I could have never imagined a day like that one. The ranch had never looked better, the fields sparkling beneath the sun, the air warm but not too hot, and all the people that mattered most to me in the world gathered in one place. Laura had somehow even tracked down Mr Buchanan, the ranch owner who'd taken me in and given me a home and sparked my love of working on the land, and he had come too, along with his wife, who apologized to me for her daughter's actions. Apparently, the young woman had eventually come clean about the fact that I never did anything to her, and I accepted the apology with no hard feelings. On that day of all days, I couldn't find it in me to hold a grudge, not when everything had worked out so perfectly.

The only people who had ever meant anything to me who weren't there were my family, my mother, my father and my sister, but it felt like if they could have been, they'd have been happy for me. They'd especially be happy that I no longer let their loss stop me from living.

We couldn't choose who left us and when, but we could choose who we loved while they were there, and as I told Laura when I proposed, I would never regret loving her.

As befitted the ranch, our banquet was a massive cookout, with half the men gathered around the big grill we used for the holiday groups and the other half taking the kids on horse rides around the near pasture. I made a trip to the barn to get some water for the horses at one point and surprised Tonia and Cam who were just coming out of it.

"Hey, Jesse." Cam gave me a smile that somehow looked sheepish and satisfied at the same time. "Do you need help with anything?"

"Sure, if you don't mind." As his wife walked past us to head back to the reception, I had to try not to laugh. "You've, uh, got some hay in your hair, Tonia."

"Oh. Thanks." She reached up and pulled it out, not looking embarrassed in the least as she gave Cam a wink. "See you later."

"You bet, Sugar." He watched her go with as much appreciation as if it were their wedding day rather than mine, and when he turned back to me, he could only shrug. "Something about the country air, I guess."

"Or maybe just the Callahan women." I clapped him on the shoulder in solidarity as we headed in to grab the water pails.

After dinner, the local band set up and everyone danced on the back lawn for hours. I lost track of Laura while I two-stepped with Mrs Callahan, Tonia, Billie, Mary-Beth, and half the women in town, it felt like. I did catch sight of Laura dancing with Dex at one point, which made me glad. He seemed to be struggling a bit lately, and that day couldn't have been easy for him, no matter how happy he was for us.

Billie grabbed me for another dance as the sun set and we switched the outdoor lights on to keep the party going. "I can create a distraction if you and Laura want to slip away. Just say the word."

"We'll be fine," I assured her. Laura would have no problem announcing when she was ready to go, but I appreciated that Billie wanted to help. I really liked all of Laura's family, but Billie and I had developed a younger sister/big brother dynamic that meant a lot to me. Almost the same age my own sister would have been, Billie helped me imagine what it might have been like if I'd gotten to know my sister as an adult. "I overheard Laura and Tonia talking about how they could reuse half this stuff for your wedding if you want to do it out here on the ranch too. Is there a man in your life I don't know about?"

Billie groaned in exasperation. "No, there isn't, and I don't want to get married here anyway. No offense, Jesse, but it just ain't my thing."

"None taken. You've got to do what's right for you."

Billie had just started her final year of college and after that, she'd have a year of teacher training before she could start working. Just like Laura, she'd always known what she wanted to do, but rather than working with animals, Billie wanted to work with kids.

And speaking of women who knew what they wanted, my wife appeared at my side a moment later. "Sorry, Billie, I'm cutting in."

"Be my guest." She gave us both a sincere smile as she stepped back. "Congratulations, guys."

As soon as Laura was in my arms, the rest of the world disappeared. "Are you doing okay?" she asked, her blue eyes looking up at me affectionately.

"I'm doing great. Today's been a lot, but in a good way. Have you had fun?"

"It's been perfect, Jesse." She sighed contentedly as she rested her head against my chest. With her body so close to mine, looking as unbelievable as she did in her dress, it didn't take long for my body to react, or for her to notice. "Are you ready to call it a night?"

"I've been ready since I got a look at you walking up the aisle," I told her truthfully, making her laugh. "I'm ready when you are."

"Let's go, then." With a wink, she pulled me towards the back door of the house. Climbing the steps, she called out to all our guests. "The bride and groom are leaving the party. Y'all stay as long as you like."

"Don't forget the bouquet!" Tonia called out, grabbing it off a nearby table and running it over to Laura. My new wife obligingly turned her back on the crowd as all the eligible women gathered nearby, and tossed it over her shoulder with impressive force.

It sailed right over most of the women who had gathered, and landed at Billie's feet instead, who stood further back, next to Dex.

"That's yours, Billie!" Laura called out as Billie rolled her eyes. "Good night, everyone!"

Cheers and shouts of congratulations followed us as we headed back into the house, closing the door behind us and shutting the rest of the world out too.

Just like the first night we slept together, I couldn't wait a second longer. I pushed her back against the door, kissing her as my hands ran over her beautiful dress, before picking her up and carrying her down the hall to our bedroom.

"I can't decide if I want you in that dress or out of it," I admitted as I placed her down on the bed and started pulling my boots off.

"Why not both?" Laura suggested, her blue eyes bright with desire. "I know you've got the stamina."

"You say that like I'm not right on the edge already from watching you all day."

"I say it because I know you can do anything, Jesse. You've never let me down yet."

With a groan, I managed to get the rest of my clothes off and pulled her panties off before hiking her skirt up, spreading her legs with her cowboy boots still on, and sinking my hard cock into her waiting warmth. "Fuck, Laura. It shouldn't be possible that this keeps feeling better."

"It shouldn't be," she agreed breathlessly as her legs wrapped around me, the heels of her boots digging into my ass. "But it does. I love you, Jesse."

"I love you too," I replied without hesitation. "With all my heart, for as long as we have."

~THE END~

The Callahans

You can read about the other Callahan siblings in their own books:

A Matter of Time - Tonia's Story

A Change of Heart - Billie's Story

A Work of Art - Dex's Story

More from the Author

<u>Contemporary Romance – 18+</u>

Callahan Series
A Matter of Time
A Piece of Land
A Change of Heart
A Work of Art

Christmas in the City Series
Mistletoe Mistake
Candy Cane Challenge
Tinsel Temptation
Gingerbread Gamble
Stocking Standoff

Standalones
Leading Lady
A Set of Three
Charity Case
Hired Lover

Contemporary Romance – New Adult/Clean

It Figures duet
It Figures
Figuring It Out

Historical Romance – 18+

Lady in Waiting Series
Lady in Waiting
King in Training
Princess in Hiding

Paranormal Romance – 18+

Cold Lake Pack Series
The Curse and the Prophecy
The Spell and the Legacy
The Dream and the Destiny

Mismatched Mates Series
Mismatched Mates
Misguided Motives
Mistaken Meanings

Serena's Story
The Alpha's Second Chance
The Returned Mate
The Vampire's Consort

Sacrifice Series
Blood Donor
Life Giver

Paranormal Romance – New Adult/Clean

The Alpha's Prey

My Patreon account has daily updates from my works-in-progress, bonus chapters and more – join me there to comment and read along as my next books are being written:
www.patreon.com/melodytyden

You can find and follow me on Facebook at:
facebook.com/melodytyden

Join the Facebook group Melody's Romance Corner for fun games, interaction with the author and exclusive news and excerpts.

You can also sign up to my newsletter at www.melodytyden.com for all the latest news.

www.ingramcontent.com/pod-product-compliance
Lightning Source LLC
Chambersburg PA
CBHW071143180726
48291CB00007B/2310